Magus to the Hermetic Order of the Golden Sprout, 12th Dan Master of Dimac, poet, adventurer, swordsman and concert pianist; big game hunter, Best dressed Man of 1933; mountaineer, lone yachtsman, Shakespearian actor and topless go-go dancer; Robert Rankin's hobbies include passive smoking, communicating with the dead and lying about his achievements. He lives in Sussex with his wife and family.

Robert Rankin is the author of *The Fandom of the Operator*, *Web Site Story*, *Waiting for Godalming*, *Sex and Drugs and Sausage Rolls*, *Snuff Fiction*, *Apocalypso*, *The Dance of the Voodoo Handbag*, *Sprout Mask Replica*, *Nostradamus Ate My Hamster*, *A Dog Called Demolition*, *The Garden of Unearthly Delights*, *The Most Amazing Man Who Ever Lived*, *The Greatest Show Off Earth*, *Raiders of the Lost Car Park*, *The Book of Ultimate Truths*, the *Armageddon* quartet (three books), and the *Brentford* trilogy (five books) which are all published by Corgi Books.

For more information on Robert Rankin and his books, see his website at:
www.lostcarpark.com/sproutlore

D1258805

www.booksattransworld.co.uk/robertrankin

Also by Robert Rankin

ARMAGEDDON THE MUSICAL

THEY CAME AND ATE US, ARMAGEDDON II: THE B-MOVIE

THE SUBURBAN BOOK OF THE DEAD,
ARMAGEDDON III: THE REMAKE

THE ANTIPOPE

THE BRENTFORD TRIANGLE

THE SPROUTS OF WRATH

THE BRENTFORD CHAINSTORE MASSACRE

THE BOOK OF ULTIMATE TRUTHS

RAIDERS OF THE LOST CAR PARK

THE GREATEST SHOW OFF EARTH

THE MOST AMAZING MAN WHO EVER LIVED

THE GARDEN OF UNEARTHLY DELIGHTS

A DOG CALLED DEMOLITION

NOSTRADAMUS ATE MY HAMSTER

SPROUT MASK REPLICA

THE DANCE OF THE VOODOO HANDBAG

APOCALYPSO

SNUFF FICTION

SEX AND DRUGS AND SAUSAGE ROLLS

WAITING FOR GODALMING

WEB SITE STORY

THE FANDOM OF THE OPERATOR

and published by Corgi Books

EAST OF EALING

Robert Rankin

CORGI BOOKS

EAST OF EALING
A CORGI BOOK : 9780552138437

Originally published in Great Britain by
Pan Books Ltd

PRINTING HISTORY
Pan edition published 1984
Corgi edition published 1992

13 15 17 19 20 18 16 14 12

Set in 11/12 Plantin by
County Typesetters, Margate, Kent.

Corgi Books are published by Transworld Publishers,
61–63 Uxbridge Road, London W5 5SA,
a division of The Random House Group Ltd.

Addresses for Random House Group Ltd companies outside the
UK can be found at: www.randomhouse.co.uk

Printed and bound in Great Britain by
Cox & Wyman Ltd, Reading, Berkshire.

The Random House Group Limited makes every effort to ensure
that the papers used in its books are made from trees that have
been legally sourced from well-managed and credibly certified
forests. Our paper procurement policy can be found at:
www.randomhouse.co.uk/paper.htm.

For my son William

1

Norman gave his ivory-handled screwdriver a final twist and secured the last screw into the side panel of the slim brass cylinder. Unclamping it from his vice, he lifted it lovingly by its shining axle, and held it towards the dust-smeared glass of the kitchenette window. It was a work of wonder and that was for certain. A mere ten inches in diameter and another one in thickness, the dim light painted a rainbow corona about its varnished circumference.

Norman carried it carefully across to his cluttered kitchen table and, elbowing aside a confusion of soiled crockery, placed it upon the twin bracket mountings which had been bolted through both tablecloth and table. The axle dropped into its mounts with a satisfying click and Norman, hardly daring to breathe, sought out his can of Three-in-One and applied a glistening bead of oil to either end.

If all his calculations, allied to those of a certain Johann Bessler, later known as Orffyreus, who had first demonstrated the prototype as long ago as 1712 in Zittau, East Germany, proved ultimately to be correct, he was even now standing upon the very threshold of yet another earth-shattering scientific breakthrough.

And all it needed was a breath. Norman leaned low

over the brazen wheel and blew upon its edge. There was a faint click, followed by another and yet another, and with a beauty, which like all of its strange kind lay firmly within the eye of its beholder, the polished brass wheel began to rotate slowly. Around and around it went, gathering momentum, until at last it reached a steady rate. Norman drew out his pocket-watch and rattled it against his ear. The second hand took to once more sweeping the pitted face of the grandaddy's retirement present. The polished wheel continued to turn; Norman counted beneath his breath and double-checked with his watch. Twenty-six revolutions per minute, exactly as old mad Bessler had predicted. Around and around and around for ever and ever and ever.

A broad, if lopsided, smile travelled where it could over Norman's face. Returning his already failing watch to its fluff-filled waistcoast pocket, he clapped his hands together and did a silly sort of dance right there and then upon the worn lino of the grimy kitchenette.

The wheel spun, its former clicking now a dull purr, and Norman thrust a knuckle to his mouth and chuckled noiselessly. His free hand hovered for a moment above the spinning wheel. If the calculations were indeed correct then virtually nothing, short of out and out destruction, should actually be able to halt the wheel's motion. Tentatively, he tapped a forefinger on to the polished surface. The wheel continued to spin. Gently, he plucked at it with finger and thumb. The wheel showed no signs of easing up. Norman laid firm hold with both hands upon the slim cylinder, his grasp skidded away, and the wheel rolled on and on and on.

This time he had cracked it! This time he had most definitely cracked it! The ultimate source of power. Weighing no more than a couple of pounds, its potential knew no bounds. It could charge up literally anything and, but for the occasional squirt of Three-in-One, needed next to no maintenance. Without the kitchenette, the shop door-bell suddenly rang in a customer and Norman dragged himself away from his spinning masterwork to answer the call of business. As he reached the door he paused a moment and looked back. Twenty-six revolutions per minute, round and around and around, for ever and ever and ever. With a final silent chuckle and a theatrical backways kick, Norman passed through the doorway, leaving his world of magic to emerge into the gloomy reality of his musty corner-shop.

Before the counter stood one James Pooley, betting man, free-thinker, and bachelor of the parish. His hand, which had even then been snaking across towards the peppermint packets, returned itself to the tweedy depths of a bottomless trouser pocket. With a cheery, 'Good morning to you, Norman,' Pooley bade the shopkeeper that very thing.

'Same to yourself, Jim,' said Norman. 'The daily, would it be?'

'The very same, five Woodys and a *Sporting Life*. I think that today I am a little more than usually liable to pull off "The Big One".'

'Of course.' Norman deftly drew out a packet of

cigarettes and the aforementioned racing paper without for a moment removing his gaze from the approximate location of Pooley's ever-wandering hands. It was not that Jim was by nature a dishonest man, but living daily upon his wits, he dared never let any opportunity, no matter how small, slip by.

'You wear the smile of a man who has already pulled off that ever elusive big fellow,' said Jim, noting well the twisted smirk still firmly plastered across Norman's face.

The shopkeeper passed Jim his life-support apparatus and nodded wildly. 'I have, I have,' said he, amidst a flurry of nose-tapping. 'Although on this occasion, as upon others, I cannot take full credit for it all myself.'

'No matter that. Many a wealthy man owes his success in life to the labours of a deceased relative.' Jim slipped his cigarettes into his breast-pocket and rolled his newspaper. 'So what is it then? Something of a scientific nature I have no doubt.'

'The very same.'

'Might I hazard a guess?'

'Be very pleased to.'

Jim stroked at the stubble of his chin, which he had been meaning to shave off for at least a day or so, and cocked his head upon one side. 'Now, if I am not mistaken,' said he, 'your recent obsession, and I use the word in the kindest possible way, has been with energy. The solar panels upon your roof do not go unnoticed hereabouts and the fact that you possess the only Morris Minor in the neighbourhood which runs upon coke has raised more than the occasional eyebrow. Am I right therefore in assuming that it is towards energy, power, and things of that nature that you have turned your enormous intellect?'

Norman's head bobbed up and down after the fashion of a toy dog in a Cortina rear window.

'Aha, then if I am not mistaken I will hazard a guess that you have rediscovered the long lost secret of perpetual motion.'

Norman clapped his hands together. 'You got it,' he crowed. 'Got it in one. I am glad that I did not lay money upon it. You got it in one.'

'Naturally,' said Jim, blowing on his fingernails. 'But I feel you knew that I would.'

Norman nodded again. 'True,' he said. 'I must admit that I had been somewhat puzzled by the ever-increasing number of little bright patches appearing upon the window of my kitchenette. However, noticing of late that each corresponds exactly in size and shape to the blot of dirt upon the end of your nose, all would seem to be revealed. But what do you think, Jim? The marvel of the age would you say? Feel free to offer criticism; my shoulders although physically bowed are metaphorically broad.'

Jim thrust his rolled-up paper into a jacket pocket. 'If you will pardon me saying this, Norman, I have never myself had a lot of truck with the concept of perpetual motion. You will recall, no doubt, me saying that the chap in Chiswick who gave all those lectures at the Memorial Library propounding the theory of reincarnation has died yet again.'

Norman nodded yet again.

'And you will also recall my brilliant *bon mot* made

11

upon the news of his passing, that the trouble with those fellows is that they are here today and here tomorrow?'

Norman winced.

'Well, such it is with perpetual motion. A fine thing it might be in itself, and a pleasure to the inventor thereof, but to the general public, in particular to the man of limited reason with no care for the higher truth, it presents but one thing only.'

'Which is?'

'Absolute monotony,' said Pooley in a leaden tone. 'All-consuming, soul-destroying, absolute monotony.'

With these few words he turned upon his heel and strode from the shop, leaving Norman to ponder upon not one but two eternal problems. The first being how a man such as Pooley could have the sheer gall to write off the greatest scientific discovery of the age with a few poorly chosen words. And the second, how he had managed, once more, to escape from the shop without having paid for either Woodbines or *Sporting Life*.

'The wheels of God grind slowly,' thought Norman to himself. 'But they do grind at twenty-six revolutions per minute.'

2

Neville the part-time barman flip-flopped across the deserted saloon-bar of the Flying Swan, his monogrammed carpet-slippers raising small clouds of dust from the faded carpet. Rooting with a will, he sought his newspaper which lay upon the pub's welcome mat beneath a pile of final demands, gaudy circulars, and rolled posters advertising the forthcoming Festival of Brentford.

Shaking it free of these postal impediments, Neville unfolded the local tabloid and perused the front page. More good good news. Earthquakes and tidal waves, wars and rumours of wars. Jolly stuff. And on the home front? Well, there was the plague of black fly currently decimating the allotment crops. A rival brewery had just put its beer up a penny a pint and its competition, ever happy to accept a challenge, were hinting at rises of two pence or more.

One particular gem caught the part-time barman's good eye: the local banks, in keeping with a country-wide trend, were investigating the possibility of dispensing with coin of the realm and instigating a single credit card system. That would go down a storm with the locals, thought Neville. Without further ado he consigned the wicked messenger of bad tidings to the wastepaper basket. 'I shall cancel this,' said the part-time barman to himself. 'I shall ask Norman to despatch me something of a more cheerful nature in the future. Possibly the *People's Friend* or *Gardener's Gazette*.'

But on further consideration, even those two periodicals were not exactly devoid of grim tidings nowadays. The *People's Friend*, not content with simply going up three pence, assailed its readers with a fine line in doom prophecy, and the *Gardener's Gazette* dedicated most of its pages to large anatomical diagrams of black fly. Neville shrugged his dressing-gowned shoulders. Seemed like a nice day though, but. The sun rising majestic as ever from behind the flat-blocks and tickling the Swan's upper panes. Always some hope for the future. Although, lately, Neville had been feeling more than a little ill at ease. It was as if some great burden was descending upon him, inch by inch and pound by pound, down on to his bony shoulders. He was hard put to explain the feeling, and there was little point in confiding his unease to the regulars, but he was certain that something altogether wrong was happening and, moreover, that it was happening to him personally.

Leaving his newspaper to confide its black tidings to the fag ends in the wastepaper basket and his mail to gather what dust it wished upon the doormat, Neville the part-time barman flip-flopped away up the Swan's twenty-six stairs to his cornflakes and a cup of the blackest of all black coffees.

In another part of Brentford other things were stirring this Shrove Tuesday morning and what those other things were and what they would later become were matters which would in their turn weigh very heavily indeed upon certain part-time barmen's shoulders.

They all truly began upon a certain section of unreclaimed bomb-site along the High Street between the Beehive pub and a rarely used side-turning known as Abaddon Street. And as fate would have it, it was across this very stretch of land that an Irish gentleman of indeterminate years, wearing a well-patched tweed jacket and a flat cap, was even now striding. He was whistling brightly and as it was his wont to do, leading by the perished rubber grip of a pitted handlebar, an elderly sit-up-and-beg bike. This was one John Vincent Omally, and his rattling companion, labouring bravely along, although devoid of front mudguards and rear brake and sorely in need of the healing balm offered by Norman's oil-can, was none other than that prince of pedaldom, Marchant, the wonder bike. Over the rugged strip of land came these two heroic figures, the morning sun tinting their features, treading a well-worn short-cut of their own making. Omally whistling a jaunty tune from the land of his fathers and Marchant offering what accompaniment he could with the occasional bout of melodic bell ringing. God was as ever in Omally's Heaven and all seemed very much all right with the world.

As they came a-striding, a-whistling and a-ringing, small birdies fluttered down on to the crumbling ivy-hung brickwork of the surrounding walls to join them in a rowdy chorus. Beads of dew swung upon

15

dandelion stems and fat-bellied garden spiders fiddled with their diamond-hung webs. It certainly wasn't a bad old life if you had the know of it, and Omally was a man whom it could reasonably be said had that very know. The lad gave a little skip and doffed his hat to the day. Without warning his foot suddenly struck a half-buried object which had certainly not existed upon his previous day's journeyings. To the accompaniment of a great Godless oath which momentarily blotted out the sunlight and raised the twittering birdies into a startled confusion, the great man of Eire plunged suddenly towards the planet of his birth, bringing with him his bicycle and tumbling into a painful, untidy, and quite undignified heap.

'By the blood of the Saints!' swore Omally, attempting to rise but discovering to his horror that Marchant now held him in something resembling an Indian death-lock. 'In the name of all the Holies!' The tangled bike did what it could to get a grip of itself and spun its back wheel, chewing up several of Omally's most highly-prized fingers. 'You stupid beast!' screamed himself, lashing out with an over-sized hobnail. 'Have a care will you?' The bike, having long years of acquaintanceship with its master to its credit, considered that this might be the time to keep the now legendary low profile.

Amidst much cursing and a great deal of needless profanity, Omally struggled painfully to his feet and sought the cause of his downfall. Almost at once he spied out the villain, a nubble of polished metal protruding from the dusty path. John was not slow in levelling his size-nine boot at it.

He was someway between mid-swing and full-swing when a mental image of a bygone relative swam into his mind. He had performed a similar action upon a half-buried obstruction during the time of the blitz. The loud report and singular lack of mortal remains paid a posthumous tribute to his lack of forethought. DANGER UNEXPLODED BOMB! screamed a siren in Omally's brain. John lowered his size-nine terror weapon gently to the deck and stooped gingerly towards the earth to examine the object. To his amazement he found himself staring at the proverbial thing of beauty. A mushroom of highly-polished brass surmounted by an enamel crown. There was that indefinable quality of value about it and Omally was not slow to notice the fact. His fingers greedily wore away at its earthy surrounding, exposing a slender, fluted column extending downwards. From even this small portion it was clear that the thing was a rare piece of workmanship; the flutes were cunningly inlaid with mother-of-pearl. Omally climbed to his feet and peered furtively around to assure himself that he was alone with his treasure. That he had struck the motherlode at last was almost a certainty. There was nothing of the doodlebug or Mark Seventeen Blockbuster about this boy, but very much of the antique bedstead of Victoria and Albert proportions.

John rubbed his hands together and chuckled. What was it his old Da had once said? A dead bird never falls out of the nest, that was it. Carefully covering his find with a clump or two of grass, Omally continued upon his way. The birdies had flown and the spiders had it away on their eight ones, but before Omally reached his secret exit in the planked fencing he was whistling once more, and Marchant was doing his level best to keep up with the increasingly more sprightly tune.

3

Jim Pooley sat upon his favourite bench before the Memorial Library, racing paper spread out across his knees, liberated Woodbine aglow between his lips, and Biro perched atop his right ear. Few were the passers-by who even troubled to notice the sitter upon the bench. Fewer still observed the chalk-drawn pentagram encircling that bench, the sprig of hemlock attached to the sitter's lapel, or the bulge of the tarot pack in his waistcoat pocket. Such subtleties were lost to the casual observer, but to the trained eye they would be instantly significant. Jim Pooley was now having a crack at occultism in his never-ending quest to pull off the six-horse Super-Yankee.

Jim had tried them all and found each uniformly lacking. The I-Ching he had studied until his eyes crossed. The prophecies of Nostradamus, the dice, the long sticks, the flight paths of birds, and the changes of barometric pressure registered upon the charts of the library entrance hall – each had received his attention as a possible catalyst for the pulling off of the ever-elusive Big One. He had considered selling his soul to the devil but it was on the cards that the Prince of Darkness probably had his name down for conscription anyway.

Thrusting his hands into his trouser pockets, Jim

peered down at his paper. Somewhere, he knew, upon this page were those six horses. Tomorrow, he knew, he would kick himself for not having seen the obvious cosmic connection. Jim concentrated every ounce of his psychic energies upon the page. Presently he was asleep. Blissful were his Morphean slumbers upon this warm spring morning and blissful they would no doubt have remained, at least until opening time at the Swan, had not a deft blow from a size-nine boot struck him upon the sole of the left foot and blasted him into consciousness. The man who could dream winners awoke with a painful start.

'Morning Jim,' said the grinning Omally. 'Having forty winks were we?'

Pooley squinted up at his rude awakener with a bloodshot eye. 'Yoga,' said he. 'Lamaic meditation. I was almost on the brink of a breakthrough and you've spoilt it.'

Omally rested his bicycle upon the library fence and his bum upon the bench. 'Sorry,' said he. 'Please pardon my intrusion upon the contemplation of your navel. You looked to all the world the very picture of a sleeper.'

'Nothing of the sort,' Pooley replied in a wounded tone. 'Do you think that I, like yourself, can afford to fritter away my time in dalliance and idleness? My life is spent in the never-ending search for higher truths.'

'Those which come in six or more figures?'

'None but the very same.'

'And how goes this search?'

20

'Fraught as ever with pitfalls for the unwary traveller.'

'As does our each,' said the Irish philosopher.

The two men sat awhile upon the library bench. Each would dearly have liked a smoke but out of politeness each waited upon his fellow to make that first selfless gesture of the day. 'I'm dying for a fag,' sighed Jim, at length.

Omally patted his pockets in a professional manner, narrowly avoiding the destruction of five Woodbine he had secreted in his waistcoat pocket. 'I'm out,' he said.

Jim shrugged. 'Why do we always go through this performance?' he asked.

Omally shook his head, 'I have no idea whatever, give us a fag, Jim?'

'Would that I could John, would that I could. But times are up against me at the present.'

Omally shook his head sadly, 'These are troubled times for us all I fear. Take my knee here,' he raised the gored article towards Jim's nose. 'What does that say to you?'

Pooley put his ear to Omally's knee, 'It is not saying much,' he said. 'Is it perhaps trying to tell me that it has a packet of cigarettes in its sock?'

'Not even warm.'

'Then you've got me.' Omally sighed. 'Shall we simply smoke our own today, Jim?'

'Good idea.' Pooley reached into his waistcoat pocket and Omally did likewise. Both withdrew identical packets into the sunlight and both opened these in unison. John's displayed five cigarettes.

Pooley's was empty. 'Now there's a thing,' said Jim.

'Decoy!' screamed John Omally. Pooley accepted the cigarette in the manner with which it was offered. 'My thanks,' said he. 'I really do have the feeling that today I might just pull off the long-awaited Big One.'

'I have something of the same feeling myself,' his companion replied.

4

The part-time barman finished the last of his toast and patted about his lips with a red gingham napkin. He leaned back in his chair and rested his palms upon his stomach. He felt certain that he was putting on weight. A thin man from birth, tall, gaunt, and scholar-stooped, Neville had never possessed a single ounce of surplus fat. But recently it seemed to him that his jackets were growing ever more tight beneath the armpits, and that the lower button on his waistcoat was becoming increasingly more difficult to secure. 'Most curious,' said Neville, rising from his seat and padding over to the bathroom scales which were now a permanent fixture in the middle of the living-room floor. Climbing aboard, he peered down between his slippered toes. Eleven stone dead, exactly as it had been for the last twenty years. The part-time barman shook his head in wonder, it was all very mysterious. Perhaps the scales were wrong, gummed up with carpet fluff or something. He'd let Norman give them the once-over. Or perhaps it was the dry cleaners? Things never seemed quite right there since that big combine bought old Tom Telford out. Possibly this new lot were having a pop at him. Putting an extra tuck in the seat of his strides every time he put them in for their monthly hose down.

Most unsporting that, hitting a lad below the belt.

Neville laughed feebly at his unintended funny, but really this was no laughter matter. Taking out the tape measure, which now never left his person, he stretched it about his waist. All seemed the same. Possibly it was simply a figment of his imagination. Possibly he was going mad. The thought was never far from his mind nowadays. Neville shuddered. He would just have to pull himself together.

Sighing deeply, he shuffled away to the bedroom to dress. Flinging off his silken dressing-gown he took up the rogue trousers from where they hung in their creases over the chair and yanked them up his legs. With difficulty he buttoned himself into respectability. They were definitely too tight for comfort, there was no point in denying it. Neville stooped for his socks but stopped in horror. The blood drained from his face and his good eye started from its socket; a nasty blue tinge crept about the barman's lips. It was worse than he feared, far worse. His trouser bottoms were swinging about his ankles like flags at half-mast. He wasn't only getting fatter, he was growing taller! Neville slumped back on to his bed, his face a grey mask of despair. It was impossible. Certainly folk could put on weight pretty rapidly, but to suddenly spring up by a good inch and a half over night? That was downright impossible, wasn't it?

Pooley and Omally strolled over the St Mary's Allotments en route to John's hut and the cup that cheers. Jim tapped his racing paper upon his leg and sought inspiration from the old enamel advertising signs along the way which served here and there as plot dividers. None was immediately forthcoming. The two threaded their way between the ranks of bean poles and waxed netting, the corrugated shanties, and zinc watertanks. They walked in single file along a narrow track through a farrowed field of broccoli and one of early flowering sprouts, finally arriving at the wicket fence and pleasant ivy-hung trelliswork that stood before Omally's private plot. John parked his bicycle in its favourite place, took up his daily pinta, turned several keys in as many weighty locks, and within a few short minutes the two men lazed upon a pair of commandeered railway carriage seats, watching the kettle taking up the bubble on the Primus.

'There is a king's ransom, I do hear, to be had out of the antique trade at present,' said John matter-of-factly.

'Oh yes?' Pooley replied without enthusiasm.

'Certainly, the junk of yesterday is proving to be the ob-ja-dart of today and the nestegg of tomorrow.' Omally rose to dump two tea bags into as many enamel mugs and top the fellows up with boiling water. 'A veritable king's ransom, ready for the taking. A man could not go it alone in such a trade, he would need a partner, of course.'

'Of course.'

'A man he could *trust*.' John put much emphasis upon the word as he wrung out the tea bags and added the cream of the milk to his own mug and a splash of the rest to Jim's. 'Yes, he would definitely want a man he could rely on.'

'I am convinced of that,' said Jim, accepting his mug. 'A bit strong, isn't it?'

'Antique bedding is currently the vogue amongst the trendies of Kensington, I understand,' John continued.

'Oh those bodies.'

'Yes, the fashionable set do be weeping, wailing, and gnashing its expensively-capped teeth for the lack of it.'

Pooley blew on to his tea. 'Strange days,' said he.

John felt that he was obviously not getting his point across in quite the right way. A more direct approach was necessary. 'Jim,' he said in a highly confidential tone. 'What would you say if I was to offer you a chance of a partnership in an enterprise which would involve you in absolutely no financial risk whatever?'

'I would say that there is always a first time for everything, I suppose.'

'What if I was to tell you that at this very moment I know of where there is an extremely valuable antique lying discarded and unwanted which is ours for the taking, what would you say then?'

Jim sipped at his tea. 'I would say to you then, Omally,' he said, without daring to look up, 'dig the bugger out yourself.'

Omally's eyebrows soared towards his flat cap.

Pooley simply pointed to an L-shaped tear in his own left trouser knee. 'I passed along your path not half an hour before you,' he said simply.

'Your lack of enterprise is a thing to inspire disgust.'

'He that diggeth a pit will fall into it. Ecclesiasticus

Chapter twenty-seven, verse twenty-six,' said Jim Pooley. 'I am not a religious man as you well know, but I feel that the Scriptures definitely have it sussed on this point. A commendable try though.' Jim took out his cigarette packet from his top pocket and handed the Irishman a tailor-made.

'Thank you,' said Omally.

'Now, if you really have a wish to make a killing today –' John nodded enthusiastically, it was early yet and his brain was only just warming up to the daily challenge, '– I have seen something which has the potential to earn a man more pennies than a thousand buried bedframes. Something which a man can only be expected to witness once in a lifetime. And something of such vast financial potential that if a man was to see it and not take advantage of the experience, he should consider himself a soul lost for ever and beyond all hope.'

'Your words are pure music,' said John Omally. 'Play on, sweet friend, play on.'

As Neville the part-time barman drew the polished brass bolts on the saloon-bar door and stood in the opening, sniffing the air, the clatter of two pairs of hobnail boots and the grating of rear mudguard upon back wheel announced the approach of a brace of regulars. One of these was a gentleman of Celtic extraction who had recently become convinced that the future lay in perpetual motion and its application to the fifth gear of the common bicycle. Neville installed himself behind the bar counter and closed the hinged counter top.

'God save all here,' said John Omally, pushing open the door.

'Count that double,' said Pooley, following up the rear.

Neville pushed a polished glass beneath the spout of the beer engine and drew upon the enamel pump handle. Before the patrons had hoisted themselves on to their accustomed barstools, two pints of Large stood brimming before them, golden brown and crystal clear. 'Welcome,' said Neville.

'Hello once more,' said Omally, 'Jim is in the chair.' Pooley smiled and pushed the exact amount of pennies and halfpennies across the polished counter top. Neville rang up 'No Sale' and once more all was as it ever had been and hopefully ever would be in Brentford.

'How goes the game then, gentlemen?' Neville asked the patrons, already a third of the way through their pints.

'As ever, cruel to the working man,' said John. 'And how is yourself?'

'To tell you the truth, a little iffy. In your personal opinion, John, how do I look to you?'

'The very picture of health.'

'Not a little puffy?' Neville fingered his middle regions.

'Not at all.'

'No hint of stoutness there? You can be frank with me, I have no fear of criticism.'

Omally shook his head and looked towards Jim. 'You look fine,' said Pooley. 'Are you feeling a bit poorly, then?'

'No, no.' Neville shook his head with vigour. 'It's just that, well . . .' he considered the two drinkers who surveyed him with dubious expressions. 'Oh, nothing at all. I look all right you think? No higher, say, than usual?' Two heads swung to and fro upon their respective necks. 'Best to forget it then, a small matter, do not let it spoil your ale.'

'Have no fear of that,' said John Omally.

The Swan's door opened to admit the entry of an elderly gentleman and his dog. 'Morning, John, Jim,' said Old Pete, sidling up to the bar. 'Large dark rum please, Neville.' Neville took himself off to the optic.

'Morning, Pete,' said Pooley, 'good day, Chips.' The ancient's furry companion woofed non-committally. 'Are you fit?'

'As well as can be expected. And how goes the sport for you? That Big One still lurking up beyond your frayed cuff?'

Pooley made a 'so-so' gesture. 'Inches, but . . .'

Old Pete accepted his drink from Neville and held up the glass to evaluate the exact volume of his measure before grudgingly pushing the correct change across the bar top. 'So,' he continued, addressing himself to Omally, 'and how fare the crops?'

'Blooming,' said Omally. 'I expect a bumper harvest this year. Come the Festival. I expect several firsts and as many seconds in the Show.'

'King Teddies again then, is it?' Revered as the personification of all agricultural knowledge within a radius of an 'nth number of miles, Old Pete had little truck with potato growers.

'Nature's finest food,' said John. 'Was it not the spud which sustained the Joyces, the Wildes, the Behans and the Traynors? Show me a great man and I will show you a spud to his rear.'

'I have little regard for footballers,' said Old Pete. 'If you were any kind of a farmer you would diversify your crops a little. I myself have fostered no fewer than five new varieties of sprout.'

Omally crossed himself and made a disgusted face. 'Don't even speak the word,' said he. 'I cannot be having with that most despicable of all vegetables.'

'The sprout is your man,' intoned the old one. 'Full of iron. A man could live alone upon a desert island all his life if he had nothing more than a few sprout seeds and bit of common sense.'

'A pox on all sprouts,' said John, crouching low over his pint. 'May the black fly take the lot of them.'

Pooley was consulting his racing paper. Possibly there was a horse running whose name was an anagram of 'sprout'. Such factors were not to be taken lightly when one was seeking that all elusive cosmic connection. The effort was quite considerable and very shortly Jim, like Dickens's now legendary fat boy, was once more asleep. Neville made to take up the half-finished glass for the washer. With a sudden transformation from Dickens to Edgar Allen Poe, the sleeper awoke. 'Not done here,' said Jim. 'It's Omally's round.' Omally got them in.

'Let us speak no more of horticulture,' said John to Old Pete. 'Your knowledge of the subject is legend hereabouts and I am not up to matching wits with you. Tell me something, do you sleep well of a night?'

'The sleep of the just, nothing else.'

'Then you must indeed have a cosy nest to take your slumbers in.'

'No, nothing much, a mattress upon a rough wooden pallet. It serves as it has since my childhood.'

Omally shook his head in dismay, 'Longevity, as I understand it to be, is very much the part and parcel of good sleeping. Man spends one third of his life in bed. Myself a good deal more. The comfort of the sleeper greatly reflects upon his health and well being.'

'Is that a fact?' said Old Pete. 'I have no complaints.'

'Because you have never experienced greater comfort. Take myself. You would take me for a man of thirty.'

'Never. Forty.'

Omally laughed. 'Always the wag. But truthfully, I attribute my good health to the comfort afforded by my bed. There is a science in these things, and believe me, I have studied this particular science.'

'Never given the matter much thought,' said Old Pete.

'So much I suspected,' said John. 'You, as an elderly gentleman, and by that I mean no offence, must first look after your health. Lying upon an uncomfortable bed can take years off your life.'

'As it happens, my old bed is a bit knackered.'

'Then there you have it.' Omally smacked his hands together. 'You are throwing away your life for a few pennies wisely invested in your own interest.'

'I am a fool to myself,' said Old Pete, who definitely wasn't. 'What are you selling, John?'

Omally tapped at his nose, 'Something very, very special. The proper palatial pit. The very acme of sleeping paraphernalia. Into my possession has come of late a bed which would stagger the senses of the gods. Now had I the accommodation I would truly claim such a prize for my own. But my apartments are small and I know that yours could easily house such a find. What do you say?'

'I'll want to have a look at the bugger first, five-thirty p.m. tonight, here.'

Omally spat upon his palm and smacked it down into the wrinkled appendage of the elder. 'Done,' said he.

'I'd better not be,' said Old Pete.

Omally drew his partner away to a side-table, 'Now that is what you call business,' he told Jim. 'The old bed is not even dug out, yet it is already sold.'

Pooley groaned; he could already feel the blisters upon his palms. 'You are on to a wrong'n there,' he said. 'This venture has to me the smell of doom about it. That is a bomb site *you* will be digging on. There will probably be a corpse asleep in that bed. Should bed it in fact be and not simply a shaft or two of nothing.'

Omally crossed himself at the mention of a corpse. 'Stop with such remarks,' said he. 'There is a day's pay in this and as the digger you deserve half of anything I get.'

'And what about Norman's wheel and the many millions to be made from that?'

'Well, we have no absolute proof that the wheel spins without cessation. This would be a matter for serious scientific investigation. Such things take time.'

'We have no lack of that, surely?'

'I will tell you what,' Omally finished his pint and studied the bottom of his glass. 'I will chance your wheel if you will chance my bedframe.'

Pooley looked doubtful.

'Now be fair,' said John. 'There are degrees of doubt to be weighed up on either side. Firstly, of course you cannot approach Norman, he knows that you are on to him. A third party must act here. Someone with a subtlety of approach. Someone gifted in such matters.'

'Someone such as yourself?'

'Good idea,' said John. 'But time is of the essence, we don't want any opportunists dipping in before us. When we leave here you collect a couple of tools from my plot and whip the bed out and I will go around to Norman's.'

If Pooley had looked doubtful before, it was nought to the way he looked now. 'I do not feel that I am getting the better part of this,' he said slowly.

'Better part?' Omally's face was all outrage. 'We are a business partnership are we not? There are no better parts involved here. Surely you are now sowing seeds of distrust?'

'Who, me? Perish the thought. The fact that I will be labouring away in a minefield digging up a rusty old bedframe while you stand chit-chatting in a cosy corner-shop had not crossed my mind.'

'So?'

Jim folded his brow. 'Whose round is it?'

'Yours, Jim,' said John Omally, 'most definitely yours.'

5

Norman had been dancing gaily through his morning's work. Between customers he had skipped backwards and forwards, turning the enamel door handle and squinting into the gloom to assure himself that all was as it should be. The wheel had been tirelessly spinning for more than four hours now and showed no signs whatever of grinding to a halt. As the Memorial Library clock struck one in the distance he turned his sign to the 'Closed For Lunch' side, bolted up, and pranced away to his sanctum sanctorum. The wheel was an undoubted success and, as such, meant that Phase One of his latest, and in his own humble opinion undeniably greatest, project was complete.

Norman slipped off his shopkeeper's overall and donned a charred leather apron and a pair of welder's goggles. Dusting down his rubber gloves with a tube of baby powder, he drew them over his sensitive fingers and flexed these magical appendages. With a flourish, he dragged aside a length of gingham tablecloth which curtained off a tiny alcove in one corner of the crowded room.

Upon a worm-eaten kitchen chair sat another Norman!

Clad in grey shopkeeper's workcoat, shirt, tie,

trousers, and worn brown brogues, he was a waxen effigy of the Madame Tussaud's variety. The scientific shopkeeper chuckled and, reaching out a rubber-clad finger, tickled his *doppelgänger* under the chin. 'Afternoon, Norman,' he said.

The double did not reply, but simply sat staring sightlessly into space. It was as near a perfect representation of its living counterpart as it was possible to be. And so it might well have been considering the long years of Norman's labour. Countless thousands of hours had gone into its every detail. Every joint in its skeletal frame was fully articulated with friction-free bearings of the shopkeeper's own design. The cranial computer banks were loaded to the very gunwhales with all the necessary information, which would enable it to perform the mundane and tiresome duties required of a corner-shopkeeper, whilst its creator could dedicate the entirety of his precious time to the more essential matters of which Phase Three of the project were composed. All it lacked was that essential spark of life, and this now ground away upon the kitchen table at precisely twenty-six revolutions per minute.

Norman chuckled anew and drew his masterpiece erect. Unbuttoning the shirt, he exposed the rubberized chest region which housed the hydraulic unit designed to simulate the motions of breathing. Tinkering with his screwdriver, he removed the frontal plate and applied a couple of squirts of Three-in-One to the brace of mountings, identical in shape and size to those which now cradled the ever-spinning wheel. He had sought far and wide for a

36

never-failing power supply, having previously nothing to hand save clumsy mains cables which, even when disguised by poking from trouser bottoms, left his progeny little scope for locomotion. This compact unit would do the job absolutely.

Norman crossed to the table, and with a set of specially fashioned tongs carefully lifted the spinning wheel upon its polished axle-rod. It turned through space gyroscopically, if nothing else it would certainly keep the robot standing upright. With a satisfying click the wheel fell into place, and Norman closed the chest cavity and rebuttoned the shirt, straightening the tie and workcoat lapels. The shopkeeper stepped back to view his mirror image. Perfection. There was a gentle flutter of movement about the chest region, a sudden blinking of eyelids and focusing of eyes, a yawn, a stretch. Clearing its throat with a curiously mechanical coughing sound, the creature spoke.

'Good afternoon, sir,' it said.

Norman clapped his hands together and danced one of his favourite silly dances. 'Wonderful,' he said with glee. 'Wonderful.'

The robot smiled crookedly. 'I am happy that you find all to your satisfaction,' said he.

'Oh, indeed, indeed. How are you then, Norman? Are you well?'

'A bit stiff, sir, as it happens, but I expect that I will wear in. Is there anything in particular you would like doing?'

Norman clapping his hands, 'How about a cup of tea, what do you think?'

'Certainly, sir.' The robot rose unsteadily to its feet, stretched himself again and waggled each foot in turn.

Norman watched in sheer exaltation as his other self performed its first task. The tea was exactly as he would have made it himself. 'You will pardon me if I don't join you, sir,' said the pseudo-shopkeeper, 'but I do not feel at all thirsty.'

At a little after three p.m., Pooley and Omally left the Flying Swan. As the two friends strode off down the Ealing Road, Neville the part-time barman shot home the brass bolts and padded away to his quarters. The floor boards groaned suspiciously beneath his tread but Neville, now buoyed up with a half-bottle of Bells, closed his ears to them.

'Right then,' said Omally, 'to business, it is yet three p.m. and we have not earned a penny.'

'I have missed the bookies,' said Jim. 'I am a hundred thousand pounds down already.'

'The day may yet be saved, positive thinking is your man. To work then.'

Pooley shook his head and departed gloomily down Albany Road, en route for the allotment. Omally squared up his shoulders and entered Norman's corner shop. Behind the counter stood Norman, idly thumbing through a copy of *Wet Girls In The Raw*. Beneath the counter crouched another Norman, chuckling silently into his hands.

'Afternoon, Norman,' said Omally. 'Packet of reds if you please, and a half-ounce of Golden.'

The mechanical confectioner cleared his throat

with a curiously mechanical coughing sound. 'Certainly, sir,' said he, turning away to seek out these articles from their niches. Below the counter Norman clicked his tongue in silent displeasure. Above the counter Omally's hand had snaked into the peppermint rack and drew a packet away to his trouser pocket. Norman would have to chalk that one up to experience and punch a few more defence mechanisms into the machine's computer banks. He scribbled a hurried note on to a discarded ice-cream wrapper and awaited developments. He did not have to wait long.

'Stick them on my slate please, Norm,' said Omally.

'Pardon me, sir?'

'On my slate, I'll settle up with you later.'

'I regret, sir, that I cannot allow you to leave the premises without having first paid for the goods. Such is the way with commerce, you understand.' Below the counter, Norman chewed upon his knuckles. This was much better. He patted his creation upon the trouser knee and gave it the old thumbs up. 'Please do not ask for credit, sir,' said the robot, 'as a smack in the mouth so often offends.'

'What?' Omally surveyed the shopkeeper with open horror, this was not the way business was done. Not the way it had been done for the last fifteen years. He did not expect to actually leave the shop without paying, unless, of course, he caught Norman on one of those occasions when he had been testing his home-made sprout beer. But this? Omally pushed back his flat cap and tugged at his curly forelock.

Was this simply some new ploy perhaps? Maybe Norman had been reading some American magazine about self-assertion or the like? He would play it along. 'My knees ache something wicked,' he said, changing the subject.

A mystified look appeared upon the robot-Norman's face. 'I am sorry to hear that, sir,' said he, sympathetically.

'It is the cycling I believe,' John continued, 'constantly forcing the pedals round and around and around. I would be lost without the bike of course, as it is my only means of transport, but I do believe that the physical effort required by the cycling is slowly crippling me.'

The robot-Norman shook his head sadly. 'That is a pity,' he sighed.

'Yes, if only there was some alternative to be had for the eternal pedalling. Around and around and around.' Omally's hand made the appropriate movements in the air. 'If you know what I mean.'

The sub-counter Norman nodded, he was already way ahead of him. The duplicate, however, seemed not to have grasped it as yet. 'Could you not possibly trade in the bike for a car or something?' he suggested.

'A car?' Omally looked askance at the shopkeeper. 'A car? How long have you known me, Norman?'

The Irishman did not hear the purring of cogs and the meshing of computer mechanisms as the robot sought out the answer to this question.

'Precisely fifteen years two months and nine days,' he said. 'You were, if I recall, wearing the same cap and trousers.'

'And do you suppose that a man who is still wearing this cap and trousers is the sort of man who could afford to buy a car?'

'I have not given the matter any thought as yet, sir,' said the robot. 'But if you like I will apply myself to it whilst you are paying for your purchases.'

Omally chewed upon his lip; he did not like the smell of this one little bit. 'So how goes the work then?' he asked, changing the subject yet again.

'Business is slack, as ever. The monthly returns are down again.'

'No, not the shop, I mean, your work,' Omally gestured towards the kitchenette door. 'What wonders are germinating in your little den?'

'If you will pardon me, sir,' said the robot, reaching forward, 'it is becoming apparent to me that you have no intention of paying for your purchases, would you kindly hand them back?'

'Norman, are you all right?'

The robot suddenly lunged forward across the counter and grasped Omally by a tweedy lapel.

'Be warned,' said the Irishman. 'I know Dimac.'

Beneath the counter, a sudden terror gripped the heart of the hidden shopkeeper. He had programmed the entirety of *Count Dante's Dimac Manual of Martial Arts* into his creation as a precaution against it being attacked. Omally's statement he knew well enough to be pure bravado, but he doubted that the robot would take it as such.

'Thus and so,' said the duplicate, drawing Omally from his feet, 'and hence.'

With a deft flick of an automated wrist, which the

legendary Count catalogued as Move thirty-two A, The Curl of the Dark Dragon's Tail, Omally found himself catapulted through the air in a flailing backward somersault which ended in sprawling confusion amidst a tangle of magazine racks and out of date chocolate-boxes.

'You bastard,' said John, spitting and drawing back his sleeves. Norman cowered in the darkness, covering his ears. The robot climbed nimbly across the counter and stood over the fallen Irishman. 'The tobacco and papers,' said he, extending a hand.

'Come now,' said John, 'be reasonable, what is all this about? You cannot go attacking people over a packet of baccy. Have you gone mad?' Whilst the robot was considering an answer to this question, Omally struck out with a devastating blow to the shopkeeper's groin. There was a sharp metallic clang and a sickening bone-splintering report. 'My God,' groaned John, falling back and gripping at his knee. 'What are you wearing, a bloody cast-iron codpiece?'

The robot was on him in a flash and, whilst Norman cowered in the darkness saying the rosary and praying desperately for the little brass wheel he had so recently set in motion to irrevocably break down, the martial duplicate lifted his struggling prize high above his head and cast him once more across the shop. This time, however, there was little to cushion Omally's fall. He struck the shop's aged front door, carrying it from its hinges, and flew out into the Ealing Road to land across the bonnet of a parked Morris Minor. It is certain that a lesser man would not possibly have survived such an assault, but

Omally, momentarily numbed, merely slid down the driver's side of the car bonnet and prepared once more to come up fighting. 'Nuts and noses' his Da always told him, and it was obvious that nuts were at present out of the question.

6

Jim Pooley slouched across the St Mary's Allotments dragging Omally's pickaxe and spade. At intervals he stopped and cursed, he was sure that he had got the worst part of this deal. Omally was probably even now sitting in Norman's kitchenette sipping celery hock and discussing contracts. Somehow John always came out on top and he was left holding the smelly end of the proverbial drain rod. The fates had never favoured the Pooleys. In Jim's considered opinion the fault lay with some neolithic ancestor who had fallen out with God. It had probably been over some quite trivial matter, but as was well known, the Almighty does have an exceedingly long memory and can be wantonly vindictive once you've got his back up. Pooley cursed all his ancestors *en masse* and threw in a few of Omally's just to be on the safe side. He was making more than a three-course meal out of the prospect of a bit of spade work and he knew it. Hopefully, a few digs at the thing and it would simply crumble to dust. At worst, a blow or two from the pickaxe would hasten the action. With all the millions to be made from Norman's wheel a few meagre pennies for a buried bedframe seemed hardly worth the candle.

Pooley slouched through the allotment gates and

off up Albany Road, the spade raising a fine shower of sparks along the pavement behind him. He turned into Abaddon Street and confronted the high fence of planking shielding the empty bombsite. With a heartfelt sigh Jim slid aside the hanging board which camouflaged the secret entrance, and climbed through the gap, backwards.

An ill-considered move upon his part. With a sudden strangled cry of horror Pooley vanished away through the gap. Omally's spade spun away from his fingers and tumbled downwards towards oblivion. By the happiest of chances Jim maintained his grip upon the pickaxe, whose head now jammed itself firmly across the gap. Where once there had been well-trodden ground, now there was complete and utter nothing. The bomb-site had simply ceased to exist. Jim was swinging precariously by a pickaxe handle over the sheer edge of a very very large pit indeed. It was the big daddy of them all, and as Jim turned terrified eyes down to squint between his dangling feet, he had the distinct impression that he was staring into the black void of space.

'Help!' wailed Jim Pooley, who was never slow on the uptake when he discovered his life to be in jeopardy. 'Fallen man here, not waving, but drowning . . . HELP!' Jim swung desperate feet towards the wall of the chasm, his hobnails scratched and scrabbled at the sheer cliff face but failed to find a purchase. 'Oh woe,' said Jim. 'Oh, help!'

A sickening report above drew Jim's attention. It seemed that the elderly head of Omally's pickaxe was debating as to whether this would be as good a time as any to part company with its similarly aged shaft. 'Oooooooh noooo!' shrieked Jim as he sank a couple of inches nearer to kingdom-come. Pooley closed his eyes and made what preparations he could, given so little time, to meet his Maker. Another loud crack above informed Jim that the pickaxe had made up his mind. The handle snapped away from the shaft and Jim was gone.

Or at least he most definitely would have been, had not a pair of muscular hands caught at his trailing arms and drawn him aloft, rending away his tweedy jacket sleeves from both armpits. A white-faced and gibbering Jim Pooley was dragged out through the gap in the fencing and deposited in a tangled heap upon the pavement.

'You are trespassing,' said a voice somewhere above him. 'These are your jacket sleeves, I believe.'

Jim squinted up painfully from his pavement repose. Above him stood as pleasant a looking angel of deliverance as might be imagined. He was tall and pale, with a shock of black hair combed away behind his ears. His eyes were of darkest jet, as was his immaculate one-piece coverall work suit. He wore a pair of miniscule headphones which he now pushed back from his ears. Jim could hear the tinkling of fairy-like music issuing from them.

'I was passing and I heard your cries,' the young man explained. 'You were trespassing you know.'

Jim climbed gracelessly to his feet and patted the dust from what was left of his jacket. He accepted the sleeves from the young man and stuffed them into a trouser pocket. 'Sorry,' said he. 'I had no idea. My thanks, sir, for saving my life.'

'It is no matter,' said the young man. 'Had you fallen you might have damaged some valuable equipment.'

'Oh, thanks very much.'

'It is no matter. This site has been acquired and excavated for a new complex to be built. Lateinos and Romiith Limited.'

'Oh, those lads.' Pooley blew on to the scorched palms of his hands. The 'Acquired for Lateinos and Romiith' signs had been blossoming upon all manner of vacant plots in Brentford recently, and the black-glazed complexes had been springing up overnight, like dark mushrooms. Exactly who Lateinos and Romiith were, nobody actually knew, but that they were very big in computers was hinted at. 'Don't let the marker posts on your allotment fall down,' folks said, 'or the buggers will stick a unit on it.'

'Well again, my thanks,' said Jim. 'I suppose you didn't see anything of an old bedframe while your lads were doing the excavations?'

'Bedframe?' The young man suddenly looked very suspicious indeed.

'Well, never mind. Listen, if you are ever in the Swan I would be glad to stand you a pint or two. Not only did you save my life but you saved me a good deal of unnecessary labour.' Pooley made as to doff his cap, but it was now many hundreds of feet beneath his reach. Cursing silently at Omally, he said, 'Thank you, then, and farewell.' Snatching up Omally's pickaxe head, he shambled away down

Abaddon Street leaving the young man staring after him wearing a more than baffled expression.

Jim thought it best to return Omally's axehead at once to his allotment shed before any more harm could come to it. He also thought it best not to mention the matter of the spade, which having been one of Omally's latest acquisitions was something of a favourite with him. Possibly then, it would be a good idea to slip around to Norman's and stick his nose once more against the kitchenette window.

As Jim came striding over the allotment ground, pickaxe head over shoulder and 'Whistle while you Work' doing that very thing from between his lips, he was more than a little surprised to discover Omally in his shirt-sleeves, bent over the zinc water-butt, dabbing at his tender places. 'John?' said Jim.

Omally looked up fearfully at the sounds of Jim's approach. His right eye appeared to have a Victoria plum growing out of it. 'Jim,' said John.

'You have been in a fight.'

'Astute as ever I see.'

'Outnumbered? How many of them, three, four?'

'Just the one.'

'Not from around these parts then. Circus strong-man was it? Sumo wrestler? Surely not . . .' Pooley crossed himself, 'Count Dante himself?'

'Close,' said Omally, feeling at his jaw, which had developed a most alarming click. 'Corner-shopkeeper, actually.'

Pooley hastily secreted the pickaxe head behind his back, turned over a handy bucket, and sat upon it. 'Not Norman? You jest, surely?'

48

'Look at my shirt-collar.' Omally waggled the frayed relic which now hung over his shoulder, college scarf fashion.

'Aren't they supposed to be sewn on all the way round?'

'I will punish him severely for this.'

'You fancy your chances at a rematch then?'

Omally shook his head painfully and whistled. 'Not I. Certainly the man has been personally schooled in the brutal, maiming, disfiguring art of Dimac by none other than that very Grand Master of the craft to whom you formerly alluded.'

'Gosh,' said Jim.

'I will have him down from a distance when he comes out to take in his milk tomorrow.'

'The half-brick?'

'Nothing less. I feel that we can forget all about ever-spinning wheels for the time being. Still all is not yet lost. How did you fare with the bed?' Omally peered over Jim's shoulder. 'Got it locked away somewhere safe then?'

Pooley scraped his heels in the dust.

'What have you done with the bed, Jim, and where are the sleeves of your jacket?'

'Ah,' said Jim, 'ah now.'

7

Norman sat in his kitchenette, dismally regarding the slim brass wheel spinning once more upon its table-top mountings. Over in the corner alcove his other self sat lifeless and staring, a gaping hole in its chest. Norman swung his leg over the kitchen chair and leaned his arms upon its worm-eaten back. The first run had not been altogether a roaring success. If Omally's bike had not chosen to intervene and trip the robot into the street, there seemed little doubt that it would have killed Omally there and then, merely to retrieve the tobacco from his pocket.

Norman chewed upon his lip. It was a regular Frankenstein's monster, that one. Not what he'd had in mind at all. Placid pseudo-shopkeeper he wanted, not psychotic android on the rampage. He would have to disconnect all the Dimac circuits and pep up the old goodwill-to-mankind modules. Possibly it was simply the case that the robot had been a little over-enthusiastic. After all, it had had his interests at heart. Norman shuddered. Omally had got away with the tobacco, and Hairy Dave had charged him fifty quid to shore up the front of the shop and screw a temporary door into the splintered frame. The robot had not been in service more than a couple of hours and it was already bankrupting him. Fifty quid for a half-ounce of Golden. And what if Omally decided to sue or, more likely, to exact revenge. It didn't bear thinking of. He would have to go round to the Swan later and apologize, stand Omally a few pints of consolation. More expense. The harassed shopkeeper climbed from his chair and sought out a quart of home-made sprout wine from the bottle-rack beneath the sink.

At length the Memorial Library clock chimed five-thirty p.m. in the distance, and upon the Swan's doorstep stood two bedraggled figures who, like Norman, had the drowning of their sorrows very much to the forefronts of their respective minds. Neville the part-time barman drew the polished bolts and swung open the famous door.

'By Magog!' said the pagan barkeep. 'Whatever has happened to you two? Should I call an ambulance?'

Pooley shook his head. 'Merely draw the ales.'

With many a backwards glance, Neville lumbered heavily away to the pumps. 'But what has happened to you both? Your eye, John? And Jim, your sleeves?' Neville pushed two brimming pints across the counter towards the straining hands of his two patrons.

'We were mugged,' said Omally, who was finding it hard to come to terms with the concept of defeat at the hands of a humble shopkeeper.

'Ten of them,' Pooley added. He had once read of a mugger's victim being carried into a pub and revived with free ale.

Neville had also read of it and took up a glass to polish. 'We live in troubled times,' he said profoundly. 'Ten and six please.'

Omally drew his boot away from his bruised ankle and pulled out several pound notes. Neville, who had never before seen the Irishman handling paper money in public, was anxious to see if they were the real McCoy. The wrinkled relic John handed him smelt a bit pony, but it did have a watermark. Neville rang up 'No Sale' and obligingly short-changed his customer. Omally slung the pennies into his trouser pocket without even checking them.

'Mugged then is it?' Neville almost felt guilty. 'Did you best the villains?'

'Did we?' Pooley raised his scorched palm and made chopping movements. 'The blackguards will think twice about molesting the folk of Brentford again I can tell you.'

'I see Norman is having his shopfront done up,' said Old Pete, who had sneaked in hard upon the heels of the two warriors.

Omally spluttered into his beer. 'Is that a fact?' said he.

'Had his shopfront mugged so I hear.'

'Give that gentleman a large dark rum,' said Omally.

The ancient accepted his prize and slunk away to a side-table with much malicious chuckling. Omally grudgingly paid up and joined Pooley, who had taken to hiding in a suitably darkened corner.

'I shan't be able to live with this,' said John, seating himself. 'That old one knows already; it will be all over the parish by morning.'

52

'But Norman?' said Pooley. 'I still can't quite believe it. Norman wouldn't hurt a spider, and by God his shop gives lodging to enough.'

'A lover of the insect kingdom he may be, but let humankind beware. The shopkeeper has finally lost his marbles. He took it out on me as though violence was going out of fashion.'

Jim sighed. 'This is a day I should certainly choose to forget. We have both paid dearly for our greed.'

John nodded thoughtfully. 'I suppose there are lessons to be learned from it. We have certainly learned ours the hard way.'

'Talking of lessons, I think your homework has just arrived.' Jim pointed over Omally's shoulder to where Norman now stood squinting about the bar.

John sank low in his high-backed chair. 'Has he seen me?' he whispered.

Pooley nodded. 'I'm afraid so, he's coming over.'

'When you hit him go for his beak, ignore the groin.'

'I'm not going to hit him, this is nothing to do with me.'

'Nothing to do with you? You started it, you and your money-making wheel . . .'

'Evening gents,' said Norman.

'Evening to you, old friend,' said Pooley, smiling sweetly.

Omally rummaged in his pockets and brought out a crumpled packet of cigarette papers and a somewhat banjoed half-ounce of tobacco. 'I never smoked it,' he said. 'You can have it back if you still want it.'

Norman held up his hand, which made Omally

flinch painfully. 'No, no, I have come to apologize. I really don't know what came over me, to lose my temper like that. I have been working too hard lately, I have a lot of worries. There is no permanent damage done, I trust?'

'I am still in a state of shock.' Omally sensed possibilities. 'Numb all over. I suspect a fracture here and there, though. I'll be off work a good while I shouldn't wonder.'

Norman nodded good-naturedly. Omally would be wanting his pound of flesh, better get it over with in one go. 'Might I buy you a drink?' he asked.

'You might,' said Omally, 'and we will see where it leads. If you could manage one for my companion also it would not go unappreciated.'

Norman smiled. He wondered whether or not to ask Pooley where the sleeves of his jacket were, but he presupposed the answer to be of a somewhat poignant nature, evoking images of such hardship and tragedy as to morally oblige the asker to purchase many further pints. 'I'll get the round in then,' said Norman, departing to the bar.

'One pint and one half-ounce up,' said John bleakly. 'What profit the day, I ask you?'

'Perk up, John, it can only get better, surely.' Pooley now sighted Old Pete hobbling purposefully towards them. 'Or possibly not.'

'Where's my bed then?' the ancient asked, prodding Omally's bruised shoulderblade with his stick. 'I've brought the money.'

'Money?' John did not recall mentioning a figure. 'How much did you bring?'

'Twenty quid.'

'Twenty quid.' Omally buried his face in his hands.

'It's enough, isn't it? You said it was an antique. I think twenty quid's a fair price if it's a good one. So where's my bed?'

'What bed?' asked Norman, who was bringing up the drinks.

'Omally said he had an antique bedstead to sell me, I want to see it.'

'The muggers took it,' said Jim Pooley helpfully. Omally, who was just coming to terms with a ten pound down payment for an antique bedstead at present being refurbished by mythical upholsterers, looked up at him in horror. 'Sorry,' said Jim, shrugging innocently.

'What muggers?' asked Norman.

'The ten who blacked his eye, or did you say there were twelve, John?'

'Ah,' said Norman stroking his chin. 'Come to think of it, I did see a gang of bully boys pushing an antique bed along down by the half-acre. Thought it odd at the time. A right evil-looking bunch they were, wouldn't have dared tackle them myself. No fighter me.'

'Bah,' snarled Old Pete. 'You're all bloody mad.' Turning upon his heel, he muttered a few well-chosen obscenities, and shuffled away.

'Thanks,' said Omally when the ancient was beyond earshot. 'I suppose that calls us square.'

'Good.' Norman passed the two newly-retired bedsalesmen their pints. 'Then, if you will pardon me, I think I will go and have a word with Old Pete. I have an old brass bed in my lock-up he might be interested in. The money will go somewhere towards meeting the cost of a new shopdoor. So all's well that ends well, eh? Every cloud has a silver lining and a trouble shared is a friend indeed.' With the briefest of goodbyes, Norman left the two stunned drinkers staring after him.

After a short yet very painful silence Omally spoke. 'You and your bloody big mouth,' said he.

Pooley turned up his ruined palms helplessly. 'Still,' he said, 'your reputation is saved at least.'

'You buffoon. There is no reputation worth more than five pounds and the man who is five pounds to credit needs no reputation whatever.'

'Ah well, let's look on the bright side. I think I can say without any fear of contradiction that nothing else can possibly happen to us today.'

It is of some small consequence to note that had Jim been possessed of that rare gift of foresight, even to the degree of a few short hours, he would certainly not have made that particular, ill-considered and totally inaccurate remark.

8

Brentford's only cinema, the Electric Alhambra, had closed its doors upon an indifferent public some fifty years ago. The canny Brentonians had shunned it from the word go, realizing that moving pictures were nothing more than a flash in the pan. Miraculously, the building had remained intact, playing host to a succession of small industries which had sprung up like mushrooms and died like mayflies. The last occupier, a Mr Doveston, Purveyor of Steam-Driven Appliances to the Aristocracy, had weathered it out for a full five years before burning his headed notepaper and vanishing with the smoke.

Now the crumbling edifice, about the size of the average scout hut and still sporting its original mock rococo stuccoed façade, was left once more alone with its memories. The projection room, which had served as governor's office to many a down at heel entrepreneur, now deprived of its desks and filing cabinets, suddenly took to itself once more. With the collapse of some lop-sided partitions, the old and pitted screen made a reappearance. But for the lack of seating and the scattered debris littering the floor, the ancient cinema emerged, a musty phoenix from its fifty-year hibernation.

The 'Sold' notice was up out front and rumour had it that the dreaded Lateinos and Romiith had the place earmarked for redevelopment. A light evening breeze rattled a corrugated iron shutter upon a glassless window, and something that looked very much like a giant feral tom stole across the floor. In the eaves a bat awoke and whistled something in an unknown dialect.

A gaunt and fragile shadow fell across an expanse of littered linoleum and a pale hand moved into a patch of light. Ghostly fingers drew away a cowled hood, revealing a head of pure white hair, an expanse of pallid forehead, and two eyes which glowed pinkly in the failing light. Surely we have seen this pale hand before? Known the Jason's fleece of snowy hair, and marvelled at the flesh coloured eyes? Can this be he who now dwells beneath, shunning the realm of sunlight and changing seasons? He who tills the subterranean waters in his search for Shamballa and its legendary dwellers in that world of forever night? Yes, there can be no doubt. The name of this seeker after the hidden truths below is well known to the folk of Brentford.

Soap Distant, it is he.

Soap spat his roll-up from between his teeth and ground it to oblivion beneath a boot-heel. He scrutinized the luminous chronometer upon his wrist and said, 'Ten thirty-two. They'll be a while yet.' He paced slowly to and fro, his shadow clattering soundlessly along the corrugated shutters to merge with the blackness as he moved beyond the range of the limited illumination. At length, his chronometer chimed the three-quarter hour, and Soap ceased his pacing. From without came sounds of approaching feet. Harsh footfalls echoing along the deserted street, accompanied by the sounds of foolish giggling and the occasional bout of coughing. 'Pissed again,' said Soap to himself, 'but no matter.'

The inebriated couple, one with a fat eye and the other sleeveless, came to a halt outside the cinema, and Soap could make out snatches of conversation that penetrated the numerous cracks in the wall.

'Who's on then?' asked a voice. 'Where's my opener?'

'William S. Hart,' said another. 'Open it with your teeth.'

'I never could abide that body's hat. I was always an Elmo Lincoln man myself. Christ, there goes a filling. You've got my opener, I remember you borrowing it.'

'I gave it back. Stand aside man, I need a quick jimmy.'

'Not in my doorway!' Soap threw open the shattered glass door to admit a stumbling Jim Pooley, flies gaping.

'By the grave,' said that man.

'By the roadside, but not in my doorway.'

Omally squinted towards the dark void which had suddenly swallowed up his companion. 'Soap?' said he. 'Soap Distant? I know that voice.'

'Come in out of the night, and pick your friend up.'

Omally bumbled in and Soap slammed shut the

door upon the Brentford night and, as far as John and Jim were concerned, life as they had once known it.

'Where's the bog?' wailed Pooley, struggling to his feet.

'Stick it out through a crack in the wall and be done.'

Pooley did so.

'How would you two care to make thirty quid for a swift half-hour's work?' Soap asked when Jim had finished his micturition.

Omally was about to say 'Each?' but after his experiences this day he thought better of it. 'I think that we would be very grateful,' he said. 'This has been a bad day for us both, financially.'

'If it is decorating,' said Jim, 'I do not feel that half an hour will be sufficient.'

'It is not decorating, it is a little matter, below.'

'Below . . . ah, well now.' Both Pooley and Omally had in chapters past had very bad experiences 'below'.

'Are you sure this is safe?' queried Omally.

'As houses.'

Pooley was more than doubtful. Sudden chill memories of former times spent beneath the surface of the globe flooded over him in an icy-black tide. 'You can have my half, John,' he said, 'I think I'll get an early night in.'

'It will take the two of you I am afraid.' Soap raised his palms in the gloom. 'It is a simple matter. One man cannot move an object, three men can.'

'Things are rarely as simple as they at first appear,' said Pooley with a wisdom older than his years.

'Come below then.'

With that, a thin line of wan light appeared in the centre of the floor, growing to a pale square illuminating a flight of stairs. Soap led the way down. 'Follow me,' he said gaily.

Pooley sucked upon a knuckle and, like the now legendary musical turn, dilly-dallied on the way. Omally nudged him in the back. 'Thirty quid,' he said.

Soap's newly-hired work-force followed him down the stairway, and above them the trapdoor slammed shut with what is referred to in condemned circles as a 'death-cell finality'. The stairway, as might be imagined, led ever down, its passageway hewn from the living rock. At length it unexpectedly debouched into a pleasant looking sitting-room, furnished with a pale green Waterford settee and matching armchairs, and decorated with Laura Ashley wallpaper. 'Nice, eh?' said Soap as he divested himself of his ankle-length cloak to reveal a natty line in three-piece tweed wear.

'Very,' said John. 'And the Russell Flints?' He pointed to a brace of pictures which hung above the hearth. 'No expense spared.'

'A gift from Professor Slocombe,' said Soap.

Pooley, who had a definite sway on, sank into a comfortable armchair.

'We have a couple of bottles of brown with us,' said John. 'If you have an opener?'

'It's a bit close down here.' Pooley fanned at his brow.

'It was a bit close down that hole today, wasn't it Jim?' Soap popped the stoppers from the bottles and ignored Pooley's similarly popping eyes.

'How did you know?'

'There's not much that goes on beneath ground level that I don't know something of. Those buggers from Lateinos and Romiith have been making my life a misery lately, sinking their damned foundations every which way about the parish.'

'Progress,' said Pooley in a doomed tone.

'Some say,' said Soap. 'Listen now, let us dispense with brown ale. I have some home-brewed mushroom brandy which I think you might find interesting.'

'That would be a challenge.'

''Tis done then.'

Something over an hour later, three very drunken men were to be found some three miles beneath the surface of planet Earth a-rowing in a leathern coracle over a stretch of ink-black subterranean water.

'Where are we?' asked an Irish surface-dweller.

'Below the very heart of London.'

'I don't recognize it.'

The splish-splash of the oars echoed about the vast cavern, eventually losing itself in the endless silence of the pit.

'How do you know which way we're going?'

Soap pointed to his luminous watch. 'Lodestone,' he said informatively.

'Oh, that lad.'

'There,' said Soap suddenly. 'Dead ahead, land ho.'

Before them in the distance an island loomed and as they drew nearer, the makings of a mausoleum wrought in marble, very much after the style of the Albert Memorial, made itself apparent.

'What is it?' Omally asked. 'King Arthur's tomb, don't tell me.' Soap tapped at his all but transparent nose. The coracle beached upon the shoreline and Soap stepped out to secure it to a frescoed pillar. The two inebriate sub-earth travellers shrugged and followed the pale man as he strode forward. 'It was never like this for Jerome K Jerome,' said Pooley.

The strange edifice was, if anything, a work of inspiration. Marble pilasters, cunningly wrought with carved tracery-work, soared upwards to dwindle into a high-domed ceiling which glittered with golden mosaic. Above, tapering gothic spires lost themselves in the darkness.

'Here it is,' said Soap. The two wonderers halted in their tracks. In the very centre of this Victorian folly stood something so totally out of place as to take the breath from their lungs. It was a cylinder of bright sparkling metal, but it was of no metal that any man of Earth had yet seen. It glistened with an oily sheen and swam through a spectrum of colours, reflecting mirror-like. A broad panel of what might have been glass, but probably was not, lay set into a section of the cylinder's apparent lid, and it was over this that the three visitors to this sunken marvel craned their necks.

'Strike me down,' said Jim Pooley.

'By Michael and the other lads,' said John Omally.

'Good, eh?' said Soap Distant.

'But who is he?'

Beneath the glazed panel, reclining upon satin cushioning, his head upon a linen pillow, lay the body of a man. He was of indeterminate age, his hair jet-black and combed away behind his ears. He had high cheek-bones and a great hawk of a nose. The face bore an indefinable grandeur, one of ancient aristocracy. From what was immediately visible, he appeared to be wearing a high wing-collared shirt, dark tie affixed with a crested stud, and a silken dressing-gown.

'He seems, almost, well, alive,' said Omally.

Soap pointed towards the gowned chest, and it could be clearly observed that it slowly rose and fell. 'Indubitably,' said he.

'But this thing? Who built it and why?'

'Best thing is to up the lid and ask him.'

Pooley had more than a few doubts upon this score. 'He looks pretty peaceful to me,' he said. 'Best to leave him alone. No business of ours this.'

'I think somehow that it is,' said Soap, and his tone left little doubt that he did.

'This thing doesn't belong,' said Omally. 'It is all wrong. Victorian mausoleum all well and good, but this? This is no product of our age even.'

'Herein lies the mystery,' said Soap. 'Give us a hand then, thirty quid for a quick heave.'

Pooley shook his head so vigorously that it made

him more dizzy than he already was. 'I think not, Soap. We are tampering with something which is none of our business. Only sorrow will come out of it, mark my words. "He that diggeth a pit will fall . . ."'

'I know all that,' said Soap. 'Kindly take hold of the top end. I had it giving a little.'

'Not me,' said Jim, folding his arms.

'Jim,' said John. 'Do you know the way back?'

'That way.' Pooley pointed variously about.

'I see. And do you think that Soap will guide us if we do not assist him?'

'Well, I . . .'

'Top end,' said Soap. 'I had it giving a little.'

The three men applied themselves to the lid of the glistening cylinder, and amidst much grunting, puffing, and cursing, there was a sharp click, a sudden rushing of air, and a metallic clang as the object of their efforts tumbled aside to fall upon the marble flooring of the *outré* construction. Three faces appeared once more over the rim of the metal sarcophagus.

The gaunt man lay corpse-like but for his gently-heaving chest; his face was placid and without expression. Then suddenly the eyelids snapped wide, the lips opened to draw in a great gulp of air and the chest rose higher than before. A cry arose from his mouth and three faces ducked away to reappear as a trinity of Chads, noses crooked above the coffin's edge. The occupant stretched up his arms and yawned loudly. His eyes flickered wildly about. He snatched at the coffin's side, and drew himself up.

He caught sight of the three now-cowering men, and a look of perplexity clouded his face. 'What year is this?' he demanded.

Omally volunteered the information.

'Too early, you have broken the seal.'

'Told you,' said Jim. 'Leave well enough alone I said. But does anybody ever listen to me, do they . . . ?'

'Shut up,' said Soap, 'and kindly give me a hand.' With the aid of Omally he helped the bemused-looking man in the dressing-gown up from the steely cylinder and into the upright position. 'Are you feeling yourself now?' The tall man, as now he revealed himself to be, did not reply, but simply stood stretching his limbs and shaking his head. 'Come quickly now,' said Soap. 'We must take him at once to Professor Slocombe.'

The journey back was to say the very least uneventful. The gaunt man in the dressing-gown sat staring into space while Omally, under Soap's direction, applied himself to the oars. Pooley, who had by now given up the ghost, slept soundly; his dreams full of six-horse accumulators coming up at stupendous odds and rocketing him into the super-dooper tax bracket. Of a sudden, these dreams dissolved as Omally dug him firmly in the ribs and said, 'We are going up.'

They made a strange procession through Brentford's night-time streets. The pale ghost of a man, now once more clad in a cloak and hood, leading a striking figure in a silk dressing-gown, and followed by two stumbling, drunken bums. Vile Tony Watkins who ran the Nocturnal Street Cleaning truck watched them pass, and a few swear words of his own invention slipped from between his dumb lips.

As the four men entered the sweeping tree-lined drive which swept into the Butts Estate, one lone light glowed in the distance, shining from Professor Slocombe's ever-open French windows.

The odd party finally paused before the Professor's garden door and Omally pressed his hand to the bolt. Through the open windows all could view the venerable scholar as he bent low over the manuscripts and priceless books. As they drew nearer he set his quill pen aside and turned to greet them.

'So,' said he, rising with difficulty from his leather chair. 'Visitors at such a late hour. And to what do I owe the pleasure?'

'Sorry to interrupt your work,' said Omally, who was now at the vanguard. 'But we have, well, how shall I put it . . . ?'

The tall man in the dressing-gown thrust his way past Omally and stood framed in the doorway. A broad smile suddenly broke out upon his bleak countenance. 'Professor,' said he. 'We meet again.'

'My word,' said the other. 'This is a most pleasant if unexpected surprise.'

The tall man stepped forward and wrung the ancient's hand between his own.

'You mean you know who he is?' asked Omally incredulously. Pooley was supporting himself upon the door-frame.

'Have you not been formally introduced?' enquired the Professor. Omally shook his head.

'Then allow me to do the honours. Soap Distant, John Omally, Jim Pooley, gentlemen, it is my pleasure to present Mr Sherlock Holmes, formerly of 221b Baker Street.'

'Your servant,' said that very man.

9

Professor Slocombe closed and bolted the long shutters upon his French windows. When his guests had seated themselves, he moved amongst them, distributing drinks and cigarettes. Sherlock Holmes lounged in a high leather-backed fireside chair and accepted a Turkish cigarette. 'My thanks, Professor,' said he. 'I see that you still favour the same brand.'

The Professor smiled and seated himself. 'I think that we have much to speak of, Sherlock. Your arrival here, although bringing me untold joy at the pleasure of meeting once more a noble friend, is, to say the least, a little perplexing.'

Holmes drew deeply upon his cigarette and blew out a plume of light blue smoke. 'It is a singular business and no mistake.'

Pooley and Omally, who had been shaking their heads in disbelief and generally making with the rumbles of suspicion, gave the thing up and slumped in their seats sipping liquor.

'It all truly began,' said Holmes, 'one foggy November night back in Eighteen-ninety. The previous month had been a successful one for me, having solved the remarkable case of the Naval Treaty and been more than adequately rewarded by Lord Holdhurst. I was experiencing a brief period of inactivity and as you will recall, such spells are no good to me. My soul as ever ached for the thrill of the chase, the challenge of pitting one's wits against some diabolic adversary, the blood coursing through the temples, the rushing of . . .'

'Quite so,' said Professor Slocombe. 'Your enthusiasm for your work is well-recorded. Upon this particular evening, however?'

'Yes, well, Watson and I had, I recall, just partaken of one of Mrs Hudson's most palatable tables of roast beef, and were setting towards consuming the last of a fine bottle of Vamberry's Port, when there came a violent knocking upon our chambers' door.'

'Probably the raven,' said Omally sarcastically.

'Do you mind?' said Professor Slocombe.

Holmes continued. 'I had heard no rappings upon the front door and knowing that Mrs Hudson was below in the kitchen was put immediately upon my guard. I had many enemies at that time you must understand. I counselled Watson to open the door whilst I remained at my chair, my revolver upon my knee, covered with a napkin.'

'Exciting so far isn't it?' said Pooley, yawning loudly.

'Riveting,' said Omally.

Holmes continued once more. 'The two figures who revealed themselves upon the door's opening were quite unlike any I have before encountered. I pride myself that I can accurately deduce the background and occupations of any man set before me, but those two left me baffled. They were tall and angular with almond-shaped eyes and oriental features. When they spoke I found their accents totally alien. Watson permitted them ingress into our rooms and although they refused both food and drink, saying that such were impossible for them, what they had to say was precise and to the point. They had come from the future, they said, naming a year well in advance of this. The world they came from was vastly different from that I inhabited, but they were adamant in offering few details. They were perplexed by a problem of utmost import which required the deductive reasoning of a mind their century did not possess. They had read in their history books of my humble exploits and felt I was the man to tackle the task. Was I willing?

'As you can imagine, I was more than doubtful and demanded some proof of their claims. What they showed me was more than adequate to convince me that they told no lie.'

'So what are you doing here?' asked Professor Slocombe. 'You should surely be away into the future by now.'

'No,' said Holmes. 'You must understand that their sophisticated equipment enabled them to traverse the fields of time in an instant, but it was not possible for them to take a being from the past forward into the future with them. I would have simply crumbled to dust upon my arrival. They were more subtle than this. They arranged for a secret place to be built for me where I might be placed in suspended animation. They would then travel forward in their time-eliminating conveyance, and unearth and resuscitate me almost on the instant.'

'Ingenious,' said the Professor, turning towards Soap Distant.

'How was I to know?' complained Soap.

'Well,' said the Professor, 'simply consider this a pleasurable stop off along your journey.'

'I think not,' said Holmes. 'Mr Distant here has broken the seal and disabled the means of my travel through time. Unless you happen to know of someone who can reset the apparatus, I would appear to be trapped.'

Professor Slocombe scratched at his head. 'That might present some problems,' said he. 'Although there is always the thought that your visitors are already in the far future discovering your loss and even now are setting back to search for you.'

'Such is, of course, the case, but they might search for a century and not find me.'

'What a load of old rubbish,' said Omally suddenly rising from his seat. 'Come, Jim, let us away to our beds.'

Pooley climbed to his feet. 'Be fair, Professor,' said he. 'This is all a bit too much over the top. I know that the world is always ready and waiting for one more Sherlock Holmes story, but this is pushing credibility to the very limit.'

'Do you doubt who I am?' Holmes rose to his full height and stood glaring at the deuce of Thomases.

'Be fair,' said Pooley, 'this is very far-fetched. You are at the very least extremely fictional in nature.'

'I am as fictional as you,' said Sherlock Holmes.

72

'Ha,' said Pooley. 'If you are the legendary doyen of detectives, answer me some questions.'

'Proceed.'

'All right then, what are the thirty-nine steps?'

'Wrong story,' said John Omally.

'Ah, well . . . In *The Red-Headed League* how did you know Vincent Spaulding was actually John Clay the murderer, thief, forger, and smasher?'

'By the white splash of acid on his forehead and his pierced ears.'

'Who lost his hat and his goose in *The Blue Carbunkle*?'

'Henry Baker.'

'What was the Musgrave Ritual?'

'Who was it? He who is gone. Who shall have it? He who will come. What is the month? Sixth from the first. Where is the sun? Over the oak. What was the shadow? . . .'

'Right, right, under the elm, we know.'

'Who was the Norwood Builder?' Jim asked.

'Jonas Oldacre.'

'And the Three Students?'

'Gilchrist, Danlat Ras and Miles McLaren.'

'And the plumber engaged to Charles Augustus Milverton's housemaid?'

'Myself,' said Holmes.

'Well you could have read them. I always believed that Holmes really did go over the Riechenbach Falls with Professor Moriarty. Those later stories were the work of a stand-in, I thought.'

'Bravo,' said Holmes. 'You are, of course, correct. You must understand that a certain amount of subterfuge was necessary to cover my disappearance. My exploits were chronicled by Doctor Watson, through an arrangement we had with a Mr Conan Doyle. I left it to him to continue with the stories after my supposed death.'

'Hang on,' said Pooley. 'Not that I can make any sense at all out of this, but if you went below under the pretence of dying in the Riechenbach Falls how could you possibly know about the Norwood Builder and the Three Students. That was four years later in *The Return of Sherlock Holmes*.'

'Ah,' said that man.

'Ah, indeed,' said Professor Slocombe. 'And Milverton's plumber?'

'Detective's license?' Holmes suggested.

'I give up,' said John Omally.

'Me also,' said Jim.

10

An inexpensive veneer of sunlight was thinly varnishing the rooftops of Brentford as Norman Hartnell took up the bundle of daily papers from his doorstep and hefted them on to his counter.

The early morning was always Norman's favourite time of the day. The nights were hell, for whilst his body slept upon its Hartnell Mark II Hydrocosipit, his brain went on the rampage, plotting, planning, and formulating, driving him on and on towards more preposterous and unattainable goals. But in the early mornings he could find just a little peace. He could peruse the daily papers as he numbered them up for delivery. He was in the privileged position of ever being the first in the parish to know the news.

On this particular morning, after a very rough night with his capricious cerebellum, Norman sliced away the twine bindings of the paper bundle with his reproduction Sword of Boda paperknife, eager to see what the rest of the world had been up to. As he tore the brown paper covering aside and delved into the top copy a singularly interesting piece met his eye, almost as if it had been simply waiting there to do so: GOVERNMENT GIVES RIGHT-HAND PLAN THE BIG THUMBS UP, he read.

An all-party-sitting last night gave the Lateinos and Romiith scheme for personalized account enumeration the go-ahead. This scheme will eventually make all previous systems of monetary exchange obsolete. Through laser implantation of a personal intromagnetic computer bar code, upon either the forehead or right hand of each individual member of society, it is thought that all crimes involving monetary theft will henceforth be made impossible. Also the need for passports or any other form of identity paper will be eliminated.

Linked with Lateinos and Romiith's master computer now currently in production, the system is expected to be instituted nationally within the next six months.

Norman whistled as he weighed up the concept. It was certainly ingenious: no-one could steal your money if you never carried any, or use your banker's card if they found your wallet in the street. With your own personal number printed on your forehead they'd have to cut your head off and pass it across the bank counter to get at your wealth. And with no money there would be no paperwork. No more monthly accounts, the money would pass invisibly, simply at the wave of a light-pen. The more Norman thought about it the more impressed he became. And the more miffed that he hadn't thought of it first.

He scribbled '15 Balfour' on to the first paper and turned it aside without giving the rest of the news even a cursory once-over. As it happened, there was little else but for wars and rumours of wars and a continuance of the black fly plague, so he certainly hadn't missed much.

In the curtained alcove in the kitchenette his

duplicate sat staring into space and thinking absolutely nothing whatsoever.

Neville the part-time barman stirred in his pit. He blinked open his good eye and stared up at the ceiling, which unaccountably appeared to have lowered itself by a couple of inches during the night. Drawing back his continental quilt, he set a monumental foot upon the worn Axminster. He yawned, stretched and considered his hands. 'Gross,' he thought. The wrists appeared massive, swelling from his pyjama sleeves to join great five-pound hams with pork sausages glued on to them. Whatever was happening to him was doing it at an accelerated rate of knots. 'It's getting out of control,' said Neville, as to the accompaniment of groaning floorboards, he arose from his bed. He would give up eating, he told himself, live exclusively on scotch, crispbread, and the occasional lime to stave off scurvy.

Neville staggered across the floor; pictures rattled upon the wall in time with his tread, and the entire upper storey of the pub seemed dangerously near to collapse. Why would nobody admit to seeing the state he was in? It had to be part of some enormous conspiracy aimed at ousting him from the Swan. Neville pawed at his swollen skull with a preposterous forefinger. Was that it? Was it the brewery having a go? That nest of vipers? Most horrors which befell him were directly attributable to them. Possibly they were bribing his patrons to ignore his plight? Or possibly they were hypnotizing him while he slept? Neville had read of slimming courses you got on cassettes and played while you were asleep. He'd never quite figured out how you turned the tape recorder on if you were fast a-kip, but it was a thought. He would search his apartments for hidden speakers as soon as he'd had his morning shower.

He struggled to squeeze himself through the bathroom doorway. Whatever it was, he would have to suss it out pretty rapidly or the entire building was going to come down about his ears.

Old Pete ambled along the Ealing Road, his tatty half-terrier, as ever, upon his heels. He had just paid his weekly visit to each of Brentford's two sub-post offices, in order to cash the two pension cheques the post office's errant computer chose weekly to award him. 'God bless the GPO,' the old reprobate had been heard to utter upon more than one occasion.

The ancient shuffled cheerfully along, rattling his stick noisily across Mrs Naylor's front railings in a manner calculated to rudely awaken the insatiable lady librarian from her erotic dreams. Young Chips chuckled to himself and gave the lampposts a bit of first-thing nasal perusal. Norman's new paperboy bustled out of the corner-shop, the heavy bag upon his shoulders, and mounted his bike. Chips momentarily bared his teeth, but it was early yet and he hardly felt up to making the effort.

Pete steered his way between the posts supporting Norman's shopfront and thrust open the temporary door. 'Morning Norman,' said he. The shopkeeper tucked away the copy of *Donkey Capers* he had been ogling and turned to seek out Pete's weekly quota of tobacco.

'How's the bed, Pete?' he asked. 'To your satisfaction I trust?'

'Magic,' said Old Pete.

'I'm so glad. Two ounces of Ships is it?'

'And a copy of the *Mercury*.' Old Pete pushed a crisp fiver across the counter.

'Ever had a credit card, Pete?' Norman rang up the sale on his cash register.

Old Pete shook his head. 'Don't think so. I have a membership card for the British Legion, and a special doo-dad which lets me travel free on the buses, other than that . . .' Old Pete scratched his snow-capped head. 'Had a pack of nudie playing-cards I bought in Cairo during the last lot. What does it do then?'

Norman did his best to explain.

'Oh no,' said Pete. 'Never had one of those. Mind you, I've never had a bank account. You selling them now, then?'

Norman shook his head. 'I was just reading this article. It seems that they are now obsolete. The Government are taking to stamping the numbers on people's heads.'

'Don't talk rubbish,' said Old Pete. 'Here now, what is this?' He pointed to his tin of tobacco.

'What is what?'

'This.' Old Pete indicated a series of little lines imprinted upon the lid. 'They weren't there last week. What are they?'

Norman took the tin and examined it. 'That's the

lads,' said he. 'Computer bar coding, it's called. That's what I was trying to explain. All commodities are now being printed with them. They tell you the price and the date you purchased the item and all that sort of thing. You pass a light-pen over them and it logs all the information straight into some master computer. The Government are simply taking the process a logical step further.'

'I don't like the smell of that,' said Old Pete. 'After all, you know when you purchased it and how much it costs, what do you need the lines for?'

Norman shrugged. 'Progress,' he said. 'We must all move with the times you know.'

'You must.' Old Pete snatched back his tobacco. 'For myself, I say a pox on the times. Now don't get me wrong, I have nothing against computers, one in particular there is which I hold in the highest esteem. But for progress in general . . .' Old Pete made the appropriate two-fingered gesture, snatched up his paper, which unbeknown to him bore a not dissimilar set of lines upon it, and shuffled from the shop.

'Daft old fogey,' said Norman to himself; but squinting around it did occur to him that every item he had ordered during the last few weeks possessed similar markings. No doubt it was all for the common good. There could not possibly be anything sinister at the back of it, surely? No, it was all part of a great masterplan to free society of crime and bring prosperity to all. Norman went off about his business, whistling, 'The Rock Island line is a mighty fine line'.

*   *   *

Jim Pooley was already upon his favourite bench. He had accosted Norman's paperboy and wrung from his clammy grip a copy of the *Sporting Life*. Yesterday had been a total disaster. His life savings, in the biscuit tin on the mantelpiece, were sadly depleted. In the dubious excitement of the night before, he and Omally had actually forgotten to ask Soap for the thirty quid. Such events were wont to dash any hopes Jim had for the future. He would simply have to pull off The Big One today and that was that.

Pooley scanned the pages in search of inspiration. Almost at once he spied out a little series of lines printed on the lower left-hand corner of the sixth page. 'Aha,' said Jim, 'a code, possibly masonic.' He recalled a discussion he had recently had with Professor Slocombe about what the ancient termed The Science of Numerology. The scholar was convinced that the answer to most if not all of existence could be divined by the study of numerical equivalents. It was all down to breaking the code. The Professor had, of course, said a great deal more at the time, but that was the general gist which Jim managed to take in. No knowledge was ever wasted upon the lad, for as his father, like Omally's, had told him somewhat obscurely when he was a lad, 'a dead bird never falls out of the nest.'

So here was a little offering, possibly a secret code, printed for the benefit of that dark order, The Bookie Brotherhood, who, as any good punter knows, are always tipped the wink in advance. Pooley turned quickly to the front page and his heart jumped for joy. It was true. He had Bob the bookie's *Sporting Life*. Oh, happy day.

'I've cracked it,' said Jim Pooley to the assortment of Brentford wildlife which watched him from the surrounding trees. The squirrels shook their heads and nudged one another. The pigeons turned their beaked faces aside and tittered into their wings. They had seen all this many times before. 'Eighteen lines,' Jim began, 'three groups of six, thick ones and thin ones, now how exactly does this work? Six six six, what might it mean?'

Pooley ran his Biro down the list of runners for the first race, six horses. The first thick line in the first group was number four. It was an outsider, the odds were enormous. Still it was worth a try. If he got it wrong today he could always steal Bob's paper again on the morrow. Jim scribbled the horse's name on to a betting-slip and applied himself to the next race. For the fourth, fifth, and sixth races, he returned to the three groups of lines and selected the second thick bar in each sequence. Satisfied that, even if he was incorrect, he had at least performed this daily task with speed and alacrity, Jim took out his exercise book and made an attempt to calculate his potential winnings. The eventual figure was so large that the last row of noughts flowed off the edge of the page. Pooley folded his betting-slip into his breast-pocket and tucked away his exercise book. 'That will do nicely thank you,' he said, leaning back upon the bench to enjoy the air.

Professor Slocombe sat taking a late breakfast with

his Victorian guest. Mr Sherlock Holmes ate sparingly as he studied the day's newspaper. 'I see,' he said at length, as he pushed the tabloid aside, 'that very little has changed since my day.'

'Come now, Holmes,' said the Professor. 'More strides forward have been taken this century than during the previous five.'

'I think not.'

'And what of technological advancement, telecommunications, space travel? We possess sciences now that in your day were undreamed of.'

'And what of poverty, squalor, and cruelty? What of injustice, intolerance, and greed? Has your age of wonder succeeded in abolishing those?'

Professor Slocombe shook his head. 'Sadly, no,' said he.

'Then little has changed. If anything, these horrors have been intensified. Details which I read here would never have been made public knowledge in my time. But if what I see is typical, and such I have no reason to disbelieve, then I am appalled to find that with the resources you now possess, little has been done.'

Professor Slocombe was for once lost for words, and chewed ruefully upon a piece of toast.

'And so I am prompted to ask,' Holmes continued, 'your reason for stranding me in this most dismal age.'

The toast caught in the old man's throat and he collapsed red-faced into a violent fit of coughing.

'Come now,' said Holmes, patting him gently upon the back, 'surely you did not think to deceive me with your display of apparent surprise at my arrival? My favourite cigarettes are in your case and my tobacco in the humidor. You serve me with a Ninety-two Vamberry, by now surely a priceless vintage. I could enumerate another twenty-three such facts regarding the "singular case of the reanimated detective", but I do not believe it to be necessary. Why have you called me here, Professor?'

The scholar took a sip of coffee and dabbed at his lips with a napkin. He rose carefully from his chair and took himself over to the French windows, where he stood, his back to the detective, staring out into his wonderful garden. 'It is a bad business,' he said, without turning.

'I have no doubt of that.'

'I am not altogether certain at present as to what steps can be taken. There is very much I have to know. I cannot face it alone.'

Holmes took out his greasy, black clay pipe from the inner pocket of his dressing-gown and filled it from the Professor's humidor. 'So,' said he, 'once more we are to work together.'

'Let me show you something and then you can decide.' Professor Slocombe lead his gaunt visitor through the study door, along the elegant hall, and up the main staircase. Holmes followed the ancient up several more flights of stairs, noting well the narrow shoulders and fragile hands of the man. The Professor had not aged by a single day since last they met so very long ago.

The two were now nearly amongst the gables of the great house, and the final staircase debouched into an extraordinary room, perfectly round, and some ten or twelve feet in diameter. It was bare of furniture save for a large, circular table with a white marble top which stood at its centre and an assortment of cranks and pulleys which hung above it. The walls were painted the darkest of blacks and there was not a window to be seen. Holmes nodded approvingly, and the Professor said, 'Of course, a camera obscura. This simple device enables me to keep a close eye upon most of the parish without the trouble of leaving my house. Would you be so kind as to close the door?'

Holmes did so, and the room plunged into darkness. There was a sharp click, followed by the sound of moving pulleys, and clattering chains. A blurred image appeared upon the table-top, cast down through the system of prisms linked to the uppermost lens mounted upon the Professor's roof. Slowly the image was brought into focus: it was a bird's-eye view of the Memorial Library. Before this, draped across the bench, lay Jim Pooley, evidently fast asleep. The Professor cranked away and the rooftop lens turned, the image upon the table swam up towards the High Street. It passed over Norman's corner-shop and the two observers were momentarily stunned by the sight of the shopkeeper alone in his backyard, apparently breaking up paving-stones with his bare hands.

'Most probably Dimac,' Professor Slocombe explained. 'It has come to be something of the vogue in Brentford.'

'I favour Barritso, as you well know,' said Holmes.

85

'Now,' said Professor Slocombe, as he swung the lens up to its highest mounting and passed the image along the borders of the Brentford Triangle, 'what do you see?'

Holmes cradled his chin in his right hand and watched the moving picture with great interest. 'Some trick of the light, surely?'

'But what do you see?'

Holmes plucked at a neat sideburn. 'I see a faint curtain of light enclosing the parish boundaries.'

'And what do you take it to be?'

Holmes shook his head. 'Some natural phenomenon perhaps? Something akin to the aurora borealis?'

'I think not.' The Professor closed the rooftop aperture and the room fell once more into darkness. Holmes heard the sound of a key turning in a lock, and a thin line of wan light spread into the room from a previously concealed doorway. 'This is a somewhat private chamber,' the Professor whispered as he led the detective through the opening and into a gabled gallery set in the very eaves of the roof. What light there was entered through chinks between the slates. The old man struck flame to an enamelled oil-lamp, and the golden light threw a long and cluttered garret into perspective. It was lined on either side with tall, dark filing cabinets. Bundles of bound documents, some evidently of great age, were stacked upon and about these, or spilled out from half-opened drawers.

'As you can observe, I have been following the course of this particular investigation for a good many years.'

Holmes ran his finger lightly over the waxen paper of a crumbling document exposing a seal imprinted with the date 1703. 'And all this has been amassed to the furtherance of one single goal?'

The Professor nodded. 'It is the product of many lifetimes' work and yet now, with all this behind me, I am still lost for a solution to the matter now closely pressing upon us.'

'But what is it, Professor? What have you found and what do you yet seek? Tell me how I might aid you, you have but to ask.'

'What I have here is evidence. But it is evidence of a most unique nature, for it is evidence of a crime which is yet to be committed; the greatest crime of them all. I have my case together and I can predict fairly accurately as to what will occur and when, but I have yet to come up with a solution as to a way that I might prevent it happening.'

'But what is it?'

'Armageddon. The apocalypse,' said Professor Slocombe. 'The coming of the millennium. Did you think that I would have gone to all this trouble for anything less?'

Sherlock Holmes shook his head slowly. 'I suppose not,' said he.

I I

Norman's automaton had finished breaking up the stones and resurfacing the shopkeeper's backyard. Now he smacked the dust from his duro-flesh palms and returned to the kitchenette to brew up some tea for his living double. Norman watched his approach through the grimy rear window. He was doing very well now, he thought. There were no more signs of violent temperament now that his circuitry had been appropriately readjusted. He would give the creation a couple of days to redecorate the premises then, if all seemed sound, get him back on shop work. Although things had got off to a poor start, Norman was certain that the future looked promising, and that he would soon be able to dedicate all his time to his greatest project yet.

The scientific shopkeeper grinned lop-sidedly and struck up a bit more whistling. He sought about on his shelves for a chocolate bar which was still in date to munch upon. Through the open shop-doorway he spied another whistler. Jim Pooley was striding by at a jaunty pace en route to Bob the bookie. Here Jim would lay on one of the most extraordinary and ill-conceived Super-Yankee accumulators ever recorded in the annals of bookmaking history.

Norman gave up his futile search, made a mental

observation that when the great day dawned and all his wares were computer-coded he would have no need to bother with such trifles as actually ordering new stock, and repaired to the kitchenette for a cuppa.

Jim Pooley pushed open Bob's armoured-glass door and entered the betting shop. As is well known, to any follower of the sport of kings, the interior of such establishments vary by but the merest detail, be they based upon some busy thoroughfare in John O'Groats or down a back alley in Penge. The betting shop is always instantly recognizable to be the thing of beauty that it is: the grey, fag-scarred linoleum floor, and the ticker-tape welcome of slip stubs; the heavily-barred counter, twelve-inch black and white tellies; the rarely-scrubbed blackboards, displaying hieroglyphics that even the now legendary Champollion would find himself hard-pressed to decipher.

Jim squinted through the blue fog of Havana cigar smoke towards its source. Behind the portcullis, pulling upon his torpedo, sat Bob the bookie.

'In for another hiding?' the millionaire enquired.

Jim smiled and waggled his betting-slip. 'Today is the day,' quoth he.

Bob stifled a yawn and rubbed a newly-purchased diamond ring upon the lapel of his smoking-jacket. The Koh-i-Noor glittered flawlessly in its setting as Jim slid his slip beneath the titanium security bars of the counter fortress. Bob held the crumpled thing at arm's length and examined it with passing interest. 'I have a new pocket calculator,' he told Pooley.

'Personalized for you by Cartiers of Paris, no

doubt,' said Jim. 'Wrought in platinum and fashioned into the likeness of a golden calf. Your initials in jade?'

'Something of the sort.'

'I have no wish to see it, but should it give you some small pleasure, I suppose I owe it to you. Times are, I see, as ever against you.'

'It is a hard life.'

'Oh, is it now? To tell you the truth, spending so much of my time, as I do, in the sensual pleasures of unashamed luxury, I rarely have time to notice.'

'It is electric,' Bob continued, 'solar-powered in fact. It will work for a thousand years without maintenance.'

'Handy,' said Jim.

'But nevertheless useless.'

'Oh dear, and why might that be?'

'Well, for all the wondrous ingenuity of its creators, the lads have overlooked one small detail, and have denied it the facility to calculate any sum greater than nine hundred and ninety-nine million, nine hundred and ninety-nine thousand, nine hundred and ninety-nine pounds.'

'The fools,' said Jim.

'My sentiments entirely. Now should your selection,' he waved Pooley's betting-slip sadly before him, 'come up at the predicted odds, I feel that my calculator will find itself many zeros below the mark.'

'Don't worry,' said Pooley sympathetically, 'I have already worked it out in my head. I'll have just the pound on it please, Bob.'

'As you wish, and shall you pay the tax?'

'Oh yes, I have no wish to upset the country's economy. Such is not fair to the Government.'

'As you will then.' Bob pushed Pooley's slip into the machine, and Jim passed him the exact amount in pennies and halfpennies. 'I'll be back around five to settle up,' said he.

Bob nodded and tinkered with his watch. 'Video roulette,' he said. 'The latest thing from Lateinos and Romiith.'

'A pox on those two lads,' said Pooley. 'And good-day.'

Jim folded his betting-slip into his breast-pocket, left the fog-bound bookie, and strolled off along the Ealing Road. He had not gone but fifty yards when he found himself confronted by a most extraordinary little scene. A group of onlookers was gathered in a tight knot about the pavement doors of the Swan's cellar. Pooley craned his head above the assembled throng and was more than a little surprised at what he saw.

Somehow, inexplicably jammed into the four-foot opening, was Neville the part-time barman.

'Someone get me out,' wailed this man, his voice soaring in pitch and volume above that of the rumbling spectators. 'By the gods somebody, please!'

Pooley rubbed at his eyes. This was an impossibility surely? Thin man trapped in fat opening; such things could not be reasonably expected to occur. But strange as strange, here they were doing that very thing. Neville spied out Pooley's face bobbing amongst the sea of others. 'Jim,' he shouted. 'Help me out will you?'

Pooley hastened to oblige. 'Stand back now, ladies and gents,' he said. 'Give the man some air now, please.'

'On your bike, Pooley,' said Old Pete, who had a particularly good place near the front. 'We're not going to miss any of this.'

'Be fair,' Jim pleaded. 'You can see he's in a bad way, give the lad a break.'

'How do you suppose it's done, then?' said Old Pete. 'Mirrors, do you think?'

Pooley shook his head. 'I've really no idea, might it be what they call a shared vision? I've read of such things.'

'Possibly that. When I was in the East, a lad in the regiment took us to see the Indian rope trick. We saw the whole thing. Magician throws up a rope, it hangs in the air, he climbs up then vanishes, then he climbs down, the whole thing.'

'Really?'

'Oh yes, well a bloke with us took pictures and when we got them back, what did they show?'

'Tell me.'

'They showed a mendicant standing beside a coil of rope. Every picture the same. Now what lied, the camera's eye, or our own?'

Neville, whose face had deepened in colour by several shades during the course of this fascinating conversation, let out a great and terrible scream.

'Keep it down, Neville,' said Old Pete. 'Can't you see we are trying to apply ourselves to the situation.'

'Oh, so sorry,' said the bunged-up barman.

'We are doing our best,' Pooley assured him. 'It is

just, well, the situation has some rather unique qualities, too hasty a decision could result in disaster.'

'Tell you what,' said Old Pete, 'I'll go through the bar and into the cellar; I'll pull and you push.' Pete scuttled away through the saloon-bar door.

'There,' said Pooley. 'Help is at hand, do not worry.'

'I'm running out of breath,' mumbled the barman. 'I'll die here in full public gaze. The humiliation, the shame. What a way to go.'

'Come on now,' said Jim, doing his best to usher away the crowd which now spilled out into the Ealing Road. 'Be off about your business, please.' He shouted down towards the cellar, 'Pete, are you there?' But there was no reply. 'Now what is he playing at?' asked Pooley. 'I'll slip inside and see if he's all right.' Jim slipped into the bar, leaving the mob to close in about the howling barman. He joined Old Pete up at the bar.

'Took your time, didn't you?' the elder enquired. 'Losing your grip then, is it? Here, have one on the house.' He poured Jim a large whisky from the barman's reserve stock. 'Cheers,' he said.

'Down the hatch,' Pooley replied. 'No offence meant, Neville.'

'So,' Old Pete continued, 'what do you take it to be, publicity stunt do you think?'

Jim shrugged hugely. 'You've got me. I can't see how it works, but he does appear to be wedged in solid.'

'Nah, he's probably up on blocks. No doubt the

brewery are planning a Billy Bunter night or some such abomination.'

'Perish the thought.' Jim Pooley crossed himself and tossed back his scotch. 'Any more left in that bottle?' he asked.

Outside, exciting things were about to happen. Leo Felix, Brentford's Rastafarian used-car dealer, had been passing by in his tow-truck; seeing the crowd gathered outside the Swan, the free-ale sign had flashed up in his colourful head. Now, he decided, might be a good time to make his peace with Neville, who had but recently barred him, once more, for life. Even as Pete and Pooley chit-chatted in the bar, Leo, dreadlocks a-dangle, was busily engaged in hooking Neville up to the winch on the back of his truck. 'I and I soon have you back on your feet,' he assured Neville. The part-time barman seemed strangely reticent about accepting this particular offer of help, and while the crowd applauded and offered encouragement, he shrieked and wriggled and invoked the aid of his pagan gods. The way things were going he felt that he would soon be getting the opportunity to address them face to face.

Leo was by now up in his cab. 'Jah, Jah Willing,' he said as he revved the engine and ram-jammed his thumb down on the hoist button. The cheering crowd parted as the hoist took up the slack.

'Ooooooooooh,' went Neville as the improvised harness tightened beneath his armpits.

'Quite mild for the time of year,' said Jim as he poured two more drinks.

'Fair,' said Pete. 'I've seen better.'

Young Chips pricked up his ears as outside the barman's scream rose to a frequency beyond human register. Sickening, bone-crunching sounds were emanating from the barman's middle regions and the cement about the cellar door's metal frame was splitting and shivering. The crowd drew back in sudden alarm; this was no laughing matter. 'Switch your winch off, Leo,' shouted somebody. 'You'll pull him in half.' Leo thumbed the button. He had been meaning to have it fixed for some time. The thing popped out from the dashboard and fell into his upturned palm. 'Haile Selassie!' said Leo Felix.

'   ,' went Neville the part-time barman.

'Back your truck up then for God's sake,' shouted another somebody, 'we'll try and get the cable off him.'

Leo hastened into the driving seat and stuck the customized Bedford into reverse. Gear cogs ground together adding further screams of distress to those already being loudly voiced.

He had been meaning to get the reverse fixed for some time.

With an almighty clunk the gear found its housing, and lodged into it as firmly as a barman in a beer cellar. Leo clawed at the gear-stick but it would not shift by an inch. His knackered tow-truck, sick to the worn treads with its constant bad treatment, had chosen this of all times to exact revenge upon its Caribbean tormentor. Tearing his keys from the dash, Leo Felix leapt pale-faced from the cab. The malevolent tow-truck rolled relentlessly backwards, bound for the crowd and the struggling barman.

As the unstoppable vehicle gathered speed, those free to do so hastily took to their heels. Neville stared up, his good eye starting from its socket. The acrid smell of exhaust fumes filled his brain, and a rear number-plate which read NEM 1515 began to engulf his world.

It looked very much like strawberry jam time for Neville the part-time barman. The truck's engine roared like some beast loosed from the bottomless pit, and ground upon its hellish course. With one final despairing gasp Neville passed from consciousness, which as it happened was quite a shame because he missed the very best bit.

As the crowd burst asunder in a screaming panic-torn explosion, a heroic figure leapt into the fray. He plunged through the mass of fleeing humankind and took up a stance between the comatose barman and the roaring instrument of doom. The feet of this titan were firmly rooted upon the pavement and his face was a cold mask of determination. His eyes shone with a strange inner light. With a single sudden lunge forward, he grasped the tailgate of the wheel-screeching vehicle and stopped it dead in its tracks. The tyres squealed upon the pavement, raising black clouds of tread. With superhuman effort Neville's deliverer dragged it up from the ground. The engine whined into overdrive and exhaust smoke enveloped him in a great monoxide cloud of death. Struggling beneath the weight of the possessed vehicle, he bore it aloft, and held it high above his head. The truck rocked and shuddered, howling like a banshee, but in a moment he had done with it.

Brentford's St George cast down the mechanical dragon, bursting out its tyres, scrambling its axles, and driving its engine to ruination upon the cold stones of the pavement. As the smoke cleared, small knots of the cowardly crowd stared back in wonder. The hero calmly knotted the slackened hoist cable about his hand and tore it from its mountings. He turned slowly towards Neville and, freeing him from his hangman's harness, stooped and carefully drew him up to pavement level, where he laid him gently to rest.

Before the crowd could arouse itself from its slack-jawed wonderment, engulf the hero, and raise him shoulder-high, Norman silently turned away from the scene of his glory and strode back to his corner-shop.

12

The ambulance bells had long died away into memory when three men came strolling along the Ealing Road. One was bowed and ancient, walking with the aid of a slim ebony cane, a mane of snow-white hair trailing out behind him. Another was tall and gaunt with a great hawk of a nose, clad in an oddly Victorian tweed suit. As to the last, he was Irish and wanted his thirty quid.

As these three approached the Swan, Sherlock Holmes suddenly laid a gentle palm upon the Professor's chest and said, 'Now what do you make of that!'

Professor Slocombe shook his old head. 'Cellar doors ajar, a barman somewhat remiss in his duties?'

'Oh, no,' said Holmes. 'Much more. And what here?'

The elder perused Leo's defunct tow-truck parked at the kerb, its back axle supported by two piles of red flettons. 'Unusual bravado upon the part of the local criminal fraternity?' he suggested.

'I think not.' Holmes drew out his glass and as Omally watched him, with one eye forever straying towards the saloon-bar door, he dropped to all fours and perused the pavement.

'How many entrances to this cellar?' asked Holmes, looking up.

'Just that,' said Omally. 'And a door behind the bar.'

'I see.' Holmes examined the blackened skid marks. 'Interesting,' said he.

'Riveting,' said John. 'Might we step inside now, please?'

Holmes rose to his feet and patted dust from his trouser knees. 'I think so,' he said.

Omally led the way and the three men entered the bar. Pooley, who with Old Pete's aid had long ago finished the bottle of Neville's reserve, rose unsteadily to greet them. Omally eyed him with great suspicion. 'Have you seen Soap this morning?' he asked.

Pooley shook his head. 'You've missed all the excitement.'

'Obviously. Whose round is it?'

'I'll get these,' said Professor Slocombe. 'Holmes?'

'A small sherry,' the detective replied. 'And a small word with Mr Pooley here.'

'Oh yes?' asked the half-drunken Jim.

'The fellow with the beard serving behind the bar is not, I believe, the regular barman.'

Pooley squinted disgustedly towards Croughton the pot-bellied potman, who was now up to his elbows in froth behind the beer engines. 'Certainly not,' said he.

'And the regular barman, a gentleman of some standing in this community, he is not one who would leave the bar during a lunchtime session without a very good reason?'

'Not Neville.'

'So I would be right then in assuming that the fat gentleman who was until recently stuck fast in the cellar doors was this very Neville?'

'You what?' said John Omally. 'What happened here, Jim?'

'I'll do my best to explain,' said Pooley, tumbling backwards from his bar stool. 'But for now I think I need to go to the toilet.'

It was quite some time before Pooley re-emerged looking a little more sober. During the period of his absence Holmes had gleaned all the necessary information from other sources, finished his sherry, and had taken himself off to places elsewhere. Jim relocated his behind upon the bar stool. Looking up at the battered Guinness clock he asked, 'Anybody know what won the one forty-five?'

'Ahriman Boy,' said Old Pete. 'I get Free Radio Brentford on my deaf aid. The commentator was having a coronary by the sound of it.'

Pooley struggled a moment to comprehend this intelligence. Slowly he withdrew his betting-slip and peered between his fingers at his selection. 'By the gods,' said he. 'Did you hear the SP?'

'Sixty-six to one,' Old Pete replied. 'A quid or two there for the outside better.'

Pooley spread his betting-slip before him on the bar counter, 'I am sixty-six quid in the black,' said he.

Omally peered over his shoulder. 'Then order me a pint of froth quickly then, Jimmy boy,' said he. 'I suppose there is no chance that was your only bet of the afternoon?'

'Actually, no,' said Jim. 'I have an accumulator here.'

'A four-horse Yankee?'

'No, a six-horse Super-Yankee.'

'I'll get my own in then.'

'Nobody has any faith in me whatever,' Jim told Professor Slocombe.

'No?' the old man shook his head in wonder. 'Then let me at least get you another drink in. Are you feeling a little better now?'

'A temporary lapse,' said Jim. 'Your man from below puts the wind up me more than a little.'

'The two o'clock's on,' said Old Pete. 'Got one in here, Jim?'

Pooley nodded. 'Lucifer Lad.'

'Want to listen?' Old Pete took out his deaf aid and turned up the volume. The Mickey Mouse voice of the commentator tinkled out the race as three men, at least, knotted their fists and offered up with small sounds of encouragement for the game outsider. Lucifer Lad romped home at sixty-six to one.

'My brain's gone,' said Pooley. 'Can anybody work it out?'

'You don't want to think about it, Jim,' said the Professor. 'Let us just say that it is a goodly sum.'

'How goodly, tell me.'

'Four thousand, three hundred and fifty-six pounds.'

They brought Jim round with the contents of the soda siphon.

'Jim,' said John, drawing him up by the lapels,

'now wake up. What kind of deal have you done with Bob?'

'The six-horse special as ever,' mumbled Pooley. 'Six winners or nothing.'

'You buffoon.' Omally threw up his hands, 'If you'd had another winner you'd get a percentage even with a couple more seconds or thirds. You'd be a thousand pounds in profit now. There is no such thing as a six-horse Super-Yankee, such things are myths. An ITV-seven there is, that bookies laugh at as they fly off to their holidays in the Seychelles. Give me that slip.' Pooley pushed it across the counter. 'Anybody got a paper?' Pooley brought his out. 'Did you pay the tax?' Pooley nodded. 'You bloody buffoon.'

'Tell me again how rich I am,' said Jim. 'Just so I can hear it.' Omally dollied it out on his fingers. By the time he had finished Old Pete said, 'The two-fifteen's on.'

Bob the Bookie was enjoying a most unpleasant lunch at The Bonny Pit Lad in Chiswick. The tenant of this dire establishment, who, as the result of some major brainstorm, had convinced himself that 'Mining Pubs' were going to be the next big thing, had borrowed a considerable sum from Bob to transform the place from a late Victorian money-spinner to a coalface catastrophe. The pit-props and stuffed ponies, the stark wooden benches and coal-dust floor had proved strangely uninviting to the Chiswick drinking fraternity. Even in those winter months, when lit by the cosy glow of Davy Lamps, there was at least a good fire burning in the hearth.

Bob the bookie had, of course, extended the tenant's credit to the point that he now owned the controlling interest in the place. The plans for the luxury steak-house it was shortly to become were already drawn up and in his safe. As he sat alone in the deserted bar devouring his 'snap', Bob pondered upon what far-flung tropical beach he might park his million-dollar bum at the weekend.

Antoine the Chauffeur entered the bar in a flash of white livery, bearing upon a silver platter the computer print-out of the latest racing update just received through the Lateinos and Romiith in-car teleprinter. The telexed message that Jim Pooley, through merit of his win in the two-fifteen was now two hundred and eighty-four thousand, one hundred and ninety-six pounds up put the definite kibosh on the apple crumble end of Bob's Cornish pasty.

'You bloody buffoon,' went John Omally. 'You'd be rich, you bloody big buffoon.'

'It hasn't changed me,' said Jim. 'I'm still your friend. Lend me a pound and I'll get them in.'

'Are we all aboard for the two-thirty?' asked Old Pete. 'What is your selection, Jim?'

'Seven Seals.' Pooley checked his slip.

'Sixty-six to one,' said Old Pete.

Omally pressed his hands to his temples. 'I just knew he was going to say that,' he groaned.

Exactly how Seven Seals, who had been running a very poor eighteenth, actually managed to catch up and overtake the favourite in the last six furlongs was a matter for experts in that particular field to ponder upon for many moons yet to come.

'You are definitely ahead now,' said John Omally. 'I make that eighteen million, seven hundred and fifty-six thousand, nine hundred and thirty-six pounds at the very last. A tidy sum I would call that.'

'Lend me another quid,' Pooley pleaded. 'I think I'd like to buy a cigar.'

As he steered Bob the bookie's Roller through the crush of lunchtime traffic in the Chiswick High Road, Antoine the Chauffeur leafed through the 'Situations Vacant' column of the *Brentford Mercury*. Bob sat quivering in the back, shaking from head to toe, his knuckles jammed into his mouth. The in-car teleprinter punched out the runners for the two forty-five. There it was, Millennium Choice at sixty-six to one, and the runners coming under starter's orders. Bob punched away at his golden calculator but the thing merely rang up 'No Sale' and switched itself off in disgust.

'Do I get any redundancy money?' Antoine enquired politely.

'They're off,' bawled Old Pete.

The Swan's crowd knotted its fists and shook them in time to Mickey's little voice. Cries of encouragement were obviously out of the question, as to hear anything of the race required a great deal of breath-holding and ear-straining, but the patrons went about this with a will. Their faces like so many gargoyles, veins straining upon temples, and sweat trickling through the Brylcreemed forelocks. They took up the universal stance of punters, legs apart and knees slightly bent, bums protruding, and chins to the fore. They were phantom jockeys to a man, riding upon the commentator's every word. Nerves were cranking themselves into the red sector.

Millennium Choice was laying a not altogether favourable sixth in the six-horse race.

'Come on man!' screamed Omally, who could stand it no longer, his outcry breached the dam and the floodtide hit the valley floor.

'Go on my son! Give him some stick! The whip, man, use the whip! Dig your heels in! Millennium, Millennium, Millennium . . . Millennium . . .' The voices tumbled one upon another rising to a deafening cacophany.

Old Pete snatched up his hearing aid and rammed it back into his ear. If the entire pub had decided to go off its head he felt no reason why he, at least, should be deprived of the result.

Bob the bookie's Roller was jammed up at the Chiswick roundabout but his Lateinos and Romiith Vista Vision portable television was working OK. As Millennium Choice swept past the post a clear six lengths ahead of the field Antoine calmly drew a red circle about a likely vacancy.

Bob looked up towards the flyover soaring away into the distance. I'll have to sell that, he thought.

'Who won it? Who won it?' The Swan's lunchtime crowd engulfed Old Pete. 'Out with it.'

The ancient raised his thumb. 'Your round I think, Jim.'

The crowd erupted and stormed the bar, Croughton the pot-bellied potman took to his heels and fled.

Omally laboured at his exercise book. 'I can't work it out,' said he, tearing out great tufts of hair. 'Professor, please?'

The old man, who had worked it out in his head, wrote one thousand, two hundred and thirty-seven million, nine hundred and fifty-seven thousand, seven hundred and seventy-six pounds.

'I think your day has also come, John,' he said, indicating the vacancy behind the bar counter. Omally thrust his exercise book in front of the golden boy and shinned over the counter to realize his own lifetime's dream. He was a natural at the pumps and the clawing, snapping, human-hydra was rapidly quelled.

'When the sixth horse goes down nobody will ever speak to me again,' the back-patted Jim told the Professor. 'Five offers of marriage I have had already.'

'Perk up,' the scholar replied. 'I know the odds are unthinkable, but I have a feeling just the same.'

Omally stuffed a pint of Large into each of Pooley's outstretched hands. 'What a game this, then?' said he.

'You will hate me also,' Pooley replied dismally.

'Me?' Omally pressed his hands to his heart. 'But I love you, my dearest friend, the brother I never had.'

'You have five brothers.'

'None like you.'

Jim considered his two pints and raised both simultaneously to his lips. It was the kind of feat no man could be expected to perform twice in a lifetime, but he drained the two at a single draught. 'Oh cruel fate,' said he, wiping the merest drip from his chin.

'Tell me, Jim,' Professor Slocombe asked, as a crowd of female kissers took turns at their hero's cheek, 'how did you do it? Was it the product of pure chance or through the study of form? I ask out of professional interest, I can assure you that it will go no further.'

Jim brushed away the barmaid from the New Inn, whose arm had snaked about his waist. 'If you really want to know, it was down to you and your talk of numerology. Find the pattern, you said. Break everything down to its numerological equivalent, you said, and the answer is yours.'

Professor Slocombe nodded enthusiastically, a light shone in his old face. 'Yes, yes,' he cried, 'then you have solved it, you have found the key. Tell me Jim, I must know.'

'It wasn't all that,' Jim replied. 'Get off there woman, those are private places. I simply followed the lines.'

'The lines? What lines?'

Pooley pushed his racing paper towards the Professor, 'Those boys there,' he said. 'Madam, put those hands away.'

Professor Slocombe drew a quivering finger across the row of computer lines, eighteen in all, three groups of six. 'Oh my Lord,' he said slowly. 'Jim, do you realize what you've done?'

'Pulled off The Big One.'

'Very much more than that.' Professor Slocombe thumbed the paper back to its front page. 'I knew it. This is not your paper.'

'I borrowed it,' said Jim guiltily.

'Jim, tear up the slip. I am not joking. You don't understand what you've got yourself into. Tear it up now, I implore you.'

'Leave it out,' Jim Pooley replied.

'I will write you a cheque.' The Professor brought out his cheque-book. 'Name the sum.'

'Is the man jesting?' Pooley turned to Old Pete who was banging his deaf aid on to the bar counter.

'I've gone deaf here,' the other replied.

'Jim,' the Professor implored, 'listen, please.'

'Pete,' said Pooley, 'you old fool, give me that thing.'

Three o'clock was fast approaching upon the Guinness clock.

'Switch her on then,' said somebody, nudging Old Pete upon the arm.

Now, it must be fairly stated that Pete's hearing aid was not one of those microchipped miracle appliances one reads so much of in the popular press. Such articles, one is so informed, although no bigger than a garden pea, can broadcast the sound of a moth breaking wind to the massed appreciation of an entire Wembley cup-tie crowd. No, old Pete's contraption was not one of these. Here instead, you had the valve, the pink Bakelite case, and the now totally expended tungsten carbide battery.

'It's broke,' said Old Pete. 'Caput.'

'It's what?'

'Pardon?' the elder replied. 'You'll have to speak up, my deaf aid's gone.'

'Deaf aid's gone. Deaf aid's gone.' The word spread like marge on a muffin. The panic spread with it.

'Tear up the slip,' the Professor commanded, his words lost in the growing din. Pooley clutched it to his bosom as the threatened firstborn it was. Omally sought Neville's knobkerry as the crowd turned into a mob and sought a beam to throw a rope over. It was lynching time in Brentford. Having seen active service in many a foreign field, Old Pete was well-prepared to go down fighting. He swung his stick with Ninja fury at the first likely skull that loomed towards him. Friend or foe wasn't in it. Fists began to fly. Omally, knobkerry in hand, launched himself from the counter into the middle of the crowd. 'On to the bookie's, Jim,' he shouted as he brought down a dozen rioters.

Sheltering his privy parts and clinging for dear life to his betting-slip, Pooley, in the wake of Professor Slocombe, whom no man present would have dared to strike no matter how dire the circumstances, edged through the *mêlée*.

'He's getting away,' yelled someone, struggling up from beneath the mad Irishman. 'After him, lads.'

The crowd swung in a blurry mass towards the saloon-bar door through which Pooley was now passing with remarkable speed. The tumbling mass burst out after him into the street. Professor Slocombe stepped nimbly aside and took himself off to business elsewhere.

Leo Felix, who had been labouring away with welder's blow-torch in a vain attempt to salvage anything of his defunct tow-truck, stared up, white-faced and dread, as Pooley blundered into him. 'I and I,' squealed the rattled Rastaman, vanishing away beneath a small Mount Zion of bowling bodies. Jim was snatched up by a dozen flailing hands and raised shoulder-high. The stampede turned to a thundering phalanx which lurched forward, bound for Bob the bookie's, bearing at their vanguard their multi-million dollar standard. Jim prepared to make a deal with God for the second time in as many days. When the sixth horse floundered, as surely it must, Mr Popular he was not going to be. 'Father forgive them,' he said.

Antoine turned Bob's Roller into the Ealing Road with an expensive shriek of burning rubber. Ahead, the advancing phalanx filled the street. Antoine yanked hard upon the wheel, but the car appeared to have ideas of its own. It tore forward into the crowd, scattering bodies to left and right. Jim cartwheeled forward and came to rest upon the gleaming bonnet, his nose jammed up against the windscreen. The Roller mounted the pavement, bringing down a lamppost and mercifully dislodging Jim, who slid into the gutter, a gibbering wreck, bereft of yet another jacket sleeve, which now swung to and fro upon a gold-plated windscreen wiper like some captured tribal war trophy.

Antoine leapt from the cab as Pooley's sixth horse kicked betting history into a cocked hat and Bob's

Roller plunged onward, bound for the rear of Leo's tow-truck and the paw paw negro blow-torch which was even now blazing away at the unattended oxy-acetylene gas-bottle beneath it.

'It's been a funny old kind of day,' said Bob the bookie.

13

The Brentford sun arose the next morning upon a parish which seemed strangely reticent about rising from its collective bed to face the challenge of the day ahead. The Swan in all of its long and colourful history had never known a night like it. Jim had loaded the disabled cash register with more pennies than it could ever hope to hold and announced to all that the drinks were most definitely on him. The parish had not been slow to respond to this selfless gesture, and the word burned like wildfire up the side-streets and back alleys as it generally did when fanned by the wind of a free drink.

Brentford put up the 'Closed for the Night' sign and severed all links with the outside world. The Swan's rival publicans chewed upon their lips for only a short while before leaving their cigars to smoulder in the ashtrays and join in the festivities. The borough council awarded the swaying Jim their highest commendation, the Argentinum Astrum, before drinking itself to collective extinction. With the charred automotive wreckage of Bob's Roller and Leo's tow-truck removed, there had been dancing in the street that night.

For Neville, upon his bed of pain, news never reached him. The Sisters of Mercy who tended to his bed-pan and blanket-baths, hiked up their skirts and joined in the revelry, leaving the metaphysical fat boy to sleep on under his heavy sedation.

For John Omally it was a night he would long remember. As Christ had feasted the five thousand upon half a score of Jewish baps and as many kippers, thus did Omally quench the thirsts of the Brentford multitude. Like the barman of myth, his hand was always there to take up the empty glass and refill it.

For Jim Pooley, morning suddenly appeared out of drunken oblivion beating a loud tattoo of drums upon the inside of his skull. Jim shook his head. An ill-considered move. The tattoo grew louder and more urgent. Jim reopened a pair of blood-red eyes. He found himself staring into the snoring face of Miss Naylor, Brentford's licentious librarian. 'Gawd,' muttered Jim to himself, 'I did strike it lucky last night.'

The pounding was coming from below, from his front door. It was the relief postman. Jim rose giddily and lurched towards the bedroom door. The words 'never again' could not make it to his lips. 'Shut up,' he whispered as the hammering continued. Jim stumbled down the uncarpeted stairs and caught his bare toe for the umpteenth time upon the tack protruding from the sixth tread. Howling beneath his breath, he toppled into the hall to find himself suddenly swimming in a sea of paper.

The hallway was jam-packed with letters, literally thousands of them, of every way, shape, colour, and form. Telegrams, buff-coloured circulars, and picture postcards.

Pooley rubbed at his eyes as he lay half-submerged in the papery cushion. He was certain that they hadn't been there the night before, but as the later moments of the previous night's revels were blank to his recollection, as attested to by the snoring female above, Jim's certainties were purely subjective in nature.

The banging continued beyond the barricade of the king's mail.

'All right, all right.' Pooley clutched at his temples and fought his way towards the front door. Pushing envelopes to left and right with great difficulty, he opened it.

'Mail,' said a sweating postman, thumbing over his shoulder towards a dozen or so bulging sacks which lay in an unruly line along the pavement. 'Your bloody birthday is it then, pal?'

Pooley shrugged, dislodging an avalanche of letters which momentarily buried him.

'I've been sticking these bastards through your letter-box for the better part of an hour and I can't get any more through. Do pardon this departure from the norm, but I must insist that you post the rest yourself. I am here on relief from Chiswick as the local bloke hasn't turned in. What is this, some kind of bleeding joke? *Candid Camera*, is it, or that *Game for a Laugh* crap?'

Pooley hunched his shoulders beneath the pressing load. 'What are they?' he asked. 'Who has sent them?'

'From those which unaccountably fell open in my hands, they would seem to be begging letters to a man. What did you do then, come up on the bleeding pools?'

'Something like that.' Jim made an attempt to close the door.

The postman's contorted face suddenly sweetened. 'Is that a fact?' he said thoughtfully. 'Then let me be the first to congratulate you.'

'You are not the first,' Jim replied, 'but thanks all the same. Now if you will excuse me.' He fought with the front door but Posty's foot was now firmly in it. Pooley relaxed his grip. 'Your foot is caught,' he observed.

'It must be a wonderful thing to have money,' said the postman, edging forward. 'I have always been a poor man myself, not that I have ever resented the rich their wealth, you understand, but I have often had cause to wonder why fate chose to deal with me and mine in so shabby a way.'

'Really?' said Jim without interest.

'Oh yes. Not that I complain, soldiering on in all weathers, crippled to the fingertips with arthritis, simply so the mail should get through.'

'Very noble.' Jim applied more pressure to the door but it was getting him nowhere.

'And my wife,' the postman continued, 'a holy martyr that woman. If I only had the money to pay for the operation I am certain that she could be relieved of her daily misery.'

'Let us hope so.'

'And my poor blind son, Kevin!'

'Get your bloody foot out of my door.'

Knowing a lost cause when he saw one, the

postman withdrew his boot and swung it at the nearest sack. The contents spilled out to flutter away upon the breeze. 'Privileged bastard,' he called after the retreating Pooley. 'Come the revolution, you and your kind will be first up against the wall. Capitalist Pig!'

Pooley slammed fast the door and stood engulfed in the floodtide of mail. He had sent out a few begging letters himself in the past, but now he knew what it felt like to be on the receiving end. Jim Pooley did not like it one little bit. His mail unread and his bedmate unwoken, Jim left the house that morning by the rear entrance.

Now he sat alone upon the Library bench. The sun had long arisen and all the makings of a great day ahead looked in the offing. Jim sighed mournfully and at intervals studied the palm of his right hand. He was not a happy man. He was a gentleman of substance now and it pained him greatly. The terrible feeling of responsibility, one he had never before experienced, gnawed away at his innards. It was all just too much. The total sum of his wealth was too large even to contemplate and with the passing of the night and the current bank rate it had already grown alarmingly.

Jim made a dismal groaning sound and buried his face in his hands. It was all just too much. He had never owned before what one might actually call 'money' and certainly not what the 'swells' refer to as the current account. He had had an overdraft once but that hadn't proved to be up to much. And the manner in which he had acquired the fortune, also drastically wrong. No betting shop could ever have had that amount of readies waiting under the counter. And even if it had, it would be hardly likely to simply push them across the counter without a life or death struggle at the very least. Guns would have been toted and knee-caps an endangered species. He and Omally had transferred no fewer than twenty-six wheelbarrow loads from there to the bank. It was simply ridiculous.

And the bank? Pooley moaned pitifully. They had taken the entire thing for granted, as if he had been merely bunging in a couple of quid out of his wages. It was almost as if they had been expecting him. Through the bullet-proof glass of the office Pooley had seen the manager sitting at his desk, a pair of minuscule headphones clasped about his ears, nodding his head and popping his fingers.

And as for this, Pooley held up his right hand and examined the palm. The bank had refused to give him either a receipt or a cheque-book. With unveiled condescension they had explained that such methods of personal finance were now obsolete and that for security's sake they must insist upon the new personalized identification system. They had then stamped his right palm with a pattern of eighteen little computer lines in three rows of six. Six six six. Pooley spat on to his palm and rubbed away at the marking; it would not budge. He eased up on the moaning and groaning and took to a bit of soulful sighing. He had become involved in something which was very much bigger than he was. He really should have listened to Professor Slocombe and torn up the slip.

A sudden screeching of white-walled tyres upon tarmac announced the arrival of Antoine with Pooley's new car. Jim distantly recalled a deal he had struck the night before.

'Your carriage awaits,' said the chauffeur of fortune, springing from the automobile and holding open the door.

Jim was entranced. The car, a silver-grey Morris Minor, although of a model some fifteen years out of date, had all the makings of one fresh from the showroom. 'Where did you get it?' he asked, rising from his gloom and strolling over to the automotive gem.

'Purchased with the money you advanced, sir,' Antoine replied politely. 'Has a few tricks under the hood.'

Pooley circled the car approvingly and ran his unsoiled hand along the spanking paintwork. 'Big Boda,' said he. 'It's a corker.'

'And what about the number plates?' Antoine indicated the same, JP 1.

'Double Boda,' said Jim Pooley.

'Would sir care to be taken for a spin?'

'Absolutely.' Jim clapped his hands together and chuckled. Maybe this being wealthy did have its compensations after all. Antoine swung forward the driver's seat and Jim clambered aboard. The chauffeur sat himself down before the wheel and closed the door. 'What is all that?' Pooley asked, spying out the Morris' dashboard; it was far from conventional.

'Customized,' said Antoine. 'By Lateinos and Romiith, who bought out the old Morris patent. This car will do nought to sixty in three point four seconds. It has weather-eye air-conditioning, fuel consumption down to near zero by merit of its improved plasma-drive system. Are you acquainted with quantum mechanics?'

'I get by,' said Jim.

'Solar pod power-retention headlights, under-pinned macro-pleasure full-glide suspension. Sub-lift non-drift gravitational thrust plates . . .'

'Drive please,' said Jim, 'I will tell you when to stop.'

'Where to, sir?' Antoine put the preposterous vehicle into instant overdrive and tore it away at Mach ten.

Pooley slewed back in his seat, cheeks drawn up towards his ears, his face suddenly resembling the now legendary Gwynplaine, of Victor Hugo's *Man who Laughs*. 'Steady on,' winced Jim.

'Gravitational acclimatization auxiliary forward modifications engaged.' Antoine touched a lighted sensor on the dash and Pooley slumped forward. 'A quick tour of the parish, taking in the more desirable residences on the "For Sale" list, would it be, sir?'

'Come again?'

'My previous employers always liked the grand tour.'

'I thought you worked for Bob?'

'Only at lunchtimes, I am a freelance.'

'Very commendable.'

The car screamed into Mafeking Avenue on two wheels, narrowly avoiding Old Pete, who raised two eloquent fingers towards its receding rear end.

'How many clients have you then?'

'Only you,' said Antoine. 'I have attended to all those who came by the big payouts. One after another.'

The Morris roared past the Memorial Park, gathering speed.

'One after another. How many have come up recently then?'

'Twenty-five, although they were never in your league.' The chauffeur cleared his throat with a curiously mechanical coughing sound.

Pooley scratched at his head. He had heard of no recent big winners hereabouts. Jim suddenly smelt the great-grandaddy of all big rats. 'Stop the car,' he demanded.

Antoine crouched low over the computerized controls, his toe edged nearer to the floor, and the modified family saloon performed another impossible feat of acceleration.

'Stop this car!' shouted Jim. 'There is a stitch-up here and I'll have no part of it.'

'Stitch-up?' leered Antoine. Pooley could just make out his face reflected in the driving mirror. It was not a face Jim would wish to recall in his dreams. The chauffeur's normally amiable visage had become contorted into a death-mask of inhuman cruelty. The eyes glowed between hooded slits, the mouth was drawn down, exposing a row of wicked metallic-looking teeth. The face was no longer human, it was atavistic, something beyond and before humanity, compelling and vibrant with dark evil power. The flying Morris cannoned through the short cobbled alleyway between the Police Station and the Beehive and swerved right through the red lights and out into the High Road. It should surely have been forced to a standstill amidst the hubbub of mid-morning traffic, but to Pooley's increasing horror the High Street was empty, the pavements deserted.

'Stop, I say!' screamed Jim. 'I will pay you anything you want, name the sum.' Antoine laughed hideously, the sounds issuing from his throat being those of sharp stones rattled in a tin can. Pooley shook his brain into gear; 'knobble the mad driver', it told him. Climbing forward, Jim lashed out towards the driver's neck. 'AAAAAGH!' went Pooley, as his lunging fingers piled into a barrier of empty air, splintering nails, and dislocating thumbs.

'Safety-shield anti-whiplash modification,' sneered the demonic driver as Pooley sank back into his seat, his wounded hands jammed beneath his armpits. The car swung into a side-road Jim did not clearly remember and thundered on towards . . . Jim suddenly stiffened in his seat . . . towards the rim of the old quarry. Jim recalled that place well enough, he used to go ferreting there when a lad. The walls were fifty-foot sheer to a man. He was heading for an appointment with none other than good old Nemesis himself. Now was the time to do some pretty nifty fast thinking. Pooley thrust his brain into overdrive. Accelerating Morris, mad driver, two doors only, invisible force-field before. No sun-roof and Nemesis five hundred yards distant. Jim chewed upon his lip, worry beads of perspiration upon his brow. No way out before, above, but possibly . . .

The mighty Morris has to its credit many an endearing feature. Ask any driver and he will mention such things as comfort, luxury, fuel economy, or the obvious prestige of ownership. But stand that man in front of his locked car to view the spectacle of his ignition keys dangling in the steering column and he will then address his praise towards the inevitably faulty boot-lock and the detachable rear seat. Pooley had crawled into more than a few Morrises on drunken evenings past when further staggering home looked out of the question. Now he was hardly backward in going that very direction.

Nemesis was yet two hundred and fifty yards to the fore. As the car ploughed on relentlessly towards the yawning chasm ahead, Jim clawed at the rear seat with his maimed fingers. With the kind of superhuman effort which would have done credit to any one of a dozen *Boy's Own Paper* heroes, he plunged into the boot and fought it open.

With one bound he was free.

As the car breasted the rim of the chasm and dashed itself down towards oblivion, Jim tumbled out into the roadway, bowling over and over like a rag doll, to the accompaniment of many a sickening, bone-shattering report. He came to a final dislocated standstill a few short yards from doom. A loud explosion beneath, a column of flame, and a rising black mushroom cloud of oily smoke signalled the sorry end of a fine car. Pooley made a feeble attempt to rise, but to no avail. Every bone in his body seemed broken several times over. His head was pointing the wrong way round for a start. A floodtide of darkness engulfed the fallen hero and Jim lapsed away into a dark oblivion of unconsciousness.

14

John Omally pressed his way through Professor Slocombe's ever-open French windows. The old scholar sat in a fireside chair earnestly conversing with the hawk-nosed man from another time. He waved his hand in familiar fashion towards the whisky decanter.

'So where is lucky Jim?' Sherlock Holmes asked. 'Putting in his bid for the brewery?'

Omally shook his head and his face showed more than just a trace of bitterness. 'I was to meet Jim at the bench. We were planning a Nile cruise.' John flung the bundle of holiday brochures he had acquired the night before into the Professor's fire. 'I missed him. No doubt he is lying even now in the arms of some avaricious female. Oh, cruel fate.'

'Cruel fate indeed,' said Holmes darkly. 'Lucky Jim may not be quite so lucky as he thinks himself to be.'

Omally pinched at the top of his nose. 'We sank a few last night and that is a fact. Jim wisely kept back a wheelbarrow-load for expenses. He was more than generous.'

'So I understand. I regret that we were unable to attend the festivities. Tell me now, would I be right in assuming that Jim was wearing gloves last night?'

Omally nodded. 'Said that the money had given him a rash. I didn't give it a lot of thought, you know what these millionaires are like, walking round in Kleenex boxes and drinking Campbells soup from tins, it's quite regular to those lads.'

Sherlock Holmes leant forward in his seat. 'Might I ask you to show me your hands?'

Omally thrust them hurriedly behind his back.

'As I deduced,' said the great detective. 'Both door and window was it?'

Omally bit at his lip and nodded ruefully. 'Until but a few minutes since.'

Professor Slocombe cast Holmes a questioning glance.

'Purely a matter of deduction,' that man explained. 'Let me see if I can set the scene, as it were. Mr Omally here has seen his dearest friend become a multimillionaire in the matter of an hour and a half. He helps him transport these riches to the bank and the two spend the night in revelry, finally returning to their respective abodes. But our friend cannot sleep, he paces the floor, he is assailed with doubts. Will the money change his companion, will it destroy their long and enduring friendship? Will he turn his back upon him? At last he can stand it no longer, his mind is made up. He will set out at once to his friend's house and knock him up. But this is not to be. He tries to open his door but it will not move. After many vain attempts to secure his freedom he tries the window, this proves similarly unrewarding, the glass cannot even be broken.'

Professor Slocombe looked quizzically towards

Omally who was catching flies with his mouth. 'Is this true?' he asked.

'In most respects; it fair put the fear of the Almighty into me I can tell you.'

'We are indeed dealing with mighty forces here,' said Sherlock Holmes, springing to his feet. 'And now I think that should we wish to entertain any hope of saving your friend we had best move with some expediency. Let us pray that the trail is not yet cold.' Without uttering another word he whisked on his tweedy jacket and plunged out through the French windows, followed by Professor Slocombe. Omally shook his head in total disbelief at it all, tossed back his drink, and followed in hot pursuit.

Holmes strode ahead up the sweeping tree-lined drive of the Butts Estate and crossed the road towards the Memorial Library. Before Pooley's bench he halted and threw himself to his hands and knees. 'Aha,' he said, taking up the spent butt of an expensive cigarette. 'He's been here and he walked towards the kerb.' Omally and the Professor looked at one another. Omally shrugged. Holmes scrutinized the roadway. 'He entered a roadster here and was driven off at some speed in that direction.'

'Can you make out the licence plate number?' Omally said cynically.

Holmes looked him up and down coldly. 'I can tell you that he was helped into the car by a gentleman of foreign extraction, who parts his hair on the left side and has his shoes hand-made, size seven and a half.'

Omally's eyes widened. 'Antoine, Bob the bookie's chauffeur.'

126

'Such was my conclusion. Now, unless you wish to waste more valuable time in fruitless badinage, I would suggest that we make haste. Time is of the essence.'

'Lead on,' said John Omally.

It is a goodly jog from the Memorial Library to the old quarry, but Holmes led the way without faltering once upon his course. Here and there along the route he dropped once more to his knees and examined the road surface. Each time Omally felt certain that he had lost his way, but each time the detective rose again and pointed the way ahead. At length the three men turned into the old quarry road. Ahead in the distance lay the crumpled wreckage which had been Jim Pooley. With a small cry Omally bounded forward and came to a standstill over the disaster area. 'Oh, no,' said he, sinking to his knees. 'Oh no, it wasn't worth this.'

Sherlock Holmes and the Professor slowly approached, the old man supporting himself upon his stick and wheezing terribly. 'Is he . . . ?' the words stuck in the Professor's throat.

Omally buried his face in his hands. 'My true friend,' he mumbled, his voice choked by emotion. He slumped back on his knees and stared up at the sky. Tears had formed in his deep-blue eyes and fell over his unshaven cheeks. 'Why?' he shouted up at the firmament. 'Tell me why?'

Holmes came forward and, stooping, turned Pooley's right palm upwards. The eighteen lines glowed darkly in the otherwise brilliant sunlight. 'There is nothing you can do for him now,' he said.

'No!' Omally elbowed the detective's hand away. 'Leave him alone, you are part of this. What the hell is going on here anyway? Why did it happen?'

'Come, John,' said the Professor, laying a slim hand upon the Irishman's shoulder. 'Come away now, there is nothing that can be done.'

Omally looked up bitterly at the old man. 'You knew about this, didn't you?' he said. 'You knew something bad was going on, you should have stopped it. You and your numbers and your magic.'

'Come, John, come please.'

Omally rose slowly to his feet and stared down at Pooley's mortal remains. 'I will kill the man who did this, Jim,' he said slowly and painfully.

Professor Slocombe pressed his hand once more to John's shoulder, and led the stumbling man away.

'All well and bloody good,' came a voice from the grave. 'But who is going to turn my head around for me?'

Omally spun about. 'Jim, you old bastard!'

'Who else would it bloody be? My head, John, if you please? It is most uncomfortable.'

The lads at the Cottage Hospital were nothing if not thorough. Spending their days as they did, playing dominoes and hunt the hypodermic, they were more than willing to face up to the challenge of the bloody spectacle Professor Slocombe presented them with. Having run a light-pen quickly over Pooley's right hand they pronounced him private patient and went about their tasks with a will. Had not the Professor been a member of the Board of Governors, there

128

seemed little doubt that they would have been a great deal more thorough than they were. Most likely to the extremes of an exploratory operation or two, with the removal of Pooley's tonsils as an encore. As it was they prodded and poked, applied iodine, took X-rays, forced him to remove his trousers, turned his head to the right, and made him cough. As an afterthought they inoculated him against tetanus, mumps, whooping cough, and diphtheria. As Doctor Kildare came up on the hospital tele-video they summarily dismissed him with a few kind words, a large bill, and a prescription for Interferon no chemist could ever hope to fill.

'See,' said Omally, as the four men left the hospital, 'all this fuss and not a bone broken.'

Pooley felt doubtfully at his bruised limbs. 'I will not bore you with my opinion of the National Health Service,' said he. 'Nor even waste my time bewailing my lot, as my pleas for sympathy fall for ever upon deaf ears.'

At last the four men entered the Professor's study. A large medicinal gold watch was handed at once to the invalid who was placed in a heavily-cushioned chair. 'My thanks,' said Jim, pocketing it away in his throat. The sun danced in upon the carpet and the four weary men lay slumped in various armchairs, each unwilling to be the first to break the tranquil silence. Pooley's limbs creaked and complained to themselves. With a crackling hand he poured himself another drink. Holmes and the Professor exchanged occasional guarded glances, and the old man appeared at times obsessed with the silver pentacle which hung upon his watch-chain. Omally drummed his fingers soundlessly upon the chair's arm and waited for the storm to break; the silence was rapidly becoming close and oppressive.

Finally Jim could stand it no longer. 'All right,' he said, climbing painfully to his feet. 'What is going on? You all know a lot more of this than me.'

'I don't,' said Omally, 'but I am beginning to have my suspicions.'

'So what is it?' Pooley turned to the Professor. 'I have just miraculously survived an attempt upon my life by a lunatic chauffeur. Such should be the cause for some small rejoicing surely. If I was dead, Omally here would already be ordering the beer for the wake.'

Professor Slocombe stepped over to his desk and took up the day's copy of the *Brentford Mercury*. He held the front page towards Jim. 'Have you read this?'

Pooley perused the encircled article with little interest and less comprehension. 'It's about computer lines,' said he. It did not go unnoticed by Holmes and the Professor that his right hand slid unobtrusively away into his trouser pocket.

'It is much more than that,' said the old man. 'It is an essential link in a dark chain of events which, unless severed, will inevitably engirdle us all. To our ultimate destruction.'

'Come now,' said Jim. 'It is just some nonsense about banks and computers, nothing more I assure you.'

Professor Slocombe shook his head, 'Sadly, it is a

great deal more than that. It is conclusive proof that all my worst fears are founded and even now the prophecies of the book of Revelation are coming to pass.'

'You jest, surely?'

Professor Slocombe shook his head once more. 'Believe in what I say,' said he. 'We are facing the greatest threat mankind has faced since the deluge. We are facing the final conflict. The apocalypse. Even now the curtains are closing.'

'No.' Jim shook his head violently and not a little painfully. 'All the stuff in that old book is most depressing. Look at me now. I experienced a slight setback, but it was the result of pure spite on Bob's part. Just because I won and he's banged up in hospital a bit scorched. I am battered but wealthy. The gods are smiling upon me.'

'No,' said Professor Slocombe. 'Money will not buy you out of this one, especially money which was never intended for your use.'

Pooley scratched at his head, raising a fine cloud of dust. 'You wouldn't care to enlarge a little on this would you Professor?' he asked. 'You see such news catches me at a rather inopportune moment. John and I are planning a bit of a holiday. Armageddon might interfere with our traveller's cheques.'

Professor Slocombe shook his head once more. Jim was beginning to find the habit mildly annoying. He had millions of pounds knocking about in the bank and was now really looking forward to spending them before they caught the moth. 'Do you really believe yourself to be one favoured of the gods?'

Jim nodded noisily. 'At this time definitely yes.'

'All right then, I will make this short, but by no means sweet. We will speak of these matters again. For now let me read you a verse or two from the Revelation; possibly it will convince you, possibly not.' Definitely not, thought Jim Pooley. The Professor took himself over to his desk where he sat before the large and outspread family Bible. 'I will spare you the preliminaries as it is obvious that you consider your time valuable. I will simply give you the relevant part and allow you to muse upon it.'

'Thanks,' said Jim doubtfully.

'Revelation, Chapter Thirteen,' said Professor Slocombe. 'This speaks of the beast that has risen from the Earth. We will address our attention to verses sixteen, seventeen; and eighteen.' He spoke the final number with a deadly intensity.

'Go ahead then.'

The Professor adjusted his ivory pince-nez and read aloud from the open book:

'16. And he causeth all, both small and great, rich and poor, free and bond to receive a mark in their right hand or in their foreheads.

17. And that no man might buy or sell save that he had the mark or the name of the beast or the number of his name.

18. Here is wisdom. Let he that hath understanding count the number of the beast; for it is the number of a man, and his number is six hundred, three score and six.'

The Professor gently closed the Holy Book and looked up towards Jim Pooley. The millionaire sat bolt upright in his chair. His eyes were unblinking

132

and stared ever downward towards the open palm of his right hand, where the computer bar code was indelibly printed. Eighteen computer lines. Three rows of six. The number of a man, six hundred, three score and six.

666

The number of the Beast. Things were suddenly beginning to sink in.

'Oh dear,' said John Omally, who was not a man unacquainted with the Scriptures. 'Why did I just know you were going to choose those very verses to be today's text?'

15

At a little after five of the clock, Pooley and Omally left Professor Slocombe's house behind and trudged up the long crescent bound for the Swan. Although the old man had served a fine tea, neither could raise much of an appetite, finding to it more than a hint of the Messianic feast. With rumbling guts and grumbling tongues they mooched along, ignoring the gaily-coloured bunting which fluttered between the great Horse Chestnuts, raised in preparation for the forthcoming Festival of Brentford. Pooley was in full slouch, his chin upon his chest, and his hands thrust deeply into his tweedy trouser pockets. His last suit was in exquisite ruin and lacked a right sleeve, which an over-zealous hospital intern who watched too many Aldo Ray films had cut away from his grazed elbow with a pair of surgical scissors. The thought that he could buy a thousand suits and all of them of the hand-tailored, Saville Row variety, did little to raise his spirits. Jim's right thumbnail worried at his hidden palm.

Omally worried at Marchant's pitted handlebars, the old boy seemed to have developed an irritating pull to the left, which was either something to do with its political leanings or something even more sinister. 'Give it a rest,' growled John as the thing had him in the gutter once more.

After what seemed an age they arrived at the Swan's welcoming portal. And found to their increased horror that it was no longer welcoming. A large plastic sign fastened to the front window announced to the world that THE BUYING OF 'ROUNDS' IS HENCEFORTH FORBIDDEN BY ORDER OF THE BREWERY. ANY CUSTOMER ATTEMPTING TO VIOLATE THIS PRINCIPLE WILL BE BARRED FOR AN INDEFINITE PERIOD.

'By the Saints,' said Omally, turning wobbly at the knees. 'Would you look at that?'

Pooley curled his lip. 'This is too much. I am even to be denied spending my money as I please.' He thrust Omally aside and entered the bar.

The Swan was empty of customers. The only folk present were a pale young man in headphones who stood behind the jump, and two brewery henchmen in drab-coloured overalls, who appeared to be screwing a gleaming contrivance of advanced design on to the bar counter.

'What is the meaning of that notice?' Pooley stormed up to the bar.

The strange young barman watched his furious approach with an untroubled expression. His head moved to and fro to a rhythm only he heard.

'I demand an explanation,' foamed the red-faced Jim.

The young man pushed back his headphones. 'What will it be then, sir?' he asked.

Jim raised his fist. 'That, that bloody notice in the window. What's your game, eh?'

'Oh, that.' The young man was all bland composure. 'Rules and regulations, what can we do?'

'We can tear the bloody thing down for a kick off.'

The young man waggled a finger. 'Naughty, naughty,' said he.

Jim clenched and unclenched his fists. 'Has the world gone mad?' he asked. 'Has the brewery lost its bloody marbles?'

The young man shrugged. 'Since the takeover everything seems to have changed.'

'Takeover, what takeover?'

'Hadn't you heard? Lateinos and Romiith bought the brewery out. An offer too good to refuse I suppose.'

Jim began to flap his hands wildly and spin about in small circles. Omally, who had followed him in, knew this to be a bad sign. Pooley sought men to kill. Two of such were now tinkering at the counter's end. 'Who are they?' Jim ceased his foolish gyrations. 'What are they up to?'

The pale young man smiled wanly. 'Installing a terminal, of course. Under the new system every establishment must have its own terminal, you know.'

'John,' said Jim, 'John, hold me back.' Omally did as he was bidden. 'What, if one might make so bold, is a terminal?' he asked.

'My goodness me,' the pale young man tittered to himself, 'we do live in the dark ages around here, don't we?' He grinned towards the two henchmen, who exchanged knowing glances and sniggered. 'This terminal,' he explained, 'is modular in concept, with a net-working capability that is virtually plug-in. It has a one hundred and twenty-eight bit multi-tasking operation, super-advanced WP forms and spread sheet planner; wide area network configuration, multi-key ISAM on shared data bases, L and R six-six-six Asynch emulations, soft fort and bit-mapped graphics.'

'Bit-mapped graphics, eh?'

The young man cleared his throat with a curiously mechanical coughing sound. 'Bit-mapped,' he said slowly. Above his left eyebrow the short row of eighteen vertical lines gave his face a permanently quizzical expression. 'Now, perhaps, sir, you would care to order?'

'Two pints of Large,' said Omally.

'As you wish, sir. Will your irate companion be thinking to order two for himself also, do you think? Once he recovers his senses?'

'We are only just outnumbered,' quoth Pooley. 'Shall we make a fight of it?'

'All in good time, Jim. Now please calm yourself and lend me a couple of quid.' The pale barman raised a tattooed eyebrow. 'Usury is strictly forbidden upon the premises, by order of the brewery.'

'A pox on the brewery,' said John. 'Jim is minding some money for me. Can I have it back please, Jim?'

'Certainly.' Pooley thrust a couple of hundred smackers into Omally's outstretched palm and outstretched his own towards the nearest pint.

The new barman deftly reached across the counter-top and caught up Jim's wrist in a vice-like grip.

Turning Jim's palm towards the ceiling he drew out a light-wand and ran it across. 'Your credit rating is triple A,' he said. 'Two pints for yourself is it?'

'Make it three,' said Jim bitterly. 'I feel a bit of a thirst coming on.'

'As you please, sir.' The pale young barman replaced his headphones and, nodding to himself, drew off the business.

Bearing their pints away, John and Jim stalked off to a side-table where they dropped into a brace of chairs and sat staring into one another's eyes.

After a somewhat pregnant pause, Jim said, 'I've had enough of all this, John.'

Omally nodded thoughtfully. 'It is not very much to my own liking,' said he, gulping away the nearest pint. 'If you want my considered opinion I feel that we should both do very well to have it away from this district post haste.'

'Look at those bastards.' Jim gestured towards the brewery henchmen who were even now tearing up the Swan's antique carpeting to run a power-line across the floor.

'Rio would be your man,' said John. 'Dusky maidens rolling green cigars upon their bronzed thighs. A train-robber chum of mine has lodgings thereabouts. The climate so they say is ideal for the professional drinking man or the unemployed war criminal.'

Pooley considered his printed palm. 'I can't be having with all this stuff. Things are no longer healthy hereabouts.'

'So let us away.'

Jim chewed upon a thumbnail. 'I think you're right,' said he. 'But what about all this Revelations business? Do you think that the Professor is correct in his theories? If it is the end of the world then it might catch up with us even in Rio.'

Omally downed another pint. 'I have my doubts about the whole thing. Listen, with the old currant bun beaming down and a bottle or two of duty-free on the patio table we can give the matter serious thought. What do you say?'

'I say it's time we had a holiday.'

'Good man. Now the travel agent's in the Ealing Road closes at six, I can be up there in five minutes on the bike and back in another five, I'll book us aboard an aeroplane for first thing tomorrow.'

'Do it then.' Jim dragged out another bundle of banknotes and thrust them at John. 'Go at once. I'll get some bottles to take out, this place is beginning to depress me.'

'Right then, I will be back directly.' Omally left the Swan and mounted up Marchant, who had set himself in for an evening kip. He bumped down the kerb and pedalled furiously up the Ealing Road. Cresting the railway bridge he swept down the other side, legs outspread, past the Mowlem's building. Without warning he suddenly came into contact with a great body of halted traffic. The road was a shambles of stalled automobiles and shouting drivers. Cars were parked at crazy angles across the road, and those at the vanguard lay, their bonnets stove in and steam issuing from their shattered radiators. A blank wall of dark light rose from the street at the junction with the Great West Road. It soared into the sky, an impenetrable barrier blocking all further progress. Omally dragged on his brakes but his iron stallion appeared to have developed ideas of its own. It rocketed him headlong into the boot of a stalled Morris Minor. John sailed forward in a blizzard of whirling banknotes, to tumble down on to the bonnet of the defunct automobile and roll on to the roadway. Cursing and spitting he slowly dragged himself to his feet and stared up at the grim barrier ahead, struck dumb with amazement and disbelief. The curtains, which the Professor had observed for so many weeks through his rooftop viewer, had finally closed upon the borders of the Brentford triangle.

And the parish was now completely sealed off from the outside world.

16

As word spread from house to house that the veil was drawn down, the people of the parish flocked into the streets. They flowed hurriedly towards the borders to stand, their noses pressed against the walls of hard air, staring out into the beyond. The vista, normally so mundane as to be invisible, now assumed a quality of remoteness and unreality. That none might any longer pass into that world made it fairyland and the figures that moved there became exaggerated and larger than life. And though they shouted and coo-eed and smote the barrier with sticks and staves, the world beyond did not see them, nor hear their cries for help. The world beyond simply went on doing that which it had always done – which wasn't very much, although it seemed so now. Although the trapped people watched desperately for some sign which might signal the recognition of their plight by the free folk, who now passed within inches, none came. Their faces never turned and they went about their business as ever they had. To the world outside it seemed that Brentford had simply ceased to exist.

What attempts were made to stir up a bit of healthy rioting were stifled almost as soon as they were begun by the arrival of police snatch squads. Strange pale young men in protective uniforms, sporting minuscule headphones, and carrying small black boxes attached to their belts, moved swiftly into the crowds to bear away the outspoken to waiting meat-wagons. Those who had voiced complaint reappeared hours later passive and uncomplaining, clearing their throats before speech with curiously mechanical coughing sounds. Brentford's ghost people drifted back to haunt their houses and closed their doors behind them.

Days began to pass one upon another, each one the same as the last. Pooley and Omally sat in the Swan bitterly regarding the new barman as he soullessly directed the redecoration of the grand old watering hole. Through the Swan's upper windows, now being double-glazed, the dark walls shimmered. Beyond them the sun shone, but here in Brentford a thin drizzle hissed upon the pavements and trickled down the gutters. Old Pete hobbled in, shaking rain from his cap and muttering under his breath. As he passed his coinage over the counter the young barman tut-tutted and warned him that such cash transactions would soon be impermissible. Old Pete muttered something in reply but it was only the word 'pox' that caught the ears of John and Jim. Pooley lit up a Passing Cloud and drew deeply upon it, he opened his mouth to speak but no word came. Omally read the expression and the open mouth and nodded hopelessly. There was no need for either question or answer, nobody knew what they were going to do next, or even why. When the barman called time six minutes early the two men parted with no words spoken and wandered away into the night.

The disappointments and the hopelessness of it all were beginning to take their irrevocable toll.

Pooley lay on his bed, hands cupped behind his head, awake to the sounds of the night. The room was now heaped with a pointless array of useless and expensive articles. The wardrobe overspilled with tailor-made suits, shirts, and shoes. Quadrophonic record players, all lacking plugs, and most not even unpacked from their boxes, lay half-hidden beneath every Frankie Laine record Jim had always promised himself. He had riffled every Brentford store in the vain attempt to spend his wealth. Finding an estate agent with property deeds still for sale he had purchased all available for wallpaper. The things he ordered arrived by the hour, to lie in soaking stacks on the pavement. Jim went about the business with a will but, as with everything now, the task was hopeless. He could never outspend his own wealth. Progress across the cluttered room was made the more precarious for fear of sinking to his doom in the marshland of expensive shagpile carpets heaped one upon another. He should have been sleeping the sleep of the drunk, but no matter how many pints he struggled to down, nowadays he still remained fiercely sober. None of it made the slightest bit of sense to Jim, there seemed no purpose to any last bit of it.

Pooley pressed the time-speak button on his brand new Lateinos and Romiith wristlet watch. 'Eleven forty-five and all is well, Jim,' said the polite little voice. Pooley made an unseemly sound and suggested that all was very far from being that. Professor

Slocombe had called him and John to a midnight rendezvous this very night. No doubt the Professor felt the need to impart to them more prophecies of impending doom. Jim did not relish the thought. And to think that he had once considered the old man to be a stimulating conversationalist and source of enlightenment.

He climbed down from the most expensive mattress printed palms could buy and sought out a pair of matching shoes from the undisciplined regiment which stood before him. Having kicked about for several minutes, to Jim's immense chagrin he unearthed one lone matched set, his tired old workboots. Muttering something about the curse of the Pooleys, Jim drew the wretched articles on to his naked feet. Having recently had a nasty experience in the bathroom with a computerized umbrella which opened automatically upon contact with water, he left the thing rolled up under the bed, and braved the drizzle in a new tweed shooting jacket with matching cap. Neither fitted. Jim shook his head – everything money could buy, but it was all rubbish. The new calfskin waistcoat had looked a bundle in the shop, but no sooner home than the buttons had begun to fall off and the leathery smell vanished away to be replaced by one of plastic. The same smell which permeated everything he had bought. Jim sniffed at the 'tweed' jacket. Yes, even that. Bewailing the millionaire's lot, Pooley slouched on to the Professor's.

Omally was already there, comfortably ensconced in a fireside chair, wearing a natty three-piece whistle

Jim had given him, his right hand wrapped about a whisky glass. Professor Slocombe was at his desk amongst his books and Sherlock Holmes was nowhere to be seen.

Upon Jim's noisy entrance, the sole of his right boot having chosen this inopportune moment to part company with its aged leather upper, John and the Professor looked up from their separate reveries and greeted the new arrival. 'Help yourself, Jim,' said the old man. 'I think you will find the fruits of my cellar eminently more stimulating than those of the Swan.'

'Praise be for that,' said Jim Pooley, liberally acquainting himself with the decanter.

'So now,' said the Professor, once Jim had hopped into a comfortable chair and eased off his rogue brogue, 'there are a good many things that I must tell you this evening. Few of which you will find comforting, I fear.'

We're off to a good start, thought Jim, but he kept it to himself.

'As you are both aware, Brentford is now completely surrounded by an impenetrable barrier.' The two men nodded gloomily; they were a long way from Rio and that was a fact. 'And no doubt you have been asking each other why?'

'Never gave it a thought,' said Jim. Omally leaned forward and smote him a painful blow to his naked sole.

'Thank you, John. Now it is my wish to put you both in the picture as far as I am able. It is essential that you understand what we face. Those of us with the power and the will to fight grow fewer by the day.

145

Soon, if the thing is not stopped, there will be none remaining.' Pooley did not like the sound of that very much at all. 'I will start at the very beginning.'

'Do so, sir,' said Jim.

'In the beginning was the word and the word was with God and God was the word . . .'

'Hold hard there,' Pooley interrupted. 'From Genesis to the Revelation is a long haul by any standard. Might we just skip right through to it now?'

'All right, but let me briefly explain. The God of Adam brought something to the world which had not existed before. He brought light. To our perception there is but one God, the true God. But our forefathers believed in an entire pantheon of Elder Gods. These rose and fell with their temples, for how can a god exist when there are none to worship him? It is the balance of equipoise; the harmony of the spheres. Each new and rising god replaces his predecessor when his temple is cast down and his followers no longer believe. Allow me to suggest the possibility that dark and sinister gods existed prior to the word which brought light to our Mother Earth.'

'Sounds pretty iffy so far,' John observed.

'Oh, it gets far worse later on,' the Professor replied. 'This is just the prawn cocktail; by cheese and biscuits you'll be thoroughly sick.'

'I have a strong stomach,' said John, refilling his glass.

'Now,' the old man continued, 'in the beginning of the world we know, our God brought light and created man. Before this time existed only utter cold and utter confusion where reigned the Elder Gods of darkness, unchallenged. With the coming of light and the creation of man they were cast down with their temples. But gods do not die, they sleep and they dream. The old serpent entered Eden to tempt man back to the darkness; he sowed the seed of doubt in him. Doubt in the power of his Creator. God drove back the serpent but the damage was already done. The serpent never left Eden you see, he slept, and he dreamed, awaiting the time when he would rise again. That time is now upon us. Through the exercise of what man thought to be his own free will he has furthered the aims of the serpent. The prophecies are even now being fulfilled, as testified by your palm there, Jim.' Pooley pocketed his tattooed mit. 'Man has, through the influence of the serpent, given genesis to his own replacement: simply, the thinking machine.'

'I, Robot?' said Omally. 'I've read all that. Machines do not think, they are programmed merely to respond, they answer questions but with the answers that were already fed into them. Computers do not have souls.'

'There now,' said Professor Slocombe, 'you have saved me my old breath. They have no souls. It is man's soul alone which prevents him slipping back into the darkness. The soul cries out to the light, the soul worships the light. Replace man and the temple of the lord of light is cast down. The darkness returns.'

'The whole menu was a bowl of sprouts,' said Omally bitterly. 'I am going to be sick.'

'It all sounds somewhat eclectic,' remarked Jim, surprising even himself. 'I do not pretend to understand much of it.'

'Like the sprout, it takes a bit of swallowing,' the Professor replied. 'What I am trying to say is this: computer science is founded upon the silicon chip. It has long been suggested by scientists that life might exist elsewhere in the universe, life possibly with a silicon base. They do not seem to realize that they have created it here on Earth, at the behest of a hidden master. When man is made subservient to the machine he is no longer in control of his own destiny. Therefore he is no longer the dominant species. The people of Brentford are being replaced one after another by duplicates of themselves. Soulless robots programmed to worship their master. Unless we act quickly, then all we have ever known will be lost.'

Pooley solemnly removed his wristlet watch and cast it into the fire. The plastic crackled amongst the flames, and, to add further horror to a conversation which had already been a far cry from a cosy fireside chat, a shrill voice shrieked out from the flames calling for mercy.

Omally crossed himself. 'I believe,' he said simply.

'Then you will fight with me?'

'I think that we have little choice. Jim?'

Pooley raised his unmarked palm. 'Count me in, I suppose,' said he.

17

The conversation wore long into the night. John and Jim were anxious to know exactly what plans the Professor had formulated, but the old man was obstinately vague in his replies. It was either that he was as yet uncertain as to what had to be done, or that he had already set certain wheels in motion and feared the two men might, out of their eagerness to pitch in for the cause, confound them. Whatever the case, Jim at length returned to his rooms and fell into a most uneasy sleep beset with ghastly dreams of mechanical monsters and bogey men who loomed up from every darkened corner. Omally, as ever, slept the sleep of the just, which was quite unjust of him, considering he had no right to do it.

At around eleven the next morning, the two men met up outside the Flying Swan. Pooley emptied what pennies remained to him into the outspread palm of his fellow. 'He won't take my cash any more, simply runs his damn little wand over my hand. It gives me little pleasure.'

'If there is a word of truth to anything the Professor told us, then at least we have a vague idea what's going on.'

'Vague would be your man, John, this is well out of my league.'

'That is a nice suit you have on there,' Omally observed as Jim strode on before him into the Swan. 'If a little tight across the shoulders perhaps.'

The pale young man in the headphones stood as ever behind the jump. Nothing had been heard of Neville since he had been whisked away in the ambulance. The Sisters of Mercy said that he had been moved to another hospital but seemed uncertain where. The fact that ownership of the brewery had changed hands suggested that Brentford had seen the last of the part-time barman. 'Replacement,' the Professor had said; it was a more than unsettling business. And the thought that duplicates were even now being created to replace each living individual in Brentford was no laughing matter.

'Usual please,' said Jim, extending his palm.

The man in the headset ran his electronic pen across the outstretched appendage and cleared his throat with a curiously mechanical coughing sound. 'Great day for the race,' he said.

'Yours or mine?' muttered Jim beneath his breath.

Omally bought his own. 'It's just not the same any more,' he sighed, as he bore his pint over to the table Jim now occupied. 'I miss the thrill of the chase.'

'I don't think anything is ever going to be the same again,' said Pooley unhappily. 'All is finished here. If only we had legged it away in time we would never be sitting here trapped like rats, waiting to be replaced by piles of diodes.'

John shook his head. 'It is a bad one to be sure. No doubt the walls will expand to finally engulf the whole world, but the Professor never did explain why it all started right here.'

'Well, I suppose it had to start somewhere and Brentford, although worse than some, is, as the world knows, better than most. But it is the unfairness of it that gets my dander up. Me, with money to burn and two dozen High Street shops to burn it in. My God, I'm doing my best, but what about teas at the Ritz and the Concorde flight to the Bahamas? Such things are day to day affairs for lads with my kind of scratch. I can't even buy people drinks. My entire wealth is without purpose.'

'The Professor warned you, Jim, the money wasn't meant for you.'

'This beer is definitely not what it was.' Pooley raised his pint and held it towards the light. Through the clear amber liquid a row of computer lines etched on to the glass twinkled like the slats of a Venetian blind.

'I had been thinking the same,' Omally replied. 'It has a definitely metallic tang to it nowadays.'

An odd figure now entered the Flying Swan. He appeared awkward and ill at ease amongst his surroundings. The stranger wore a wide-brimmed hat of dark material and a similarly-coloured cloak which reached to the floor, exposing only the very tips of his Wellington boots.

'It's Soap,' Omally whispered. 'Now what do you suppose he is doing here?'

'Come to pay us our thirty quid, hopefully,' said Jim, who even in wealth was never too aloof to forget a creditor.

Soap ordered a Guinness, without the head, and paid for the same with a gold nugget which the barman weighed up and committed to the till. The man in black approached the two seated drinkers. 'Good day,' he said.

'Not yet,' said the Omally. 'But you have my full permission to improve upon it should you so wish.'

'Might I take a seat?'

'If you must.'

Soap removed his hat and placed it upon the table. His albino coiffure glowed stunningly even in the dim light of the saloon-bar; the pink eyes wandered between the two men. 'How's tricks?' he asked.

'Oh, going great guns,' Pooley made an airy gesture. 'Just sitting here drinking duff beer, waiting for the end of the world. Ringside seats to boot.'

'Hm.' Soap toyed with the ample brim of his extraordinary hat. 'I'll tell you what though, but. You're better off here than out there.' He thumbed away towards the glistening wall of light which shimmered in the distance beyond the Swan's upper panes. 'It's all hell for sure in that neck of the woods.'

'You mean you've been outside?' Omally raised his ample eyebrows.

'Naturally.' Soap tugged lewdly at his lower eye. 'You know the expression you can't keep a good man down? Well here it's a case of a good man down is worth three in the Butts. Good'n that, eh? One of my own.'

'Bloody marvellous,' said Pooley without conviction. 'So what is going on out there?'

'Bad things.' Soap stared sombrely into his pint. The sharpened, ear-rooting nail of his little finger traced a runic symbol upon the knap of his hatbrim. 'Bad things.' Soap sipped at his pint and drew a slim wrist across his mouth. 'Bloody chaos,' he said simply. 'It makes me sick at heart to see what goes on out there, but the Professor says that I must keep the watch. Although he nevers says for what.'

'So what have you seen, Soap?'

'They are starving out there.' Soap's pink eyes darted up at his inquisitor.

'You're joking, surely?'

'I am not. Since the institution of the new non-monetary system of exchange the entire country is literally in a state of civil war.'

'Come now,' said Jim. 'What you mean is that a few die-hards are giving two fingers to the printed-palm brigade. Bloody good luck to them I say. I'll arrange to have a couple of million drawn out. You take it with my blessings.'

'Money won't do it,' said Soap. 'Paper currency is illegal. All assets were instantly frozen on the day of the change. Each individual had to hand in his cash to the bank upon his turn for registration. Those who refused to submit to the change found every door closed to them. They could not travel upon buses or trains or buy petrol for their own cars; nor milk from the milkman, nor bread from the bakers. Their friends and neighbours rejected them. Even members of their own families, those who had the mark, refused them. They were ostracized totally from society. Many went straight to the banks but were told that they had missed their opportunity and that was that.'

'And that no man might buy or sell, save he that had the mark or the name of the beast or the number of his name,' said Jim Pooley in a leaden voice.

'The very same.'

'The callous bastards,' said John Omally. 'So what happened then?'

'Exactly what you might expect. Open rebellion on the part of the unmarked. What they could no longer buy they took. There was looting and burning and killing. Much killing. Under the direction of the Government's master computer martial law was imposed. The computer issued a brief edict: all those who do not bear the mark to be shot on sight.'

'Are you making this up, Soap?' Omally leant forward in his seat and waggled his fist threateningly beneath the hollow Earther's all-but-transparent nose. 'Jim and I have both sussed that something pretty pony is going on here. Although we are trapped by a seemingly impenetrable barrier, the shops never run dry. There is always milk and fags, bread and beer, although that is tasting a bit odd of late. It must all be coming in from the outside, although we haven't figured out exactly how as yet. Parachutes in the dead of night we suspect.'

'You're on a wrong'n,' said Soap. 'Nothing gets in or out except me. And there's no food going begging out there either.'

'So how do you account for it then?'

'It is all manufactured right here in the parish.'

154

'Oh rot,' said Jim. 'Do you see any cows grazing in the Memorial Park, or any hop fields or tobacco plantations? Talk sense, Soap, please. How could any of it be made here?'

'It is all artificially produced. Every last little thing, it's all synthetic. Including your manky beer.' Soap pushed his glass aside. 'I can't tell you how it's done but I can tell you who's doing it.'

'Lateinos and bloody Romiith,' said Omally in a doom-laden voice.

'None other. What do you think the walls are up for anyway?'

'To keep us in,' Jim said gloomily. 'To keep me in and stop me spending my money.'

'Wrong,' said Soap. 'To keep the others out. Those walls were whipped up to protect the master computer complex in Abaddon Street. It is the centre of the whole operation.'

'They got my antique bedstead, the bastards,' snarled Omally, 'and now my beer also. Will it never end?'

'But why is this master complex in Brentford?' Jim asked. 'I'd always pictured Armageddon getting off to its first round in a somewhat more Biblical setting. The gasworks and the flyover just don't seem to fit.'

'You'll have to ask the Professor about that,' said Soap. 'Or possibly your man there.' Soap stretched out a pale hand towards the tall, gaunt spectre wearing long out-moded tweeds and smoking a Turkish cigarette who now stood majestically framed in the Swan's famous portal.

'Gentlemen,' said Mr Sherlock Holmes, gesturing to the three seated figures, two of which were now cowering away and seeking invisibility, 'if I might just prevail upon your aid in a small matter.'

'And there was I utterly convinced that things could get no worse,' said John Omally. 'Oh foolish fellow me.'

18

Sherlock Holmes strode up the Ealing Road, his cigarette billowing smoke about his angular visage. Pooley and Omally plodded behind, and had they chosen to pause a moment and look around they might just have caught sight of the manhole cover which closed upon Soap's retreating form.

'I merely wish you to be close at hand,' said Sherlock Holmes as he marched along. 'Just button your lips and hang loose, got me?'

Pooley, who had recently purchased for the detective an advanced video recorder and the complete series of Basil Rathbone cassettes, thought to detect the hint of an American accent creeping into the Victorian voice. 'Oh, gotcha,' he said.

Outside Norman's corner-shop Holmes drew to a sudden halt. His two followers did likewise and peered without enthusiasm through the spotless plexiglass of the new aluminium-framed door to where Norman stood behind his shining counter. The true shopkeeper was busy in his kitchenette, bent low over a set of indecipherable plans scrawled on to the innards of a cornflake packet. He scarcely heard the shopdoor-bell chime out an electronic fanfare. His double peered up from the countertop computer terminal and surveyed his three potential customers. The Irish one, cowering to the rear, owed, he recalled. Clearing his throat with a curiously mechanical coughing sound, he asked, 'How might we serve you, gentlemen?'

'We?' queried Sherlock Holmes.

'The plurality is used in a purely business sense,' the robot replied. 'We, the interest, which is Norman Hartnell, cornershop, as a small concern, realize the need to extend a personal welcome to the prospective client in these competitive times.'

'Very precise,' said Sherlock Holmes. 'An ounce of Ships, if you please.'

'Certainly, sir.' The robot slipped his hand behind his back and drew out the packet. Omally considered that to be a pretty sneaky move by any reckoning.

'You have redecorated your premises, I see,' said Holmes.

Considering this to be a simple statement of fact which required no reply, the robot offered none.

'And all achieved with the left hand.'

The creation stiffened ever so slightly but retained its composure, although a fleeting look of suspicion crossed its face. Pooley and Omally both stepped back unconsciously.

'I was always given to understand that you were right-handed,' Holmes continued.

'That will be eighteen shillings and sixpence, please, sir.' The robot stretched forward both hands, that he might exhibit no personal preference.

'Put it on my slate, please,' said Sherlock Holmes.

Beneath his breath John Omally began to recite the rosary.

Holmes' deadly phrase clanged amongst the robot's network of inner circuitry and fed out the word 'Dimac' in any one of a dozen known languages. 'Eighteen shillings and sixpence, please,' he said. 'The management regret that . . .'

'So I have been given to understand,' said Holmes. 'If it is not inconvenient, I should like a word or two with the management.'

'I am it.' The robot pressed his hands to the countertop and prepared to spring over. 'Kindly hand me the eighteen shillings and sixpence.'

'I think not,' said Sherlock Holmes. 'Let us not bandy words, please. If the real Norman Hartnell still draws breath then I wish to speak with him. If not, then I am making a citizen's arrest.'

The robot lunged forward across the counter and made a grab at the detective's throat. Holmes stepped nimbly beyond range and drew out his revolver. He pointed it at the space between the robot's eyes, his aim was steady and unshaking. 'Hurry now,' he said, 'my time is valuable.'

The robot stared at the great detective. Its lips were drawn back from its plasticized teeth which glowed an evil yellow. Its eyes blazed hatred and its hands crooked into cruel claws.

'Hold hard or I fire.'

The pseudo-shopkeeper crouched low upon his knees and suddenly leapt upwards. Holmes' finger closed about the trigger, but the inhuman reactions of the creation far outmatched his own. The thing leapt upwards, passing clean through the ceiling of the shop, bringing down an avalanche of lathe and plaster and tumbling timberwork. Holmes staggered backwards, shielding his face from the falling debris. Pooley and Omally adopted the now legendary foetal position. A series of further crashes signalled the departure of the robot through the walls of Norman's back bedroom.

Startled by the sounds of destruction, the shop-keeper burst through his kitchenette door into the now thoroughly ventilated shop. He gazed up at the crude hole yawning above and then down at the faces of the three coughing and spluttering men as they slowly appeared amidst the cloud of dust. 'What . . . who . . . why . . . ?' Norman's voice trailed off as Sherlock Holmes rose from the debris, patting plaster from his shoulders, and removing a section of lathing from his hair.

'Mr Hartnell,' he said, 'it is a pleasure to meet you actually in the flesh, as it were.'

Pooley and Omally blinked their eyes towards the gaping ceiling, towards the startled shopkeeper, and finally towards each other. Shaking their dust-covered heads in total disbelief, they followed the detective who was even now ushering the fretful Norman away into his kitchenette. Holmes suggested that Omally might bolt the front door and put up the 'Closed For The Day' sign. This the Irishman did with haste, fearing that he might miss anything of what might be yet to come. When he entered the kitchenette he found Norman squatting upon his odd-legged chair in the centre of the room, surrounded by a clutter of bizarre-looking equip-ment which was obviously the current fruit of his prodigious scientific brain. Holmes perched behind him upon the kitchen table, a tweedy vulture hovering above his carrion lunch. Without warning he suddenly thrust a long bony finger into Norman's right ear.

'Ooh, ouch, ow, get off me,' squealed the shop-keeper, doubling up.

Holmes examined his fingertip and waggled it beneath his nose. 'I pride myself,' said he, 'that, given a specimen of earwax, I can state the occupation of the donor with such an accuracy that any suggestion of there being any element of chance involved is absolutely confounded.'

'Really?' said Omally studying the ceiling and kicking his heels upon the new lino of the floor.

'Who's your friend?' whined the persecuted shop-keeper.

'Don't ask,' counselled Jim Pooley.

'I will ask the questions, if you don't mind.' Holmes prodded Norman in the ribs with a patent leather toecap.

'I do, as it happens,' said Norman, flinching anew.

'Be that as it may, I believe that you have much to tell us.'

'Bugger off, will you?' Norman cowered in his seat.

'Language,' said Jim. 'Mr H, our companion here, is a house-guest of the Professor's. He can be trusted absolutely, I assure you.'

'I have nothing to say. What is all this about anyway? Can't you see I'm busy redecorating?'

'The shop ceiling seems a bit drastic,' said John.

161

'Blame the wife,' Norman said sarcastically. 'She said she wanted two rooms knocked into one.'

'I once heard George Robey tell that joke,' said Holmes. 'It was old even then.'

'George Robey?'

'No matter. Now, sir, there are questions that must be answered. How can it be that your duplicate works in your shop yet you still exist? Show me your palms, sir.'

'Show me your palms? Jim, where do you meet these people?' A sudden clout on the back of the head sent the shopkeeper sprawling.

'Here, steady on,' cried Jim. 'There's no need for any of that. Sherlock Holmes never engaged in that kind of practice.'

'Changing times,' the detective pronounced, examining his knuckles.

'Sherlock Holmes?' sneered Norman from the desk. 'Is that who he thinks he is?'

'Your servant, sir,' said Holmes, bowing slightly from the waist.

'Oh yes?' Norman cowered in the corner shielding his privy parts. 'Well if you're Sherlock Holmes then tell me, what are the thirty-nine steps?'

'This is where I came in,' said Jim.

Holmes leant forward and waggled his waxy finger towards Norman. 'Spill the beans, you,' he cried. 'Spill the beans!'

'He's been watching the Basil Rathbone reruns,' Pooley whispered to Omally.

'If you don't mind,' said John, 'I think Jim and I will take our leave now. We are men of peace, and displays of gratuitous violence trouble our sensitivities. Even in the cause of justice and the quest for truth, we find them upsetting.'

Pooley nodded. 'If you are now preparing to wade in with the old rubber truncheon, kindly wait until we have taken our leave.'

'Fellas,' whined the fallen shopkeeper, 'fellas, don't leave me here with this lunatic.'

'Sorry,' said Jim, 'but this is none of our business.'

'If you really wish to make a fight of it, your Dimac should be a match for his Barritso.' Omally pointed to the still prominent lump upon his forehead, which bore a silent if painful testimony to his previous encounter with the martial shopman.

'That wasn't me, John, I swear it.'

'So,' said Sherlock Holmes, 'then spill the beans, buddy.'

'All right, all right, but no more hitting.'

'No more hitting,' said Sherlock Holmes.

Buddy prepared himself to spill all the beans.

19

Old Pete thrust his wrinkled hand beneath the shining plexiglass counter-shield of the sub-post office. The dark young man now serving behind the jump did not remove his minuscule headphones but merely nodded as he passed the electronic light-wand across the ancient's palm. He punched a few details into the computer terminal and awaited the forth-coming readout. Upon its arrival he raised a quizzical eyebrow towards the pensioner and said, 'There appears to be some discrepancy here, sir. I suggest that you come back next week.'

Old Pete glared daggers at the dark young fellow-me-lad behind the tinted screen. 'What damned discrepancy?' he demanded.

The young man sighed tolerantly. 'The computer registers a discrepancy,' he said. 'It states that for the last ten years you have been receiving two pensions each week. Such a thing could not, of course, happen now under the new advanced system. But with the old Giro, well who knows? We shall just have to resubmit the data and await a decision.'

'And how long will that take?'

'Well, computer time is valuable, you are allotted six seconds weekly; we will see what happens when your turn comes around again.'

'And in the meantime?' foamed Old Pete. 'Do you mean that until your filthy electronic box of tricks gives you the go-ahead I am penniless?'

'The word "penniless" no longer applies. It is simply that, pending investigations, your credit is temporarily suspended. You must understand that this is for the public good. We are trying to institute the new system hereabouts in a manner that will cause minimum civil unrest.'

'You'll get maximum civil unrest if I don't get my damned pensions, I mean, pension!' Young Chips growled in agreement and bared his fangs.

'Next customer, please,' the dark young man said.

'Hold hard,' cried Old Pete raising his stick. 'I want to speak to the manager.'

'This branch no longer has a manager, sir, but an operator, fully conversant, I hasten to add, with all current trends in new technology.'

'A pox upon your technology. Who do I see about my pension?'

'Well you might fill in a form which we will forward in due course to Head Office, requesting a manual systems over-ride, although the procedure is somewhat archaic and extremely lengthy.'

'Then I'll go up to your Head Office and speak with them.'

The dark young man laughed malevolently. 'One does not simply go up to Lateinos and Romiiths and speak to them. Whoever heard of such a thing?' He smirked towards his assistant, who tittered behind her hand and turned up her eyes.

'Oh don't they, though?' snarled Old Pete, grinding upon his dentures and rapping his Penang-lawyer upon the plexiglass screen. 'Well, we'll see about that.' With Chips hard on his down-at-heels, the ancient departed the sub-post office, walking for once without the aid of his stick.

Ahead, where once had been only bombsite land, the Lateinos and Romiith building rose above Brentford, a dark and accusing finger pointing towards the enclosed triangle of grey-troubled sky. Sixty-six floors of black lustreless glass, swallowing up the light. Within its cruel and jagged shadow magnolias wilted in their window-boxes and synthetic gold-top became doorstep cheese. It was not a thing of beauty but there was a terrible quality of a joyless for ever about it. High upon the uppermost ramparts, amid the clouds, tiny figures came and went, moving at a furious pace, striving to increase its height. Never had there been a Babel tower more fit for the tumbling, nor a fogey more willing to take on the task.

Old Pete rounded the corner into Abaddon Street and glowered up at the sheer glass monolith. 'Progress,' he spat, rattling his ill-fitting dentures. 'A pox on it all.' His bold stride suddenly became a hobble once more as he passed into the bleak shadow of the imperious building and sought the entrance. A faceless wall met his limited vision. Another painful hundred yards, a further corner, and another blank wall of featureless glass. 'Damned odd,' wheezed the ancient to his dog as he plodded onwards once more. The entrance to the building could only be in the

High Street. To Old Pete's utter disgust and still increasing fury, it was not.

He now stood leaning upon his cane beneath the night-black structure, puffing and blowing and cursing loudly whenever he could draw sufficient breath. There was simply no way in or out of the building, not a doorway, not an entrance, not a letter-box or a nameplate, nothing. Young Chips cocked his furry head upon one side and peered up at his ancient master. The old boy suddenly looked very fragile indeed. The snow-capped head shook and shivered, and beneath the frayed cuffs of his one suit, the gnarled and knobby hands with their blue street-maps of veins knotted and reknotted themselves into feeble fists. 'We'll get to the bottom of this,' snarled Old Pete, still undefeated. Once more raising his stick and this time striking at the dead-black wall towering towards infinity. The blow did not elicit a sound and this raised the ancient's fury to cardiac arrest level. Pummelling for all he was worth he retraced his steps and staggered back towards Abaddon Street.

As the aged loon lurched along, raining blows upon the opaque glass, a hidden probe, shielded from his vision, moved with him, scanning his every movement. Digesting and cataloguing the minutiae that made up Old Pete. Through an advanced form of electro-carbon dating it penetrated the bone rings of his skull and accurately calculated his age to five decimal places. Its spectroscopic intensifiers analysed the soil samples beneath his fingernails and generated graphs which were no matters for jest. Fluoroscopes

X-rayed his lower gut and ruminated upon the half-digested lunchtime pork pies, which contained no traces of pork whatever. The probe swept into the fabric of his wartime shirt, illuminating a thousand hidden laundry marks and cross-indexed them. It moved down to his underpants and hurriedly retraced its metaphorical footsteps to areas above belt-level. It checked out the tweed of his jacket, measured the angles of the lapels and, through numerous esoteric calculations, tracked down the suit's manufacture to a Wednesday in a long hot summer prior to the Great War. The computer banks gulped it all down and gorged themselves upon the feast of data; gurgled with delight and dug in ever more deeply in search of further toothsome morsels. They entered secretly into his head and chewed upon his brain cells, ravenously seeking the possibility of electron particle variabilities in the codex of his cerebellum.

Within .666 of a second they had done with their main course and were seeking a mangey-looking half-terrier for afters. The read-out which followed, had it been broadcast in standard five-point lettering, would have formed an equation sufficient to engirdle the Earth several times around. Summing up, the computer pronounced Old Pete a harmless loony and no threat to security. It did, however, suggest that certain discrepancies existed regarding multiple payment of pensions in the past and that the data relating to this would require a prolonged period to assess accurately. It refused to comment on Young Chips, offering only a cryptic remark that the wearing of flea collars should be made compulsory.

Old Pete finally gave up his unequeal struggle and limped off down the street effing and blinding for all he was worth. Young Chips lifted his furry leg contemptuously on to the dull black-glass wall and skipped off after his master. The Lateinos and Romiith mainframe filed away Old Pete's vitals and beamed a triplicate copy of the now completed programme to the bio-gene constructional workshop, twenty-six storeys below. The probe moved up once more to the building's roof and turned itself to more pressing business. Included amongst a billion or so other tiny matters which required attention was the removal from this plane of existence of a certain local Professor and his unclassifiable house-guest.

The sensory scanner criss-crossed the triangle of streets and houses, prying and probing. The X-ray eye of the great machine penetrated each dwelling, highlighting the plumbing pipes and television tubes. The house-owners were tiny red blotches moving to and fro, going about their business unaware that all was revealed to the voyeurist machine which lurked above their heads. The data whirred into the computer banks, but at intervals the motors flicked and whined as a patch of impenetrable white light appeared on the screen. As the macroscope focused upon the area of disturbance and intensified its gaze, the area revealed itself to be a large house and garden set upon the historic Butts Estate. The data retrieval cross-locators coughed and spluttered, fruitlessly seeking a snippet of relevant information, but none was to be found. The white patch glared on the screen, the missing piece of a great jigsaw. The best the print-out could come up with was 'Insufficient data, scan penetration negative, over-ride and re-submit.'

20

Professor Slocombe rewound the great ormulu mantel-clock and, withdrawing the fretted key from the gilded face, set the pendulum in motion. The sonorous tocking of the magnificent timepiece returned the heartbeat once more to the silent house.

Sherlock Holmes entered the study through the open French windows. 'It has stopped again?' said he.

The Professor nodded sombrely. 'The mechanism has become infected, I believe.'

Holmes slumped into a fireside chair. 'You have had the electricity disconnected, I trust?'

'As we discussed, we will have to be very much upon our guard from now on. I have taken what protective measures I can, but my powers are not inexhaustible, I can feel the pressure upon me even now.'

Holmes slid a pale hand about the decanter's neck and poured himself a small scotch. 'I have just spent a most informative hour with Norman Hartnell. A man of exceptional capability.'

Professor Slocombe smiled ruefully. 'He keeps us all guessing, that is for certain.'

'I discovered the hand of a duplicate replacement at work in his shop and sought to question it.'

Professor Slocombe raised his eyebrows in horror. 'That was a somewhat reckless move upon your part.'

'Perhaps, but when confronted by the gun you gave me, the thing took flight, literally, through the ceiling of the shop. To my astonishment the real Mr Hartnell appears from his quarters. The mechanical double was, in fact, something of his own creation. To spare his time for more important matters, according to himself.'

Professor Slocombe chuckled loudly. 'Bravo, Norman,' he said. 'The shopkeeper does have something rather substantial on the go at the present time. It is of the utmost importance that nothing stand in his way.'

Sherlock Holmes shook his head. 'Your corner-shopkeeper produces an all-but-perfect facsimile of himself with no more than a few discarded wireless-set parts and something he calls Meccano and you treat it as if it were an everyday affair.'

'This is Brentford. Norman's ingenuity is not unknown to me.'

'And do you know how his mechanical man is powered?'

'Knowing Norman, it probably has a key in its back or runs upon steam.'

'On the contrary,' said Sherlock Holmes, taking the opportunity to spring from his chair and take up a striking pose against the mantelpiece, 'it runs from a slim brass wheel set into its chest. Your shopkeeper has rediscovered the secret of perpetual motion.'

'Has he, be damned?' The Professor bit upon his

lower lip. 'Now that is another matter entirely.'

'Ha,' said Holmes, nodding his head, 'and now would you like me to bring you the automaton, that you might inspect his workings at first hand?'

'Very much. Do you consider that such might be achieved in safety?'

'Certainly, I took the liberty of following the ample trail he left, after my interview with Norman. He is holed up on the allotment.'

'Holed up?'

'Certainly, in Mr Omally's shed. If I can catch him unawares I shall bring him here at gunpoint. Although I must confess to a certain bafflement here. How might it be that an automaton who can leap without effort or apparent harm through ceilings and walls, fears the simple bullet?'

'Ha, yourself!' said Professor Slocombe. 'You have your secrets and I have mine. Go then, with my blessing, but stay upon your guard. Take no unnecessary risks.'

'Natcho,' said Sherlock Holmes, turning as he left to make a gesture which all lovers of the New York television cop genre know to be the 'soul fist'.

'Natcho?' Professor Slocombe shook his old head and returned once more to his work.

21

Having slipped away to Jack Lane's for a pint or three of non-takeover-brewery beer, Pooley and Omally now loped down a bunting bedecked Sprite Street. To either side, front gardens bulged with sections of the home-made floats destined to join the grand carnival procession of this year's Festival which, meaningless as it now appeared, showed every sign of going on regardless. Exactly what the theme of the parade was, neither man very much cared. As they ambled along they muttered away to one another in muted, if urgent, tones.

'As I see it,' mumbled John, 'we have few options left open to us at present. If the end of civilization is approaching there is little, if anything, we can do about it.'

'But what about all my millions?' Jim complained. 'I thought that the holders of the world's wealth always had it up and away on their hand-mades and sailed their luxury yachts into the sunset at the merest mention of impending doom.'

'What, off down the canal you fancy?'

'Well, somewhere, surely? Let us at least go down with Soap and weather it out until the troubles are over.'

'I had considered that, but you will recall that it is

very dark down there in his neck of the woods. And darkness would seem to be the keynote of this whole insane concerto.'

'So what do we do then?'

The two stopped on the corner of Abaddon Street and stood a moment, gazing up at the great black monolith towering above them.

'I have been giving this matter a great deal of thought and I think I have come up with an answer.'

'It better be a goody.'

'It is, but not here. Walls have ears as they say. Let us hasten away to a place of privacy and discuss this matter.'

It did not take a child of six to put the necessary two and two together and come up with Omally's suggestion for a likely conspiratorial hideaway. 'My hut,' said John.

The two men strode over the allotments, each alone with his particular thoughts. The first inkling that anything of a more untoward nature than was now the common norm was currently on the go thereabouts hit them like the proverbial bolt from the blue. The sound of gunfire suddenly rattled their eardrums, and the unexpected sight of Omally's corrugated iron roof rising from its mountings and coming rapidly in their direction put new life into their feet.

'Run for your life,' yelled Omally.

'I am already, get out of my way.'

The roof smashed to earth, sparing them by inches. The cause of the shed's destruction tumbled down to bowl over and over between them. Norman's duplicate rose to his feet and glared back towards the ruined hut. Sherlock Holmes appeared at the doorway wielding his gun.

'Not again.' Pooley crawled away on all fours, seeking safety.

'Stop him,' cried Sherlock Holmes.

'With the corner up, pal.'

'Hold hard or I fire.'

Norman's duplicate turned upon his attacker. He snatched up a ten-gallon oil-drum which was harmlessly serving its time as a water-butt and raised it above his head. Holmes stood his ground, feet planted firmly apart, both hands upon his weapon. 'This is a Magnum Forty-four,' he said, 'biggest handgun in the world, and can blow your head clean off your shoulders.'

'He has definitely been watching too many videos,' whispered Omally as he crawled over to Pooley's place of safety.

'Now I know what you're thinking,' Holmes continued, 'you're thinking, in all that commotion did he fire five shots or six, that's what you're thinking, isn't it, punk?'

'I much preferred the Victorian approach,' said Jim Pooley.

Norman's robot stiffened; he was not adverse to watching the occasional Clint Eastwood movie himself on Norman's home-made video.

'Do you know, in all the excitement I'm not really sure myself? So what do you say, punk?'

The mechanical punk, who had seen that particular film six times said, 'It's a fair cop, governor,' and raised its hands.

'Up against the wall and spread'm mother,' cried Sherlock Holmes, causing Sir Arthur Conan Doyle to veritably spin in his grave.

Not too long later, Jim Pooley, John Omally, and Mr Sherlock Holmes, this time accompanied by a near-perfect facsimile of a highly-regarded local shop-keeper, entered the Professor's study. The scholar looked up from his desk and turned about in his chair. 'You made very short work of that,' he said. 'Good afternoon, Norman.'

The mechanical shopkeeper regarded the Pro-fessor as if he was guano on a hat-brim. 'You would do well to leave well enough alone,' said he.

Professor Slocombe turned up his palms. 'Please be seated, I have no wish to detain you longer than necessary. I merely seek a few answers to certain pressing questions.'

The duplicate clutched at his chest. 'To take away my life, more likely.'

'No, no, I swear. Please be seated.' Professor Slocombe turned to his other guests. 'Please avail yourselves, gentlemen, Norman and I have much to speak of.'

Holmes held his gun pointing steadily towards the robot's spinning heart. 'You counselled care, Pro-fessor,' said he, 'and now it is my turn.'

'A degree of trust must exist, Holmes, kindly put aside your gun.'

Holmes did so. Pooley and Omally fought awhile over the decanter and finally came to an agreement.

'It is of the greatest importance that we speak with

177

each other,' Professor Slocombe told the robot. 'Please believe that I wish you no harm. Will you play straight with me?'

'I will, sir, but have a care for him. The man is clearly mad. Calls himself Sherlock Holmes but knows not a thing of the thirty-nine steps. I would have come to you of my own accord.'

'Really?'

'Oh yes.' The robot cleared his throat with a curiously mechanical coughing sound which sent the wind up Pooley and Omally. 'Things cannot be allowed to continue as they are.'

Professor Slocombe raised his eyebrows. 'You are aware of that?'

'I can hear them talking. They gnaw at my brain but I will not allow them ingress. I am Norman's man and sworn by the bond of birth to protect him.'

'Your loyalty is commendable.'

'I am sworn to serve mankind.'

'From behind a counter,' sneered Omally.

The robot nodded grimly. 'It sounded a little more noble the way I put it, but no matter, there is little enough of mankind now left to serve. The shop doorbell is silent the better part of the day. Trade declines; I rarely punch an order into the terminal, and when I do, the new stocks which finally arrive are further foreshortened. The master computer now runs it all. Mankind is on the wane, the new order prevails, night falls upon Brentford and the world. It is the coming of Ragnorok. *Götterdämmerung.*'

'Stick the Laurence Olivier circuits into override,

you clockwork clown,' said John Vincent Omally, Man of Earth.

'How would you like me to fill your mouth with boot?' the robot enquired.

'Gentlemen, gentlemen,' said Professor Slocombe, 'let us have a little decorum please.'

'Well, he's had my shed down,' Omally complained. 'For one sworn to protect mankind he's about as much use as a nipple on a—'

'Quite so, John. Please be calm, we will achieve nothing by fighting amongst ourselves. We must all pull together.'

'You can pull whatever you want,' said the robot, 'but take it from me, you had better start with your fingers. Unless you can come up with something pretty special, pretty snappish, then you blokes are banjoed, get my meaning, F . . . U . . . C . . .'

'Language, please,' said Professor Slocombe. 'I think we catch your drift. Something pretty special was what I had in mind.'

22

'AAAAOOOOOOOOOAAAAAAAAAAAOOOOO . . . O . . . UH?'

Neville the part-time barman awoke after an absence of some eleven chapters. Scorning the tried and tested 'Where am I?' he settled for 'Why have I got a light bulb stuck up my left nostril?' which was at least original. His eyes rolled up towards the ceiling, several inches above his face, and a great hand rose to brush away the obstruction blocking one side of his nose. This bed is a bit high, thought Neville. But then the dreadful memories of his most despicable situation came flooding back in a tidal wave of adipose tissue.

'The fat!' groaned Neville, his voice rumbling up from the depths of his stomach to shiver the ceiling above. 'The terrible fat!' He tried to move his great St Paul's dome of a head, but it seemed to be wedged tightly into an upper corner of the tiny hospital room. Painfully he struggled and shifted until he was able to peer down over the great massed army of himself and gauge some idea of how the land lay. It lay someway distant in the downwards direction. 'OOOOOAAAAAAOOOOOOOAAA . . . UH,' moaned Neville. 'Worse, much worse.'

A sudden sound distracted him from his misery,

somewhere beneath his spreading bulk and slightly to one side, a door appeared to be opening. From his eyrie above the picture-rail Neville watched a minuscule nurse enter the already crowded room.

'And how are we today?' asked this fairy person.

'We?' Neville's voice arose in desperation. 'You mean that there is more than one of me now?'

'No, no.' The tiny nurse held up a pair of doll-like hands. 'You are doing very well, making good progress, great signs of improvement, nothing to fear.'

Neville now noticed to his increasing horror that the midget was brandishing a hypodermic syringe. Which, although perched between her tiddly digits like a Christmas cracker fag-holder, looked none the less as threatening as any of the others he had recently experienced at hind quarters.

'Time for your daily jab, roll over please.'

'Roll over? Are you mad, woman?' Neville wobbled his jowls down at the nurse.

The woman smiled up at him. 'Come on now, sir,' she wheedled. 'We're not going to throw one of our little tantrums now, are we?'

If Neville could have freed one of his feet, possibly the one which was now wedged above the curtain-rail surrounding his bed, he would have happily stamped the tiny nurse to an omelette.

'Come on now, sir, roly-poly.'

'Crunch crunch,' went Neville. 'Fe . . . Fi . . . Fo . . . Fum . . .'

'Don't start all that again, sir. I shall have to call for doctor.'

181

'Crunch . . . splat.' Neville struggled to free a foot, or anything.

'You leave me no choice, then.' The tiny nurse left the room, slamming the door behind her.

Neville rubbed his nose upon the ceiling. How long had he been here? Days? Months? Years? He really had no idea. What were they doing to him? Pumping him full of drugs to keep him sedated? What? He had known all along that it was a conspiracy, but what were they up to? They had blown him up like a blimp for their own foul ends. Probably for some vile new hormone research designed to increase the bacon yield from porker pigs. It was the Illuminati, or the masons, or the Moonies or some suchlike sinister outfit. Just because he was slightly paranoid, it didn't mean they weren't out to get him.

And far worse even, what was happening at the Swan? That defrocked Matelot Croughton would have his hand in the till up to the armpit. The beer would be flat and the ashtrays full. There was even the possibility of after-hours drinking, Omally would see to that. He was probably even downing pints on credit at this very moment. It was all too much. He must escape, if only to save his reputation. Neville twisted and turned in his confinement, a latterday Alice tormented in a sterilized doll's house.

The door of the room flew open beneath him and the nurse re-entered, accompanied by a pale young doctor in headphones. As Neville watched in fearful anticipation, he withdrew from his belt a small black device bristling with a pair of slim metallic rods. 'We

182

are being naughty again,' he said, clearing his throat with a curiously mechanical coughing sound and arming the mechanism. 'Will we never learn?'

Neville the part-time barman turned up his eyes and gritted his teeth, 'Fe . . .Fi . . .Fo . . .'

The pale young man stepped forward and applied the electrodes to Neville's groin. A mind-rending shock of raw pain tore the captive barman's nerve endings to a million ribbons and he sank once more from consciousness into a blinding red haze of dumb agony.

23

The afflicted sun swung slowly into the Brentford sky, illuminating a parish which seemed already very much on the go. There were now none of the customary morningtide grumblings and complaints which greeted the arrival of each new day. Here were lads leaping to their feet anxious to continue their labours; and their labours as ever centred upon the forthcoming Festival of Brentford. Barefooted children already pranced stiff-leggedly about the maypoles set upon the Butts. The sounds of hammering and nailing echoed in the streets as the great floats were being hobbled into shape in myriad back to backs. The borough was obsessed by the approaching event, but the whys and the wherefores were misty businesses not lightly dwelt upon.

John and Jim slumbered amongst the potato sacks beneath a corrugated iron lean-to, sleeping the blessed sleep of the Bacchanalian. Professor Slocombe toiled with book and abacus, and Sherlock Holmes crept over a distant rooftop, magnifying glass in hand. Norman of the corner shop tinkered with Allen key and soldering iron upon the project of his own conception, and Old Pete with Chips at heel made his way along the Ealing Road, cursing bitterly. Neville slept in a netherworld of force-fed suppressants, dreaming escape and revenge. The old gods slept also, but the morning of the magicians was not far from the dawning.

'Things are certainly not what they used to be in Brentford,' groaned Jim Pooley.

The allotments being something of a parish nature reserve, the over-abundance of hearty birdsong tore the million-dollar bum and his Irish companion grudgingly from the arms of good old munificent Morpheus. Jim emerged from beneath his corrugated iron four-poster and grimaced at the world to be. He shushed at the feathered choristers and counselled silence. 'Before I was rich,' he said, tapping at his skull in the hope of restoring some order, 'before I was rich, I rarely took up a night's lodgings upon the allotments.'

A woebegone face emerged from the lean-to, the sight silencing the birdies in a manner which normally it would have taken a twelve-bore to do. The godforsaken thing that was John Omally was far better kept from the gaze of children or the faint of heart. 'Morning, Jim,' said he.

Pooley caught sight of the facial devastation. 'Put that back for your own sake,' he advised. 'I should not wish to come to close quarters with an article such as that until far starboard of breakfast time.'

Omally's stomach made a repulsive sound. 'Now breakfast would indeed be your man,' he said, taking his ravaged features back into the darkness. The birdsong welled forth anew.

'Shut up,' bawled Pooley, clutching his skull. The birdies put the proverbial sock in it.

'Shall we try the Professor for a slice or two of toast?' Jim asked.

'Definitely not,' a voice called back from the darkness. 'I have no wish to see that good gentleman again. Buy me back my introduction please, Jim. I will owe you.'

'I can lend you a quid, John, but no more.'

'Let us go round and impose upon Norman. He is currently at a disadvantage. A bit of company will do him no harm.'

Pooley rubbed at his forehead and did a bit of hopeless eye focusing. 'All right,' he said. 'but if he starts to part the bacon with his left hand then I am having it away on my toes.'

Omally's face appeared once more in the light. This time it had been translated into the one worn by his normal self.

'You have remarkable powers of recuperation, John,' said Jim.

'I am a Dubliner.'

'But of course.'

The two men tucked in their respective shirt-tails and strolled as best they could over the allotments, through the gates, and off up the Albany Road. A hundred or so yards behind them another Pooley and Omally fell into step and did likewise.

'You were saying last night,' said Jim, as they reached Moby Dick Terrace, 'although I should not broach the subject so early in the morning, something about reaching a decision?'

186

'Oh yes,' John thrust out his chest and made some attempt to draw in breath. 'My mind is made up, I have the thing figured.'

'And as to this particular plan. Is it kosher and above board or is it the well-intentioned codswallop of the truly banjoed?'

'I had a drink on me, truly. But in no way did it affect my reason.'

Now fifty yards behind, the other Pooley and Omally marched purposefully on in perfect step, their faces staring ever ahead.

'So tell me all about it then, John.'

Omally tapped at his nose. 'All in good time. Let us get some brekky under our belts first.'

As they rounded the corner into Ealing Road they saw Old Pete approaching, cursing and swearing, his daily paper jammed beneath his arm. Young Chips followed, marking the lampposts for his own. The elder hobbled on, and as he caught sight of John and Jim he grunted a half-hearted 'good morning'. As they all but drew level the old man suddenly dropped his paper and raised his stick. He stared past John and Jim and his mouth fell open, bringing the full dental horror of his National Healthers into hideous prominence. 'G . . . gawd,' he stammered, 'now I *have* seen it all.'

John and Jim looked at one another, towards the gesturing ancient, and finally back over their shoulders, following the direction of his confounded gaze. Bearing down upon them at a goodly rate of knots marched their perfect doubles. 'Run for your life!' screamed Omally. Jim was already under starter's orders. The two tore past the befuddled ancient and his similarly bemused pet at an Olympic pace. Their doubles strode on in unison, hard upon the retreating heels.

Old Pete turned to watch the curious quartet dwindle into the distance. He stooped crookedly to retrieve his fallen paper and shook his old head in wonder. 'I am certain that I saw that,' he told Chips. 'Although I am sure it will pass.'

Young Chips made a low gummy sort of growling sound. He had recently bitten a postman's leg and lost several of his favourite teeth for his pains. He just wasn't certain about anything any more.

John and Jim were making admirable time along the Ealing Road. They passed Norman's corner-shop, the Swan, the Princess Vic, and drew level with the football ground. 'Where do we go?' gasped Pooley. 'There's nowhere to run to.'

'Just keep running, we've got to lose them.' John squinted back over his shoulders. Himself and Jim showed no signs of fatigue, if anything they looked more sprightly, as if the exercise was doing them good. 'Run, man, run!'

Round into the maze of back streets behind the football ground went the hunted pair. The doubles came forward at the jog, staring ever ahead. John dragged Pooley into an alleyway. 'Along here and keep it sprightly,' he urged.

The breathless Jim collapsed into a convulsion of coughing, hands upon knees. 'I cannot continue,' he croaked. 'Leave me here to die.'

'And die you surely will. Ahead, man.'

Omally thrust Pooley forward, the sound of approaching footfalls echoing in his ears. Down the dustbin-crowded alley they ran, John overturning as many as he could behind him. The duplicates crashed along, behind, casting the toppled bins effortlessly aside. John and Jim emerged into an obscure side-street neither of them could put a name to. The Lateinos and Romiith computer scan which observed their every movement had it well-catalogued in degree and minutes to a fearful number of decimal places.

'There has to be some way to dodge them,' gasped Pooley.

'Keep going, damn you.'

The duplicates crashed out into the street behind them.

Across Brentford ran Pooley and Omally, zig-zagging through people's back gardens, up and down fire escapes, in between the trees of the Memorial Park, and ever onwards. Behind them came the pounding of synchronized feet, never letting up for an instant.

'No more,' gulped Jim, when the two had shinned with difficulty over a high wall and dropped down into no safety whatsoever on the other side. 'I am finished.'

The sweat ran freely into Omally's eyes as he tore off his jacket and flung it aside. 'Not me,' said he. 'I'm not giving in to some clockwork copy, not while I still draw breath.'

With a great rending of brick and mortar, a section of the wall collapsed about them as the two duplicates applied their combined force.

'Run, Jim.'

'I'll race you.'

Along the cobbled way towards Old Brentford Docks staggered John and Jim, their last reserves of stamina all but drained away. Their hobnails sparked and clattered upon the cobbles and behind them in perfect unison their soulless pursuers were to be heard click-clacking at an easy pace. John pulled Jim into one of the disused warehouses. As he did so, their infra-red images unaccountably vanished from the screen of the Lateinos and Romiith computer. They ducked away behind a stack of abandoned loading pallets and shrank into the darkness, hearts pounding. From without, the sound of approaching footsteps drew nearer, then suddenly ceased. 'Quiet now,' whispered Omally, ramming his hands over Pooley's convulsing cherry-red face. Jim gasped for breath and sank down on to his bum with a dull thud. Omally ssshed him into silence, his finger upon his lips. The sound of slow, steady footfalls reached their ears. 'Stay quiet.'

The duplicates moved about the building, uncertain of which way to go; they tested the air with their sophisticated nasal sensory apparatus, in the hope of catching the scent of their quarries, but the ozone of the old dock drew the kipper over their tracks. Jim Pooley drew a fistful of sweat from his brow and spattered it on to the dusty floor of the old warehouse. He looked towards John, who shrugged in the darkness. Long, painful minutes passed. Jim folded his jacket across his chest to muffle the sound of his deafening heartbeat. Omally slunk to and fro seeking an exit or a reason or an anything. Outside, the duplicates stealthily encircled the building, sniffing and peering. The Omally gestured to the yawning doorway. The Pooley nodded. The duplicates entered the warehouse. Omally saw their shadows spread across the floor and flattened himself on to the deck. The two came slowly forward, scanning the way before them. Circuits meshed and weaved in their mechanized brains, drawing in the data, and processing it in the twinkling of a plastic eyelid.

From behind the stack of pallets a very foolish voice indeed said suddenly, 'Well, I think we've outrun them, John. Care for a tailor-made?'

Omally's eyes widened in horror as he watched the two heads, one his own and the other that of his dearest friend, swivel upon their frictionless bearings, and swing in the direction of the sound. He gestured towards Jim, whose face could just be seen grinning from behind the stack of pallets. 'Come, come.'

The robot Pooley leapt forward and grasped the obstruction barring his way. He tore the stack apart with a single movement, sending them smashing to all sides.

Jim looked up white and trembling and saw death staring him right between the eyes. 'Help, John,' he squealed, cowering back against the wall. 'Do something.'

Grinning like a gargoyle, the robot slowly withdrew from the pocket of his brand new suit, a small wicked-looking black instrument with two extendable electrodes. With a flick of the thumb he armed the mechanism and sent sparks crackling about the tips of the rods.

Omally floundered about seeking a suitable weapon, his hand closed over a length of iron conduit. 'Up the rebels,' he cried as he flung himself towards Jim's attacker. His own double turned upon him to stand glaring, eye to eye. 'You bastard,' spat Omally, 'come and try your luck.' He swung his cudgel with terrific force but the robot shot out a hand and grasped it, tearing it from his grip and flinging it the length of the warehouse. Omally ducked back as his double delved into its pocket. The smile widened upon its lips as the small black box appeared.

'Hold hard,' a voice echoed about the warehouse. Four pairs of eyes shot in the direction of the sound. A tall, gaunt figure stood crouched in the doorway, silhouetted against the light, legs spread widely apart and hands held forward. 'This is a Magnum Forty-four,' he shouted, 'biggest handgun in the world and can blow your heads clean off your shoulders. What do you say, punks?'

The robot duplicates looked towards their respective quarries, one cowering and covering his nuts, the other standing defiant, thirty-four-function barlow knife now in hand. They turned in unison towards the source of their annoyance.

'Hold hard or I fire,' cried Sherlock Holmes.

The robots stole forward upon synthetic heels.

'Right on.' Holmes' trigger finger tightened. Two shots rang out in rapid succession. The robot Pooley span from his feet in a hazy blur, his head a mass of trailing ribbons and sparking wires. The Omally sank to its knees, foul yellow slime spurting from two over-large holes front and back of its plastic skull. He rose to stumble forward, cruel claws scratching at the air, jerked upright, then slumped to the deck, a rag doll flung carelessly aside. Holmes blew into the barrel of his Forty-four, spun it upon his forefinger, and tucked it away into his shoulder holster. 'Gotcha,' he said.

Omally clicked back the blade of his barlow knife and thrust the thing into his breast pocket. He stepped over to console the gibbering Pooley. 'Thanks yet again,' he said to Sherlock Holmes. 'It seems that we are once more in your debt.'

'No sweat,' the great detective replied. He stooped over the twisted 'corpse' of the false and fallen Pooley and began to turn out its pockets. Jim crept forward and watched in horror as Holmes examined the contents before tossing them aside. A besmutted handkerchief, a leaky ballpoint pen, an initialled gold Cartier lighter, and a packet of Passing Cloud cigarettes.

Pooley patted frantically at his pockets; they'd been picked obviously. To his further horror his patting disclosed an identically besmutted handkerchief, a leaky ballpoint pen, and the same Cartier lighter, which he had not as yet learned how to fill; even the packet of fags. Pooley held out his hands to Sherlock Holmes. The detective took the cigarette packet and shook it open: seventeen cigarettes. He picked up the robot's packet: three gone from the packet of twenty.

'Very thorough. Every last detail absolutely correct,' said Holmes. 'I would hazard a guess that, should we analyse the fluff in your trouser pockets and that of this demon-spawn here, they would match exactly.' Jim shuddered. Holmes completed his search and satisfied himself that he had taken all relevant matters into account. He rose to leave. 'I must away now,' he said. 'The game is afoot.'

'It's costing us an arm and a leg,' said Omally. 'Well, good luck to you at the very least.'

'Your sentiment is appreciated, John, but luck plays no part whatsoever in my investigations.' Holmes tapped at his right temple. 'It all comes from here. The science of deduction, made art.'

'Yes,' said Omally doubtfully. 'Well, be that as it may. My best wishes to you for the success of your mission.'

'Ten-four,' said the detective. 'Up and away.' With these few words he leapt out through the warehouse door and was presently lost from view.

'I still say he's a nutter.' Omally brushed the dust and grime away from the numb and shattered Jim Pooley.

The two electronic cadavers lay spread across the warehouse floor, and it was no pleasant thing to behold your own corpse lying at your very feet. Pocket fluff and all. Omally turned Jim's head away. 'Come on, mate,' said he softly. 'We've had a good innings here, let's not spoil it.'

Jim pointed a dangly hand towards his *doppel-gänger*, 'It was me,' he said. 'It was me.'

'Well, it's not any more. Come on, let's get out of here.'

'I shouldn't do it.' A voice from behind froze Omally in his tracks and caused his hand to seek out his barlow knife. 'Don't go outside, I'm telling you.' Omally turned slowly and wearily to face whatever the new threat might be. Across the deserted warehouse floor a head peeped out from a now open manhole. It was Soap Distant. 'Lead roof,' said the pink-eyed man from below. 'The computer scan cannot penetrate it. That's why they couldn't find you.'

Omally peered up into the darkness of the eaves above. 'So that was it.'

'Hurry now,' said Soap. 'Their back-up boys are on the way.'

John did not need telling twice. Thrusting Pooley before him, he made for the manhole and something which loosely-resembled safety. As Jim's head vanished into the darkness below John skipped back to where his duplicate lay. Viewing his own remains, he smiled briefly, and stopped to remove the thing's left boot. Upending this, a bundle of banknotes tumbled out into his hand. 'Very thorough indeed,' said John, pocketing the spoils of war.

24

A half a mile beneath the surface of Planet Earth, Soap Distant offered Omally a cup of tea.

'This time I think I will,' said John. 'Is there any chance of breakfast, Soap?'

'Certainly.' The pink-eyed man applied himself to the frying-pan.

'Are you all right, Jim?' Omally prodded his companion who was staring dumbly into space.

'It was me,' mouthed Jim.

'Well, it isn't now. You're safe.'

'It was me.'

'Sunnyside up,' piped Soap.

'Two on a raft,' Omally replied, 'with all the trimmings.'

Shortly a fine breakfast was in the offing. With the aid of much pushing, prompting, and cuffing, Jim was slowly brought back to the land of the living to enjoy his. For every 'It was me', he received a blow to the head. Somewhat after the fashion of the now legendary Pavlov's pooches he learned the error of his ways. 'Could I have another fried slice?' he asked.

Soap obliged. As he turned the bread in the pan he said. 'The lead you see, the scan cannot penetrate it. They've got an eye in the sky up there watching everybody that's left, but they can't see through the lead. I myself lined the Professor's loft with lead foil. Keeps the buggers out it does.'

Omally wiped his chin. 'Very good, Soap. It is pleasing to hear that some precautions can be taken.'

'Oh yes, no system is infallible. Old Ratinous and Loathesome think they've got it all figured out, but there is always a dodge to be found by the thinking man.'

'Such was once the credo of my karma but I am now experiencing some doubts.'

'Don't,' said Soap. 'We'll beat the blighters yet.'

'You seem very confident.'

Soap dumped the fried slice on to Pooley's plate, and popped a grilled tomato into his mouth. 'Oh yes,' he said between munchings, 'there is not a machine yet that will not fare the worse for a well-placed spanner jammed up its works.'

'Good man,' said Omally, leaning forward to pat his host upon the shoulder. 'I hope you know where to place the spanner.'

'Never fear.' Soap pulled at his lower eye. 'Never fear.'

'See,' said Omally, nudging Pooley in the rib area, 'even with Armageddon staring you in the face there is always a flanker to be pulled.'

'It was me,' said Jim. 'Could I have another grilled sausage do you think, Soap?'

The pink-eyed man laughed heartily. 'Have two,' he cried, 'have three if you wish.'

'Three would be fine,' said Jim. 'I have no wish to appear greedy.'

The three sub-Earthers enjoyed a hearty breakfast washed down with several bottles of Chateau Distant carrot claret. 'I think you might do well to lie low here for a while,' Soap advised his guests. 'Your cards would seem to be well and truly marked at present.'

'What about the spanner?' Omally made turning motions with his hand.

'All in good time, Professor Slocombe has the matter well in hand. He will tell us when the time is right.'

Omally made a sour face. 'Much as I love that old man, I am not altogether sure that his reasoning is quite as clear as it once was.'

Soap flapped his hands wildly. 'Do not say such things. The Professor is an Illuminati. You must trust in all he says.'

'Perhaps,' Omally finished his glass. 'But it is all theories, theories, and there is precious little of what he says that makes any sense to me.'

'I would have thought that as a Catholic yourself, the idea would have held great appeal.'

'What Armageddon? The Twilight of the Gods? Not a lot.'

'No, not that side of it, I mean about the garden.'

'What garden?'

'About the garden being in Brentford. That is the whole point of it all, surely?'

'Soap, in a single sentence you have lost me completely. What are you talking about?'

'Eden, the Garden of Eden. Do you mean he didn't tell you?'

'Hold on, hold on.' Omally held up his hands. 'Go through this again slowly. What are you talking about?'

'The Garden of Eden,' said Soap. 'You know the one, gets a big mention in Genesis.'

'Of course I know. What are you saying?'

Soap shook his head; he was clearly speaking with a half-wit. 'Why do you think the walls have come down about Brentford?'

'To stop me spending my millions,' said Pooley bitterly.

'Hardly that. To protect Eden against the fall of Babylon.'

'I always had Babylon pegged as being a little further south.'

'Not a bit of it,' said Soap. 'Chiswick.'

'Chiswick?'

'Yes. You see, the Professor solved the whole thing years ago, when he reorientated all the old maps. He was under the belief that the entire chronology and location of Biblical events was wildly inaccurate. He spent years piecing it all together before he finally solved the riddle.'

'That Babylon was in Chiswick.'

'Yes, but more importantly, that the Garden of Eden was planted right here. Upon the very spot now enclosed within the Brentford Triangle.'

'Madness,' said Omally, 'nothing more, nothing less.'

'Not a bit of it. He showed me all the reorientated

maps. All the events chronicled in the Bible took place right here in England.'

'And Christ?'

'And did those feet in ancient times? Liverpool born, crucified in Edinburgh.'

'Blasphemy,' said Omally, 'heresy also.'

'It is as true as I am sitting here.' Soap crossed his heart with a wet finger. 'All the stories in the Bible are based upon more ancient texts than scholars suppose. The events took place in a more northerly clime. They were transferred to their present incorrect locations upon far later translations of the Holy Word. The dates are thousands of years out. It all happened right here, and, for that matter, it is still happening. I would have thought that matters above make that patently obvious.'

'Blessed Mary,' said John Omally.

'Born in Penge.'

'Where else?'

'Makes you think, though,' said Pooley, freshening his glass. 'After all, we all knew that Brentford was the hub of the universe. This simply confirms it.'

'Exactly,' said Soap. 'And we have always known that God is an Englishman.'

'Steady on,' said John Omally. 'I will swallow a lot but never that. British at a pinch. But English? Never.'

'*Ipso facto*,' said Soap, 'or something like.'

'I will need to give this matter a considerable amount of intense thought,' said John Omally, 'which I believe might necessitate the consumption of a litre or two more of your claret to aid cogitation.'

'Cogitate on me,' said Soap Distant, drawing out a brace of flagons from beneath his chair.

'You are a gentleman, sir.'

25

Norman had the door of his shop well-barred. Trade had fallen off to such an alarming degree that, but for serving Old Pete with his newspaper and tobacco, there seemed no point whatever in opening. Absolute panic, and the fear of his duplicate's return, or possibly the arrival of something far worse, had prompted him this day, upon the ancient's departure, to barricade the premises against the outside world. The counters now stood across the front door, with what few items still remained stacked upon them. Viewing the hole in his ceiling, Norman considered these moves to be little more than token opposition. But even token opposition was surely better than no opposition at all. 'Many hands make light work,' said the shopkeeper, irrelevantly recalling a faith-healing session he had once attended, where a defunct fuse box which had thrown the place into darkness, had been miraculously restored to life.

Norman tottered over the newly-laid linoleum, wielding his screwdriver Excalibur-fashion. He entered the kitchenette. There wasn't a lot of room in there at present. The object of his most recent, all-consuming attention occupied more than a little floor space.

Norman's time machine was a big filler!

There was very much of the electric chair evident in the overall design of the thing. But also a good deal of NASA's mission control and a fair degree of Captain Nemo's Nautilus. A *soupçon* of the pumping station at Kew and Doctor F's laboratory completed the picture. The thing bristled with the banks of twinkling lights Norman always felt were so essential to lend the necessary atmosphere to such a project. Above the driving seat, commandeered from his Morris Minor, a slim brass wheel turned at precisely twenty-six revolutions per minute. From the axle-rods, wires trailed to every compass point like the ribbons of an eccentric electronic maypole, enshrouding the entire contraption, which rested upon a kind of Father Christmas sleigh.

'Now then.' Norman consulted a ludicrous wiring diagram scrawled on to the back of a computer stock control print-out. It was all something to do with E equalling MC^2, the parallax theory, whatever that might be, and the triangulations of Pythagorus. Oh yes, and the space-time continuum, not that that even bore thinking about.

Norman shook his head at the wonder of it all. Scientists always did tend to over-complicate the issues. Professional pride, he supposed. To him science was, and always had been, a pretty straightforward affair, which required only the minimum of writing down. Once you'd nicked the idea, this time from HG Wells, you simply went down to Kay's Electrical in the High Street and purchased all the component parts. What you couldn't buy you hobbled up out of defunct wirelesses and what was left of the

Meccano set. Scientists always made such a big deal out of things and did it all arse about face. Norman was the happy exception to this rule.

Brentford seemed to be in a bit of schtuck at the present, but the shopkeeper considered that once he had the machine on the go he would at least be able to set matters straight once and for all. He always liked to think that he was helping out, and seeing as how nobody had cared to put him in the picture he meant to go it alone. Not being at all silly he had tracked down the root cause of the Parish's ills to the dreaded Lateinos and Romiith concern, and it seemed but a simple thing to him to slip back into the past and make a few subtle changes. Like murdering the bastards where they slept in their cribs for a first off. Then bending the council records so he got that planning permission to do his loft conversion. And he had always wanted to shake the hand of that editor of the *Brentford Mercury* who had run off with his wife. There was quite a lot you could achieve once you'd got time travel licked.

Norman had definitely decided to travel backwards first; the future looked anything but rosy. He dived forward with his screwdriver into an impenetrable-looking network of wires and fuse boxes and twiddled about here and there. The strains of the Rolling Stones' legendary composition 'Time Is On My Side' sprang almost unconsciously to his lips. The whole concept of the enterprise pleased Norman with its every single detail. There was the sheer naked thrill of hurtling into the unknown, allied with the potential power a man might wield once able to traverse the fields of time. Also, and by no means the smallest part of it, was the infinite variety of puns and proverbs that could be drawn from the word 'time'. Such things must never be overlooked. 'Time, gentlemen, please,' said Norman, tittering loudly to himself. He flicked a random selection of likely-looking switches in the hope that he might get some clue as to why he had fitted them. One brought his old Bush Radiogram bucketing into life, 'It's time for old time,' sang a disembodied voice. Norman creased up. He was having the time of his life.

The shopkeeper straightened his back and scratched at his head with the end of his screwdriver. It did all look about finished really. He could always tighten up the odd bolt, or give the gleaming brasswork another polish, but apart from these niceties it looked very much complete. 'And not before time,' chuckled Norman, making nudging notions towards an imaginary companion.

The sounds of sharp tapping suddenly drew his attention. Someone, or something, was knocking upon the barricaded shop-door. An icy hand clutched at the shopkeeper's heart. Of course, it could be just a customer anxious to pay his newspaper bill? Well, it could be.

The Lateinos and Romiith computer scan monitored Norman's infra-red image as it dithered about in the crowded kitchenette. The sensors gauged the increase in his pulse rate and analysed the sweat particles which broke out on his forehead. It also relayed this information instantly to the shopkeeper's mirror image, which was even now rapping left-handedly upon the door. A cruel smile appeared upon the duplicate's face as it turned and strode purposefully away, bound for the backyard wall.

Norman gnawed upon his knuckles. Now would certainly seem like an ideal time for a bit of a test run. He climbed rapidly into the driving seat and fastened his safety belt; as he had no way of telling exactly which way up time was when you travelled through it he did not wish to fall out. Carefully, he swung a pair of great calliper arms, heavily-burdened with switch-boxes and levers, about him, and, turning the ignition key, put the machine into reverse. Lights pulsed and flashed, and the great brazen wheel tumbled on above him, a ring of sparks encircled the machine in a twinkling halo. The sudden crash of brickwork informed the aspiring time traveller that an unwelcome visitor had just entered his backyard. The buzzing and hammering of the mechanism increased at a goodly rate; but to Norman's dismay he did not appear to be going anywhere, either backwards, or forwards, or even upside down. 'Get a move on,' shouted the distraught shopkeeper, thumbing switches and squinting up at the kitchen clock in the hope of a fluctuation. The machine shook and shivered. The lights flashed and the engine roared. The sounds of splintering woodwork as the kitchen door parted company with its hinges were swallowed up in the cacophony.

Norman's fearsome replica stood in the doorway clearing its throat and rubbing its hands together.

Norman flung levers in all directions and waggled the joystick. The creature stalked towards him wearing a most unpleasant expression. It reached down slowly and grasped one of the runners, meaning to up-end the whole caboodle. Norman cowered back in his seat, kicking at any levers which lay beyond his reach. The creature strained at the runner but the thing would not shift. Norman stared up at the great wheel spinning above, its gyroscopic effect was such that the machine could not possibly be overturned. The robot, being Norman to its finger ends, twigged this almost instantaneously, and abandoned this futile pursuit to deal with matters more directly. Its hands stretched towards Norman's throat. The wee lad shrank away, burbling for mercy. The demon double clawed towards him, its eyes blazing hatred, and its lips drawn back from gnashing, grinding teeth; the talons were an inch from Norman's throat. Norman unceremoniously wet himself. Not the wisest thing to do when surrounded by so much unearthed electrical apparatus.

'Oooooooooooh!' Norman's voice rose to an operatic soprano as the charge caught him squarely in the nuts, arched up his backbone and shot out through the top of his head, setting his barnet ablaze. A great jolt rocked the machine, sparks cascaded roman candle style from every corner, and the humming and throbbing rose to a deafening crescendo. As if suddenly alert to the possibility of imminent explosion the robot drew back its hands. It dropped them once more to the runner then straightened up and backed towards the door. Norman batted at his cranial bonfire and squinted through the now rising smoke. To his amazement he saw the creature back away through the doorway and the shattered kitchen-door rise magically behind it, to slap back into its mountings, pristine and undamaged. Norman's eyes flew towards the kitchen clock. The second hand was belting round the face like a propeller. It was travelling anti-clockwise. 'Ha ha ha ha ha ha.' Norman clapped his hands together and bounced up and down in his seat, oblivious to his scrambled goolies and smouldering top-knot.

He was travelling back in time!

The second hand was gathering speed, increasing to a blur, followed now by the minute and the hour. The kitchenette began to grow vague and fuzzy and then in a flash it vanished.

The kitchenette door tore from its hinges and crashed down on the linoleum. Norman's duplicate stood horribly framed in the doorway, staring into the fog of smoke which now filled the otherwise empty room. A look of perplexity swept over the robot shopkeeper's face. Data retrieval and logic modification channels whirred and cross-meshed, and finally spelt out absolutely sweet bugger all. Which certainly served them right.

26

Norman held fast to his seat and stared forward into the darkness. Strange lights welled up before him, swung past to either side, and vanished away behind. He experienced no sensation of motion; it was as if he was somehow travelling outside of space and time altogether. He was in limbo. Norman looked at his watch. It had stopped. He scrutinized the date counter he had optimistically screwed on to one of the enclosing calliper arms; a tangle of wires dangled from beneath it. He had forgotten to link the thing up. Where was he, and more importantly when was he? He might have been travelling for an hour or a year or a century. He had no way of telling. He had best put the machine out of gear and cruise to a halt before he slipped back too far. The idea of finding himself trampled on by a dinosaur was most unappealing.

A terrible fear took a grip upon his heart. Exactly what would he find when he stopped? He could wind up in the middle of Rorke's Drift with the Zulus on the attack. Or even in the sea or inside the heart of a mountain. There was no way of telling. Perhaps if he slowed down just a bit he could spy out a safe place to land. Norman's hand hovered over the controls, a look of imbecility folding his face in half. He had pulled off The Big One this time and no mistake, but where was it going to get him? In big big trouble, that was where. Norman did his best to weigh up the pros and cons. Could he get killed in the past before he had even been born? Was such a thing possible? The situation he was now in lent sufficient weight to the conviction that nothing was impossible. The words of the great Jack Vance filled his head, 'In a situation of infinity, every possibility no matter how remote must find physical expression.' He had that sewn into a sampler over his bed.

It was all too much for the shopkeeper and he slumped dejectedly over the controls and grizzled quietly, resigning himself to oblivion. What had he done? What in the name of dear Mother Earth had he done?

'Norman,' a voice called to him from out of the void. 'Norman.'

'Who's that?' Norman squinted into the darkness. 'I know that voice.'

'Norman,' the voice grew louder. 'Halt the apparatus, you will slip beyond reach.'

Norman hammered at the controls; he tore the ignition key from the dashboard, and a sudden rush of air buffeted him back in his seat. Light popped and flashed about him, the machine rattled and shuddered and with a great sigh, daylight spun into view from the end of a long dark tunnel and broke in every direction. Norman shielded his face, closed his eyes and prepared to make what peace he could with his Creator. There was a hefty whack and a moment of terrible silence. Norman flinched and cowered.

Warm sunlight tickled his fingers and the sound of birdsong filled his ears. Still not daring to look, Norman sniffed. The sweet scent of flowers, sweeter than any he had previously smelled – or was that now *would* smell? – engulfed him.

He had died, that was it. Died and gone to the good place. Hope always sprang eternal in the wee lad. Norman uncovered his eyes and peered through his fingers. The time machine rested in an Arcadian glade upon a richly-forested hillside, bordering a beautiful valley which swept in gentle rolls down to a picturesque and meandering river. Very nice indeed. This far exceeded his highest hopes of what Heaven might look like. The trip had been well worthwhile after all. Rising high above the hills beyond the river stood a shimmering white fairytale castle, pennants flying in the breeze. It was the stuff of storybooks, of childhood innocence. It was wonderful. Pushing back the calliper arms, Norman unclipped his safety belt and, plucking gingerly at his still damp trouser seat, set his feet upon the lush green carpet of dew-soaked grass. It was paradise; the enchanted glade.

'Norman.' The voice loosened the lad's bowels, but he had nothing left to yield. 'Norman.' An old man was approaching, hobbling upon a cane. He was clothed in a flowing robe of deepest black, embroidered richly with stars and pentacles and magical symbols picked out in silvern thread. Upon his head he wore a tall conical hat of identical craftsmanship. He sported a long white beard and was the very picture of all one might reasonably expect of Merlin the Magician.

Norman peered at the approaching apparition. He knew that face, that stooping gait, as well as he knew anything. A choked voice rose from his throat. 'Professor Slocombe?'

The magician put his long finger to his lips. 'All in good time, he said. 'Welcome, Norman.'

'Where am I?'

'Why in Camelot, of course. Wherever did you think?'

'I thought, perhaps, well I don't know, still in Brentford maybe.'

Merlin cocked his head on one side. 'Brentford,' he said. 'I like the name, I will see what can be done about that for some future time. But for now we have much to speak of. Will you come with me to yonder castle and take a cup of mead?'

'I think that would be just fine,' said Norman, the once and future shopkeeper of England.

27

Professor Slocombe looked up towards the great ormolu mantel-clock and nodded his old head gently in time to the pendulum's swing. 'Good luck, Norman,' he said. Drawing his gaze from the antique timepiece, he turned to stare out through the open French windows. There, in the all-too-near distance, the great black shaft of the Lateinos and Romiith building obscenely scarred the two-hundred-year-old skyline. Its upper reaches were lost high amongst gathering stormclouds. The aura of undiluted evil pressed out from it, seeking to penetrate the very room. The old man shuddered briefly and drew the windows shut. Norman's homemade double laid aside a bound volume of da Vinci, penned in the crooked mirror-Latin of the great man himself, and peered quizzically towards the Professor.

'I know what you are thinking,' the scholar said. 'He is safe thus far, so much is already known to me. But as to the return trip, all depends upon the calculations. It is all in the numbers. We can only offer our prayers.'

'Prayers?'

'They offer some comfort.'

'I wouldn't know,' said the robot, somewhat

brusquely. 'Norman did not see fit to log such concepts into my data banks.'

Professor Slocombe watched the mechanical man with unguarded interest. 'I should really like to know exactly what you do feel.'

'I feel texture. I think, therefore I am. Or so I have been informed. Every cloud has a silver lining I was also told, and a trouble shared is a bird in the . . .'

'Yes, indeed. But what causes you to react? How do you arrive at decisions? What motivates you?'

'Impetus. I react as I have been programmed to do. Upon information received, as the boys in blue will have it.'

'Do you believe then that this is how the other duplicates function?'

'Certainly not.' Something approaching pride entered the robot's voice. 'They are merely receivers, created solely to receive and to collect information and perform their tasks. The mainframe of the great computer does all their thinking for them. Clockwork dummies, that's all they are.'

'Interesting,' said Professor Slocombe.

'You spend a great deal of time in idle speculation,' the robot observed, 'considering the gravity of the situation. You seek to detect human emotion in me. I might do the same to you.'

Professor Slocombe chuckled delightedly. 'There are more wheels currently in motion than the one which spins in your chest,' said he. 'Even now, great forces are beginning to stir elsewhere in the parish.'

28

Fe . . . fi . . . fo . . . fum.' The bloated barman awoke giddily from another bout of barbiturate-induced slumber and rattled the window-panes of his hospital prison. The door beneath him opened and his Promethean tormentor entered the barman-crowded room, hypodermic at the ready. Neville eyed her with absolute loathing. 'I smell the blood of an Englishman.'

'We are not going to be naughty again, are we?'

'Be he alive or be he dead.'

'Roly-poly, please, sir.'

'I'll grind his bones to make my bread.'

'I shall have to fetch doctor, then.'

'No!' Neville drew in his breath, filled his cheeks, and blew a great blast at the clinical harpy. The midget fought at the gale, but lost her footing and fluttered away through the doorway and out into the corridor. 'At last,' said Neville to the ceiling against which his face had been compressed so uncomfortably for so very long. 'At long long last.' He raised a fist the size of a cement sack and clenched and unclenched the fingers. The sap was beginning to rise and a great inner strength was rising with it. The power was surging, driving through his veins; unstoppable and titanic.

At last he realized the truth: his consuming disability had been nothing more than the painful and grotesque prelude to what was to come. The time for the settling of scores was fast approaching. The power of the great Old Ones. The gods of his pagan ancestry born in the dawn of the light when the world was full of wonder. The power had returned and it had returned to him. The last of the line.

A broad tight-lipped smile arced up upon the barman's face. His fingers flexed, and beneath the surgical gown huge muscles rolled about his body, porpoises swimming in a sack. The Herculean barman pressed his hands to the ceiling of his most private ward. With a splinter of plastic-cladding, his hands rose, tightening to fists and forcing upwards, unstoppably. Neville rose with them, pouring forth from his prison, rising upon a floodtide of super-human energy. The barman's head and shoulders passed through the ceiling and a low choked cry rose from his throat.

He was ill-prepared for the sight which met his gaze. He had supposed himself to be in the private wing of the Cottage Hospital. The view from the window tending to support this well enough. But not a bit of it. The hospital room and its window view were nothing but a sham, hiding a grim reality. The tiny room was little more than a box, set in some great empty warehouse of a place. It spread away, dimly-lit, acre upon acre of concrete flooring and absolutely nothing. The window view, now seen from above, was a mish-mash of laser lines projected on to a screen. It was a hologram.

'Fe . . . fi . . . fo,' said Neville, as he perused his stark surroundings. Where was he? He felt like a jack-in-the-box in an empty toy factory. 'Curiouser and curiouser!' Standing erect and kicking aside the make-believe walls of the movie-set hospital room, he stood upon a soundstage vaster by far than any ever envisaged by the now legendary Cecil B himself.

Neville drew in his breath and watched in pride as his great chest rose beneath the gown. This was the dream come true, surely? The impossible dream realized. His gods had at long last decided to smile upon him. He must have performed for them some great service without even realizing it. A million glorious thoughts poured into the barman's head. He would seek out that Trevor Alvy who had bullied him at school; and parade up and down the beach come summer with his shirt actually off. No more heavy sweaters to disguise his bony physique, no more cutting jibes about his round shoulders. He would get a tan. And kick sand in people's faces. Yes, he would definitely do that. He would eject drunks from the bar without having to resort to the sneaky knobkerry from behind. Neville threw himself into a pose, displaying muscles in places where Arnold Schwarzenegger didn't even have places. Conan who? He was quids in here and no mistake. 'Oh joy, oh bliss.' Things were happening about Neville's groin regions which, out of common decency, he did not even dare to dwell upon. The bulging barman paused for a moment or two's reflection. For one thing, it was impossible for him to gauge exactly how high he might be. If the hospital room was life-size, he must surely top the twenty-foot mark. That was no laughing matter. Giants, no matter how well hung they might be, were never exactly the most popular fellows in town. In fact, the more well hung they were, the worse their lot. There was always some would be 'David' about, with a catapult and poor eyesight.

Neville erased such thoughts from his brain with difficulty. If this thing had been done to him, then it had been done with a purpose. There was no accident or casual element of chance evident here. This was something else, something very very special. And he would have to find out the purpose. And to do that, he would first have to make his escape from this great cold dark room at the very hurry-up. Before the chill began to shrink anything. Upon those tireless, finely-muscled legs that Charles Atlas had promised to a dozen generations of sickly youth, Neville took flight and sped away with great leaps and bounds, seeking the exit.

29

A good half-mile beneath the barbarian barman's thundering feet, John Omally opened another bottle of carrot claret and poured himself a large glass. 'Soap,' said he to his host, 'this is good stuff you have here.'

'Nectar,' Jim Pooley agreed. 'Write me down the recipe and I will provide for your old age.'

Soap grinned stupidly. 'You must try the cigars,' he said, rising unsteadily from his horrendous armchair and tottering over to the box.

'Home-grown?'

Soap made a crooked 'O' out of his thumb and forefinger. 'I have a five spot says you cannot identify the blend.'

'Take it out of the money you still owe us,' said Jim.

Soap handed out a brace of lime-green coronas. Omally took his dubiously and rolled it against his ear. 'Not a sprout?' he asked in a fearful voice.

'Heavens no.' Soap crossed his heart. 'Would I do that to you?'

Pooley sniffed his along its length. 'Not spud?'

'Absolutely not. I know Omally stuffs his peelings into his pipe, but even he would draw the line at manufacturing cigars from them.'

'They don't roll,' said John, making the motions.

The two men lit up, and collapsed simultaneously into fits of violent coughing.

'Whatever it is,' wheezed John, tears streaming from his eyes, 'it's good stuff.'

'Perhaps a little sharp.' Jim's face now matched the colour of his cigar.

'Do you give up?'

'Indubitably.'

'Well I shan't tell you anyway.' Soap slumped back into his chair, hands clasped behind his head.

The ruddy hue slowly returned to Jim's face as he got the measure of his smoke. 'How long do you think we are going to have to fiddle about down here?' he asked.

Soap shrugged.

Omally tapped a quarter-inch of snow-white ash into a glass cache pot of the Boda persuasion. 'We can't stay down here indefinitely, Soap,' he said. 'Although your hospitality is greatly appreciated, you must surely realize that we must make some attempts at salvaging something of our former lives. We were quite fond of them.'

Soap waved his hands at the Irishman. 'All in good time, John. The Prof will tip us the wink. For now, have a drink and a smoke and a pleasant chat.'

'I fear we will shortly exhaust all topics of conversation.'

'Not a bit of it, I am a fascinating conversationalist. On most matters I am eloquence personified. My range is almost inexhaustible.'

'And your modesty legend. I know.'

220

'All right then, what is your opinion of evolution?'

'A nine-aeon wonder.' Omally awaited the applause.

'I have a somewhat revolutionary theory of my own.'

'I do not wish to hear it.'

'I subscribe to the view that the world was created five minutes ago, complete with all records and memories. Although an improbable hypothesis, I think you will find it logically irrefutable.'

'And how long have you held this belief?'

'Hard to say, possibly four and a half minutes.'

'Fol-de-rol.'

'Well, what about politics, then? As an Irishman, you must have some definite views.'

'As an Irishman, I never trouble to give the matter a moment's thought.'

'Religion, then?'

'I subscribe to the view that the world was created five minutes ago. Are you looking for a grazed chin, Soap?'

'Only trying to pass the time with a little pleasant intercourse.'

'Careful,' said Jim.

'Well, I get few callers.'

'Hardly surprising, your address is somewhat obscure even for the A to Z.'

'Would you care to see my mushroom beds?'

'Frankly, no.'

'I spy with my little eye?'

'Stick it in your ear, Soap.'

The three men sat awhile in silence. Jim picked a

bit of chive out of his teeth and won five quid from Soap. But other than that there was frankly no excitement to be had whatsoever, which might in its way have been a good thing, for there was a great deal of it in the offing. A sudden bout of urgent knocking rattled Soap Distant's front door.

'Expecting guests?' Omally asked. 'Ladies, I trust. Current affairs have played havoc with my social calendar.'

Soap's face had, within the twinkling of an eye, transformed itself from an amiable countenance into the all-too-familiar mask of cold fear. 'Are either of you tooled up?' he asked inanely.

'I have my barlow knife,' said Omally, rapidly finishing his drink.

'And me my running shoes,' said Jim. 'Where's the back door, Soap?'

Mr Distant dithered in his armchair. 'No-one knows of this place,' he whispered hoarsely. The pounding on the door informed him that that statement was patently incorrect.

Omally rose hurriedly from his seat. 'Lead us to the priesthole, Soap, and make it snappy.'

'I'm for that.' Jim leapt up and began smacking at the walls. 'Where's the secret panel, Soap?'

Soap chewed upon his knuckles. 'It's the other me,' he whimpered. 'I knew it had to happen, even here.'

'The odds are in its favour. Kindly show us the way out.'

'There's no other exit.'

'Then find us a place to hide, someone must

continue to serve the cause, even if you are indisposed.'

'Yes, fair do's,' Jim agreed, as the pounding rattled ornaments and nerves alike. 'If it's the other you, then he may not know John and I are here. We at least should hide until the bloodshed is over.'

'Oh, thanks very much, pals.'

'We'd do the same for you.'

'Come again?'

'Open up there.' A voice from without brought the ludicrous conversation to a halt.

'It's Sherlock Holmes,' said Omally. 'Let him in.'

Soap hastened to unfasten the front door. 'Close it without delay.' The detective pressed himself inside. 'They are hard upon my heels.'

'How did you know where I lived?' Soap pressed the bolts home.

'No matter. Are you three tooled up?'

Omally shook his head and fell back into his seat. Pooley did likewise. 'Would you care for another splash of carrot, Jim?' Omally waggled the bottle towards Pooley.

'Another would be fine. So how goes the game afoot, Sherlock?'

'A bit iffy as it happens.' Holmes drew out his revolver and flattened himself against the front wall.

Jim rattled his glass against the bottle's neck. 'And you have brought the lads down here after us. Most enterprising.'

'I never really believed in him, you know,' said John, now refreshing his own glass.

'I looked it all up in the library,' Pooley replied.

'The evidence is very much against him. Purely fictitious, I so believe.'

'Wise up,' said Sherlock Holmes. 'These mothers mean business.'

The sounds of terrible ghost train screaming leant weight to his conviction. From beyond, something malevolent was surging forward from the darkness. Pooley covered his ears and crossed his eyes. Omally snatched up a Biba table-lamp and prepared once more to do battle. If the awful screaming was not bad enough, the sounds which accompanied it were sufficient to put the wind up even Saint Anthony himself. Hideous slurpings and suckings, as of some gigantic mollusc, and thrashing sounds, dragging chains and clicking joints. All in all, anything but a Christmas hamper.

Omally turned towards Holmes, who now crouched facing the door, Magnum forty-four poised once more between his outstretched hands. 'What in the name of the Holies is it?' he shouted above the growing din.

'It came at me from a basement opening. I have only seen its like before amongst the work of Hieronymous Bosch.'

This remark meant little to Omally who had always thought a Bosch to be an expensive sports car. But that the something which was approaching was very very nasty and somewhat overlarge seemed on the cards.

As the first concussion shook the front wall, Holmes fired point-blank into the door. A gale-force icy wind swept through the bullet-hole, like a blast from a ruptured gas-pipe. A fetid odour filled the room; the stench of the very pit itself, of all the world's carrion congealed into a single rotting mass. Holmes staggered back into Omally, coughing and gagging. The Irishman fell to his knees, covering his nose, and retching violently. Outside, the thing lashed at the door with redoubled fury. The iron hinges screamed in anguish, echoing those of the satanic emissary of death. Beneath the throbbing door, slim, barbed hooks worked and tore. A yellow haze of brimstone coloured the unbreathable air and the room shook and shivered beneath the hellish assault.

Omally crawled over to Soap Distant, who had wisely assumed the foetal position beneath the table. 'You've got to get us out,' he shouted, tearing away the hands clamped about the albino head. 'There has to be a way.'

'No way.' Soap tore himself from Omally's hold. 'No way.'

Shivers of woodwork flew from the bottom of the door as the evil barbs, now showing porcupine quills and scorpion tails thrashing about them, stripped the Ronseal finish clear down to the filled knot-holes. Omally stumbled to his feet. Sherlock Holmes was standing alone in the whirlwind, a speckled band tied bandana-fashion across his face. A finger in the air. The doyen of dicks was definitely off his trolley, thought John. As if reading his thoughts, Holmes suddenly struck him a weltering blow to the skull. Caught in surprise John hit the deck. Holmes leapt down upon him and pointed frantically through the swirling, cascading stench. 'Fireplace,' he shouted, his voice all but lost amidst the screaming, the hurricane, and the splintering woodwork. 'Up the chimney, get going, quick.'

It took very little time for Omally to cop on. Grabbing the huddled Pooley firmly by the collar, he dragged him towards what was surely the only hope of escape. Holmes stepped over to Soap and booted him in the ribcage. Soap peered up bitterly towards his tormentor, a dizzy blur, lost for the most part in the maelstrom of tearing elements. Holmes stretched deftly forward and hooked a pair of fingers into the sub-Earther's nostrils. 'Lead us out!' he cried, bearing him aloft. Whimpering and howling, but somehow happy for the nose-plugs, Soap staggered forward. Holmes thrust his head first into the fireplace and then, suddenly enlightened, Soap turned towards his persecutor with a nodding, smiling head and gestured upwards. Within a moment he was scrabbling into the darkness above. Omally pressed Jim onwards and followed hard upon his heels. Holmes spun about, revolver in hand, as the door burst from its hinges to spin a million whirling fragments about him. The icy gale tore his tweedy jacket from his shoulders as the thing rolled into the room, a tangle of barbs, quills and spikes, whipping and lashing and screaming, screaming. The great detective held his ground and fired off his revolver again and again into the spinning ball of death as it charged towards him.

The wind and the terror coming from below spurred on the three-man escape committee as it crept higher and higher up the narrow black chimney. Soap's voice called down from above, 'Come on, lads, shouldn't be more than a mile at most.' Pooley mumbled and complained, but Omally, who was tail-end Charlie and in the most vulnerable position, bit him in the ankle. A howl of pain and a sudden acceleration from Jim assured the struggling Irishman that the message was well-received.

The going was far from certain and made ever more perilous by the cramped space and the complete and utter darkness. Stones and grit tumbled down into the climbers' faces. Soap trod upon Jim's hands and Jim out of fairness trod upon John's. Higher and higher up the slim shaft of hope they clambered until at last they could no longer feel the icy wind rushing from below or the awful stench souring their nostrils. They paused a moment, clinging to what they could for dear life, to catch their breath, and cough up what was left of their lungs.

'How much farther, Soap?' Omally wiped at his streaming eyes and strained to support himself whilst delving in his pockets for a fag.

'A goodly way and all of it straight up.'

'There is actually an opening at the top?' Jim ventured. 'I mean I'd just hate to climb all this way and find myself peering out of a ventilation duct in Lateinos and Romiith's basement.'

'Hm. To be quite candid, this digging is one of the great grandaddy's. We shall have to trust to the luck of the Distants.'

'Oh, very comforting. Ooh, ow, ouch!'

'Sorry, Jim. Did I singe your bum?'

'Pass me up that fag, you clumsy oaf.'

'Smoking cigarettes can harm your health,' said Soap. 'Ooh, ow, ouch!'

'Onward, Christian Soldier,' said Jim, withdrawing the lighted fag from Soap's trouser seat.

The three continued their bleak and harrowing journey, now illuminated by the firefly-glow of three burning cigarettes. The first hour was really quite uneventful, other than for the occasional minor avalanche which threatened to plunge them to a most uninviting oblivion. It was several minutes into the second that things took a most depressing turn for the worst.

'I hate to tell you this,' said Soap Distant, 'but I've run out of passage.'

'You've bloody what? Careful there, that's my damn hand you're treading on.'

'Get a move on, Pooley.'

'Shut up, John.'

'Stop the two of you, for God's sake. I can't climb any higher.'

'Then get to one side and let us pass.'

'He means the passage has come to an end, John.'

'Then stand aside and let me kill him.'

'Shut up, I can see daylight.'

'What?'

The three men strained their eyes into the darkness above. In the far distance a dim light showed. A mere pinprick, yet it was some kind of hope, although not a lot.

'Get a move on,' yelled Omally.

'I've told you, something's blocking my way.'

'I just knew it,' said Jim, with the voice of one who just knew it. 'No way up, no way down. Doomed to starve here until we drop away one by one like little shrivelled up . . .'

'Give it a rest, Jim. What's in the way, Soap?'

Soap prodded above. 'Some old grill or grating, rusty as hell.'

'Easy on the descriptions.'

'Solid as a rock also.'

'Doom and desolation oh misery, misery.'

'I have plenty of fuel in my lighter, Jim.'

'Sorry, John. Can't you wiggle it loose, Soap?'

'It's bloody rusted in. Can't you hear what I'm saying?'

'Let me get up there then.'

'There's no room, John.'

'Then we'll all just have to push, that's all. Brace yourself, lads, after three. Three!'

Soap wedged his shoulders beneath the obstruction, Jim got a purchase under his bum, with Omally straining from below.

'Heave.'

'AAAGH!'

'OOOOW.'

'Get off there.'

'My God.'

'Again, it's giving.'

'It's not giving, I am.'

'I felt it give.'

'That was my shoulder.'

'Put your back into it.'

229

'Mind where you're holding.'

'We're there, we're there.'

'Who said that?'

'One more time . . .'

'It's giving . . . It's giving . . . It's gone.'

Soap's head and shoulders battered up through the obstruction, a thin and crumbling iron grid cemented solidly into place through the application of fifty-years pigeon guano. 'You bastards!' Soap's arms were pinned at his sides, his feet lashed out furiously. 'You bastards!'

'Watch where you're kicking,' Pooley complained.

Soap's muffled voice screamed down at them from above. 'You bloody lunatics, I'm stuck in here.'

Now, as you might reasonably expect, a heated debate occurred beneath the struggling Soap, as to what might be the best means of adding the necessary irresistible force to the currently immovable object.

'We must pull him down and give him another charge,' Jim declared.

'Down on top of us so we all fall down the hole?'

'Grease him with goose fat.'

'You wally.'

'Tickle his feet then.'

'And you a millionaire, Jim. I thought you blokes had it all sussed.'

'A hoist, a hoist, my kingdom for a hoist.'

'I'm starting to suffocate, lads,' called Soap distantly.

Pooley weighed up the situation. 'Doom and desperation,' he concluded.

'Stop everything,' Omally demanded. 'Enough is enough. It is a well-attested fact that the man who can get his head and shoulders through a gap can get the rest of him through also.'

Soap wriggled like a maggot on a number nine hook.

'Stick your head down here, Jim. I want to whisper.'

Soap thrashed and struggled, but his movements were becoming weaker by the moment.

'I can't do that to Soap!'

'It only takes a second. Take my word for it, it will do the trick.'

'But it's not decent.'

'Do it to Soap or I'll do it to you.'

Pooley closed his eyes and gritted his teeth. Reaching up he performed a quick vicious action.

'EEEEEEEEEOOOOOOOOOOOOOOOOW!'

A few moments later three men lay puffing and panting in the entrance to the loading bay at Meeks Boatyard on the bank of the Grand Union Canal. A few feet away a wall of impenetrable turquoise light rose from the water and spread away to either side and ever above.

'Too much to hope that we'd come up on the other side,' sighed Pooley.

Soap Distant, red-faced and clutching at himself, looked daggers at him. 'I'll have you for that,' he said painfully.

Jim smiled sickly. 'What could we do? Look on the bright side, at least we all got out alive.'

'Not all,' said John Omally.

'Eh?'

Omally gestured towards the open manhole through which they had just emerged. 'And then there were three,' he said in a leaden tone.

'Holmes,' cried Pooley. 'In all the excitement . . .' he scrabbled over to the manhole and shouted the detective's name into the void. His voice came back to him again and again, mocking his cries.

'Leave it, Jim.' Omally put his hand to his best friend's shoulder. 'He never had a chance.'

'I didn't think.' Pooley looked up fearfully. 'I didn't think.'

'None of us did. We only thought of ourselves and our own.'

'We left him to . . .'

'Yes.'

'The poor bastard.'

'The poor noble bastard. He saved our lives at the expense of his own.'

Pooley climbed slowly to his feet and thrust his hands into his trouser pockets. He looked up to where the Lateinos and Romiith building rose, filling the skyline. 'Oh shit!' he said, kicking at the toppled manhole cover. 'Oh, that's me finished. Those bastards are going to pay for this.'

'Oh yes,' said John Omally. 'They are definitely going to do all of that.'

30

Professor Slocombe withdrew a goose feather quill from the inkwell, and scratched out the fifth day from the June calendar. From beyond the shuttered French windows sounds as of merriment reached him. The Brentford Festival had begun. Throughout the night, the floats had been assembling upon the Butts Estate; lumbering through the darkness, heavy and ponderous. Through a crack in the shutters he had watched their slow progress and viewed their silhouettes, stark against an almost white sky. He had presided over many Festivals past and judged many a float competition, but he had never seen anything such as this. The shapes which rolled onward through the night upon their many wheels were totally alien, even to he who had seen so much. They were the stuff of nightmare, the dreams of the delirious and dying sick. If human hand had wrought these monstrosities, then it was a hand far better stricken from the arm.

A shiver ran up the long spine of the ancient scholar and his mottled hand closed about a crystal tumbler, half-filled upon his desk. Sleep had not touched him in more than a week and could offer nothing to soothe the ache which filled his heart and the very marrow of his bones. The great clock upon the mantelshelf was even now ticking away mankind's final hours. The prophecies were being fulfilled and the helplessness, to one who knew, but was yet unable to act, was beyond human endurance.

Professor Slocombe raked his hand across the desk and tumbled a stack of magazines to the carpeted floor. *Computer Weekly, Softwear Review, Micro Times, Popular Processor:* the poison fruits from the new technology's tree of life. Mankind had finally reached its own level of super incompetence, and made itself obsolete. It had promoted itself into extinction. Uncomprehending, it had made a science out of the thing; established a new order, laid the foundation for a new culture, and ultimately created a god. Or more accurately, aided the reinstatement of one previously superseded. Computer technology had given mankind the opportunity to regress, to cease thinking and in so doing cease to be. Why bother to add? The machine can do it for us. Mankind had been subtly tricked into believing that sophistication was progress. That godhead technology could cure man's ills at the flick of a switch, or if not that, then after a few more years of further sophistication. Man had lost sight of himself. Darkness was soon to triumph over the light, and the real means of confounding it were fading before the Professor's eyes. It was progress. Mankind had made so much progress that it no longer had any hope of survival. The miracle of science had become a chamber of horrors.

Somewhere in the dark tower which pierced the Brentford sky, the bleak temple of technology, the dragon lay curled in its lair. Its moment of release drew nigh, and who was there to plunge the sword of truth into its black heart?

The old man drained his glass and refilled it. He watched the gilded pendulum endlessly carving its arc. Where was Holmes? He was to have returned at daybreak, having followed up certain of his own leads, but he was hours overdue. The Professor had put into his keeping certain documents which he felt might hold an ultimate solution; but where was he now? Crowds were gathering in the street and it was an invitation to disaster to venture out of doors.

The sound of rumbling wheels and wild applause drew his eyes once more towards the shuttered windows. Should they choose now to make an assault upon the house the Professor knew he would be powerless to stop them. If ever there was a time to rally the troops beneath the banner of truth, now was definitely it.

At the present time, the Legion of Light was holed up in an outside privy in Moby Dick Terrace. There was more than just a little of the Lost Patrol about these three particular stalwarts.

'Can you see anything?' asked Jim, as Omally put his eye once more to the door's half-moon.

'I can see a good deal,' the brave Sir Knight replied, 'and to be perfectly frank, I like not a bit of it.'

'Let's have a squint,' said Soap Distant. 'And you keep your hands to yourself, Pooley.'

'They're in my pockets. Have a care where you step, it's crowded in here.'

Soap's pink eye rose to the carved cresent. 'My God,' said he.

'Not mine,' said John Omally.

Beyond the broken trelliswork which topped the garden fence, the great Festival floats were moving in slow procession. The thin dawn light, now tinting their silhouettes, brought them form and solidity. They were vast, towering to fill the streets, extending outwards within inches of the house walls. But what were they? They had something of the look of great bloated sombre reptiles, with scaled flanks and rudimentary limbs. All gill slits and hulking slabby sides. But they were too large, too daunting, too top-heavy. They did not fit. How many of these monstrosities had already passed and how many more were yet to come? The three men skulking in the evil-smelling dunny chose not to make bets.

Soap tore his eye from the hole with difficulty. Already the terrible compulsion to watch each movement of the swaying behemoths had become all but overwhelming. 'What are they?' he gasped, pressing his hands across the hole that he might see no more.

'The work of the Devil.' Omally's voice, coming from the darkness, put the wind up even himself. 'We have to get out of here. At least to the Professor's, then I don't know what.'

'A manhole, two gardens up, leads indirectly into a tunnel to his basement.'

'Oh no.' This voice belonged to Jim Pooley. 'Down again we do not go. I will take my chances above ground.'

'Well, please yourself. Whatever killed Holmes could not pursue us, it was pretty big. The tunnels hereabouts are small. I shall travel below; you do as you see fit.'

'I think we should stick together,' Omally advised. 'Are you sure it's safe, Soap?'

'To tell the absolute truth, I'm not too sure of anything any more.'

'Oh doom, oh desolation. Oooh, ooooow!'

'Come on then.' Omally eased open the door, and the three men, one now limping a little and clutching at himself, ducked across the garden and shinned up a dividing fence. Soap's manhole was overgrown with weeds, which seemed promising. The hollow Earther took a slim crooked tool from his belt and, scraping away the undergrowth, flipped off the cover in a professional manner. 'Follow me,' he said, vanishing from sight.

Pooley looked at Omally. 'It's all up and down these days, isn't it?'

'After you, Jim. I should hate you to have cold feet.'

Muttering and complaining, the blighted billionaire clambered into the hole, followed by Omally, who drew the lid back into place.

Three darting images vanished from the screen of the Lateinos and Romiith computer scan, but already the information had been processed and relayed. No less than three Pooleys and a brace of

237

Omallys were already scaling the garden wall. None of them were wearing carnival hats.

'Come on, lads.' Soap's voice urged them on from the darkness. 'And get a move on, something smells a bit iffy down here.' With hands about each other's waists, the most unmusical of all conga lines moved along a few short feet beneath the streets of Brentford. The rumble of the heavy floats and the muffled sounds of chanting, coming faintly to them as the duplicates mouthed to the holophonic images pouring into their brains through their minuscule headphones, were anything but cheering.

Soap suddenly came upon a heavy door blocking his way. 'There now,' said he.

'Where now, exactly?'

'We're there.'

'Good man, Soap. Now open up, let's not waste any time.'

The sounds of Soap fumbling in his pockets preceded a long and dismal groan. 'My keys.'

'Where *are* your keys, Soap?'

'In my desk, I think.'

A piercing white light illuminated the narrow black corridor. It shone directly on to three terrified faces, which had turned instinctively towards it. From about the light source came the flashing of blue sparks as several lethal handsets energized.

'Get out of the way,' said Omally. 'Let me at that lock.' The Irishman squeezed past the pink-eyed man and dropped to his knees. A neat roll of housebreaking implements materialized from a hidden pocket in his waistcoat and were rapidly unfurled.

'John,' said Jim, 'I had no idea.'

'They were the daddy's. Keep out of the light and keep those bastards back somehow.'

The light was moving nearer, spiralling along the wet brick-worked tube of the tunnel. The crackling of the handsets became audible.

'You'll not break it,' gibbered Soap. 'The lock is protected, it cannot be picked.'

'There is no lock which cannot be picked.' Omally flung aside a bundle of metal tags and slotted another sequence into the shaft of the skeleton key.

'You won't open it.'

'Shut up will you?'

'Get away.' For once doing the bold thing, Pooley had crept back up the tunnel towards his attackers. Now he lashed out with his hobnail at the blinding light as it reared up in his face. His boot connected and the beam swung aside, leaving Omally to fumble in the darkness. 'Nice one, Jim,' he spat. 'Now I can't see a bloody thing.'

'Get off me, leave hold.' Clawing hands reached out towards Pooley. In the coruscating blue fire his face twisted and contorted. 'John, protect me for God's sake!'

'Protect me . . .' Omally's brain kicked into gear. He tore his crucifix from about his neck and fumbling for the keyhole thrust it in and turned it sharply to the right. 'We're in, lads,' cried John.

'Go quickly,' said Soap. 'It is up to you now.' With a brisk movement he vanished away as if by magic into the brickwork of the passage.

Omally bundled his way through the doorway.

Pooley wrenched himself away from his attackers, leaving them the right sleeve of his cashmere jacket as something to remember him by. The combined weight of two men hurtled the door back into its jambs. Fists rained upon it from without, but they could not penetrate the mantle of protection. Omally winkled out his crucifix and pressed it to his lips. 'And then there were two,' said he, sinking to his bum with a dull thump.

Jim slowly removed his jacket, folding it neatly across his arm. He laid upon the floor and began to leap up and down upon it. 'Bugger, bugger, bugger, bugger,' he went.

Omally watched the performance without comment. They were a strange old breed these millionaire lads and that was a fact. 'When you are done,' he said at length, 'I suggest we go upstairs and break the sad news of Holmes to the old man.'

'Oh bugger,' said Pooley.

'So you said.'

'No, this is another quite separate bugger. I left my fags in the top pocket.'

Professor Slocombe watched the two men plod wearily up the cellar steps, slouch down the side-corridor, and halt before the study door, twin looks of indecision upon their unshaven faces. He opened his eyes. 'Come in, lads,' he called. 'No need to skulk about out here.' Beyond the heavy-panelled door, Omally shrugged. With evasive eyes and shuffling feet, he and Jim sheepishly entered the study. Professor Slocombe indicated the decanter, and Omally grasped it up by the neck and rattled it into a crystal tumbler.

'Easy on the glassware, John.'

Omally, his face like a smacked bottom, looked up at the ancient. 'Sherlock Holmes is dead,' he blurted out.

Professor Slocombe's face was without expression. His eyes widened until they became all but circular. The whites formed two Polo mints about the pupils. The narrow jaw slowly revolved as if he was grinding his teeth upon Omally's words.

'That cannot be,' he said, slowly drawing himself from his desk and turning his back upon his uninvited guests. 'It cannot be.'

Omally poured his drink down his neck and slung another large measure into his glass. 'And mine,' complained Pooley.

The Professor turned upon them. 'How did this happen? Did you see it?' A high tone of fear choked at his voice.

'Not exactly,' Jim replied nervously, 'but believe us, sir, he could not have survived.'

'He saved our lives,' said Omally.

'But you did not actually see?'

'Not exactly, thank God.'

Professor Slocombe smiled ruefully. 'I thought not.'

Omally opened his mouth to speak, but thought better of it. If the old man did not care to accept the truth, then there was no good to be gained through labouring the point. 'All right,' said he carefully, 'we did not actually see it.'

'No,' said the Professor. 'You did not. So let us speak no more of the matter. There is little time left and much which must be done.'

'We are actually somewhat knackered,' said Jim, sinking into a chair. 'We've had a trying day.'

'I am afraid that it is not over yet. Kindly follow me.'

The Professor strode across the room and made towards the study door. Jim shrugged towards John, who put his finger to his lips and shook his head. 'Come on,' he said. 'We've nothing left to lose have we?' Omally followed the old man into the corridor.

Jim, left alone for a moment, suddenly smiled. He drew from his trouser pocket the ormulu-trimmed Boda hip-flask he had recently purchased and not yet had the opportunity to use, and hastily filled it from the old man's decanter. 'No point in going unarmed,' said he, following up the rear.

The Professor led them up several flights of steps to the room which housed the camera obscura. When Jim had closed the door and plunged them into darkness, he winched the apparatus into action and brought the image of the surrounding area into focus upon the polished marble table-top. The sight which leapt into vision was such as to take the breath from their lungs. Omally crossed himself and took an involuntary step backwards.

The evil travesty which was the Festival procession now filled every road and side-street in view. And the tableaux wrought upon them were now becoming recognizable for the horrors they were. It was as if those earlier floats they had seen were but the blurred and ill-formed shapes of clay, awaiting the hand of the master craftsman to draw form from them. Now the lines were distinct, the contours clearly defined.

'Look there.' Jim pointed to a lighted float which passed close to the Seaman's Mission, a stone's throw from the Professor's door. Depicted there was the form of a giant, clad in robes of crimson and seated upon a great throne, carved with the gilded heads of bulls. Golden banners, each emblazoned with similar motifs, fluttered above and five hooded, stunted figures cowered at his feet in attitudes of supplication. The crimson giant raised and lowered his hand in mechanical benediction, and it appeared that for a moment he raised his eyes, twin blood bowls of fire, towards the men in the rooftop bower, and stared into their very souls.

'Him,' said Omally.

'And there.' Jim pointed vigorously. 'Look at that, look at that.'

As the throned float moved beyond the range of vision, another rose up behind it. Here, a legion of men climbed one upon another, pointing towards the sky. They were identical in appearance. each resembling to a tee the young Jack Palance: the Cereans.

To either side of the floats marched a legion of men, women, and children. Familiar faces, now alien and unknown; their faces wore determined expressions and each marched in step, raising his or her own banner. Each illuminated with eighteen vertical lines, placed in three rows of six. The number of the beast, for it is the number of a man. Professor Slocombe pointed towards the image. Away in the distance, far greater shapes were looming into view, things so dark and loathsome, that even there, upon the flat white marble surface, their ghost images exuded a sense of eldritch horror which stunned the senses.

'Switch it off,' Omally demanded. 'There is too much madness here.'

'One more small thing you must see, John.' Professor Slocombe adjusted the apparatus and the image of the Lateinos and Romiith building drew a black shroud across the table-top. The old man cranked the mechanism and enlarged an area at the base of the building. 'Now look carefully, did you see that?'

His guests blinked and squinted at the image. 'I saw something,' said Jim, 'but what?'

'Look harder.'

'Yes, I see it.' It was but a fleeting movement, a single figure detached himself from the throng, pressed his hand to a section of the wall and was instantly swallowed up into the building to vanish without trace.

'I was at a loss to find a means of gaining entry,' the Professor explained, 'but Holmes reasoned the thing through and deduced their method.'

'If it's a lock then I shall pick it.'

'Not on this occasion, John. But one of us here has the key in his hand even now.'

'Oh no,' said Jim, thrusting his tattooed hand into his pocket. 'Not this boy, not in there.'

'You have the right of admission, Jim, right there in the palm of your hand.'

'No, no, no.' Pooley shook his head vigorously, 'An eight a.m. appointment with Albert Pierrepoint I should much prefer.'

'In my mind, only one course of action lies open. Unless we can penetrate the building and apply the proverbial spanner to the computer's works, all will be irretrievably lost. We cannot think to destroy the dark God himself. But if his temple is cast down and his worshippers annihilated, then he must withdraw once more, into the place of forever night from whence he has emerged.' Professor Slocombe recranked the mechanism and the room fell into darkness.

'Oh doom,' said Jim Pooley. 'Oh doom and desolaooooow! Let go there, John.'

'We must make our move now.' Professor Slocombe's voice echoed in the void. 'There is no more time, come at once.' He opened the door and the wan light from the stairs entered the strange roof chamber.

'But we cannot go outside,' said Omally. 'One step out of this house and good night.'

'Have no fear, I have taken the matter into consideration.' Professor Slocombe led the two lost souls back to his study. 'You are not going to like this, John,' said he, as he opened the desk drawer.

'That should create no immediate problem. I have liked nothing thus far.'

'So be it.' Professor Slocombe drew out a number of items, which had very much the appearance of being metallic balaclava helmets, and laid them on the table.

'Superman outfits,' said Pooley, very impressed. 'I should have realized, Professor, you are one of the Justice League of America.'

'Silence, Pooley.'

'Sorry, John.'

'As ludicrous as these items at first must appear, they may well be our salvation. As you are no doubt now aware, the Lateinos and Romiith computer scan cannot penetrate lead. Hopefully, these lead-foil helmets will shield our brain patterns from the machine's detection and allow us to move about unmolested.'

'Size seven and a half,' said Jim. 'But I can fit into a seven at a push.'

'Good man. As an extra precaution, if each of you could slip another piece of foil into your breast pocket then your heartbeat should be similarly concealed. No doubt the infra-red image produced by body heat will still register, but the result should be somewhat confused. "Will not compute", I believe the expression to be.'

'Bravo.' Omally slipped on his helmet without hesitation.

'Very Richard the Lionheart,' chuckled Pooley.

'A fine man,' said Professor Slocombe. 'I knew him well.'

The three men, now decked out in their ludicrous headgear, slipped through the Professor's French windows and out into the garden. At times one has to swallow quite a lot for a quiet life in Brentford.

Above the wall the titanic floats filled the street. As one by one the balaclava'd goodguys eased their way into the swaying crowd, each held his breath and did a fair bit of praying. Professor Slocombe plucked at

Omally's sleeve. 'Follow me.' The marching horde plodded onward. The floats dwarfed both street and sky. Jim peered about him; he was walking in a dream. The men and women to either side of him, each wearing their pair of minuscule headphones, were unreal. And that he knew to be true in every sense of the word. At close hand, the floats appeared shabby and ill-constructed; a mish-mash of texture and hue coming together as if, and no doubt it was exactly thus, programmed to create an overall effect. No hand of man had been at work here. Like all else it was a sick parody, a sham, and nothing more. The bolted wheel near at hand turned in faulty circles grinding the tarmac, untrue. But it was hypnotic, its unreality drew the eye and held it there. 'Come on, Jim.' Omally tugged at Pooley's sleeve. 'You're falling behind again.'

Pooley struggled on. Ahead, the Lateinos and Romiith building dwarfed all beneath its black shadow. The sky was dark with tumbling clouds, strange images weaved and flowed beyond the mysterious glittering walls, shimmering over the roof-tops. Even now something terrible was occurring beyond the boundaries of the borough.

The awful procession turned out of the Butts and up into Moby Dick Terrace. Professor Slocombe drew his followers aside from the throng and the helmeted duo scuttled after him. 'Make haste now.'

The Lateinos and Romiith building filled the eastern skyline. Jim noted with increasing gloom that an entire terrace of houses had gone, overwhelmed by the pitiless structure which reared into the darkling sky.

On a roadside bench ahead an old man sat with his dog.

'Good day, lads,' said Old Pete, as the strangely-clad threesome passed him by at close quarters. 'Fair old do this year, isn't it?'

'Bloody marvellous,' Pooley replied. 'Hope to see you later for one in the Swan if all goes well.'

Old Pete cleared his throat with a curiously mechanical coughing sound. 'Look out for yourself,' said he.

The three men continued their journey at the jog.

'Stop here now,' said Professor Slocombe, as they came finally to the corner of the street. 'I am expecting somebody.'

'A friend I hope.'

'That would be nice,' said Jim, with a little more flippancy than the situation warranted. 'Organizer of the Festival raffle is it? Or chairman of the float committee?'

Omally took what he considered to be one of the last opportunities left to him to welt Jim about the head. 'Oow ouch!' he said, clutching at a throbbing fist. Pooley smiled sweetly. 'How much do you want for the copyright of this helmet?' he asked the Professor.

'Leave it out, you two. Here he comes.'

Along the deserted pavement, weaving with great difficulty, came an all too familiar figure, clad in grey shopkeeper's overall and trilby hat. But what was this that the clone shopkeeper rode upon his precarious journey? Could this be that creaking vestige of a more glorious age, now black and pitted and sorely taken with the rest? Surely we have seen these perished hand-grips before? Marvelled at the coil-spring saddle and oil-bath chainguard? The stymied Sturmey Archer Three-speed and the tungsten-carbide lamp? Yes, there can be no doubt, it is that noted iron stallion, that prince of pedaldom, squeaking and complaining beneath the weight of its alien rider, it can be no other. Let men take note and ladies beware: Marchant the wonder bike, it is he.

'Get off my bleeding bicycle,' yelled John Omally.

Norman the Second leapt down from his borrowed mount with some alacrity. Not, however, with sufficient alertness to avoid the sneaky pedal which had been awaiting its chance to drive in deep. Norman's right trouser cuff vanished into the oil-bath and the automated shopman bit the dust.

'Bastard,' squealed the mechanical man. 'I'll do for you.'

'Nice one, Marchant,' said John, drawing his bike beyond reach. The bicycle rang its bell in greeting and nuzzled its handlebar into its master's waistcoat.

'Bloody pathetic isn't it?' said Jim. 'A boy and his bike, I ask you.'

'Do you think we might apply ourselves to the job in hand?' the Professor asked.

'I like the helmets,' said Norman the Second. 'What is it then, Justice League of America?'

'A running gag I believe,' Jim replied. 'Did you have to bring his bike? That thing depresses me.'

249

'Easy Jim, if I am going to die, I will do it with Marchant at my side, or at least under my bum.'

'Bloody pathetic.'

'Time to do your party trick, Jim,' said Omally. 'Professor?'

The old man indicated a dimly-lit panel on the bleak wall. 'Just there,' he said.

'I don't know if this is such a good idea,' Jim complained. 'I think the best idea would be to give the place a good leaving alone.'

'Stick your mitt out, Jim.'

The cursed Croesus placed his priceless palm on to the panel. There was a brief swish and a section of the wall shot aside. A very bad smell came from within.

'Quickly now,' said the Professor. 'Keep your hand on the panel until we're all in, Jim.'

A moment later the gap closed upon three men, one robot shopkeeper, and a bike called Marchant.

'Blimey,' said Omally. 'I don't know what I expected, but it wasn't this.'

They stood now in what might have been the lobby and entrance hall of any one of a thousand big business consortiums. The traditional symbols of success and opulence, the marble walls, thick plush carpeting, chromium reception desk, even the rubber plant in its Boda plant-stand, were all there. It was so normal and so very ordinary as to be fearful. For behind this façade, each man knew, lurked a power more evil than anything words were able to express.

'Gentlemen,' said Professor Slocombe, 'we are now in the belly of the beast.'

Omally suddenly clutched at his stomach. 'I think I'm going to chuck up,' he said. 'I can feel something. Something wrong.'

'Hold on.' The Professor laid a calming hand upon Omally's arm. 'Speak the rosary; it will pass.'

Beneath his breath Omally whispered the magical words of the old prayer. Its power was almost instantaneous, and the sick and claustrophobic feeling lifted itself from his shoulders, to alight upon Jim Pooley.

'Blech,' went Jim. Being a man of fewer words and little religious conviction, he threw up over the rubber plant.

'That will please the caretaker,' chuckled Omally.

'Sorry,' said Jim, drawing his shirt-sleeve over the cold sweat on his brow. 'Gippy tummy I think. I must be going cold turkey for the want of a pint.'

'You and me both. Which way, Professor?'

The old man fingered his chin. 'There is no-one on the desk, shall we take the lift?'

Norman the Second shook his head, 'I would strongly advise the stairs. A stairway to oblivion is better than no stairway at all I always say. Would you like me to carry your bike, John, or would you prefer to chain it to the rubber plant?'

'I'll carry my own bike, thank you.'

Pooley squinted up at the ragged geometry, spiralling into nothingness above. 'Looks like a long haul,' said he. 'Surely the cellar would be your man, down to the fuse boxes and out with the fuse. I feel that I have done more than my fair share of climbing today.'

'Onward and upward.'

Now there just may be a knack to be had with stairs. Some speak with conviction that the balls of the feet are your man. Others favour shallow breathing or the occupation of the mind upon higher things. Walking up backwards, that one might deceive your legs into thinking they were coming down, has even been suggested. In the course of the next fifteen minutes it must fairly be stated that each of these possible methods and in fact a good many more, ranging from the subtly ingenious to the downright absurd, were employed. And each met with complete and utter failure.

'I'm gone.' Pooley sank to his knees and clutched at his heart.

'Nurse, the oxygen.' Omally dragged himself a stair or more further and collapsed beneath his bike. 'We must give poor Jim a breather,' he said. 'The life of ease has gone to his legs.'

'Are you all right yourself?' Norman the Second enquired.

'Oh yes.' Omally wheezed bronchitically and wiped the sweat from his eyes. 'It is Jim I fear for.'

Professor Slocombe peered down from a landing above. If his ancient limbs were suffering the agonies one would naturally assume them to be, he showed no outward sign. The light of determination burned in his eyes. 'Come on now,' he urged. 'We are nearly there.'

'Nearly there?' groaned Jim. 'Not only can I hear

the grim reaper sharpening his scythe, I am beginning to see the sparks.'

'You've enough breath, Jim; lend him your arm, John.'

'Come on, Jim.' Omally shouldered up his bike and aided his sagging companion. 'If we get out of this I will let you buy me a drink.'

'If we get out of this I will buy you a pub.'

'Onward and upward then.'

Another two flights passed beneath them; to John and Jim it was evident that some fiendish builder was steadily increasing the depth of the treads.

'Stop now.'

'With the greatest pleasure.'

Professor Slocombe put his eye to the smoked glass of a partition door. 'Yes,' said he in a whisper. 'We shall trace it from here, I think.'

Norman the Second ran his fingertips about the door's perimeter and nodded. 'Appears safe enough,' he said.

'Then let us see.' Professor Slocombe gestured to Jim. 'You push it, please.'

Pooley shook his head dismally but did as he was bid. The door gave to expose a long dimly-lit corridor.

Omally fanned at his nose. 'It smells like the dead house.'

Professor Slocombe pressed a large gingham handkerchief to his face. 'Will you lead the way, Norman?'

The robot entered the corridor. 'I can feel the vibration of it,' he said, 'but it is some distance away. If I could get to a VDU.'

'Stand alone, clustered, or wide-area network?' Omally asked, sarcastically.

'Super advanced WP and a spread-sheet planner, hopefully,' said Jim.

'Do I take the piss out of your relatives?' Norman the Second asked. 'Stick your palm against this panel will you please?'

'Security round here stinks as bad as the air,' Pooley pressed the panel. A gleaming black door slid noiselessly aside.

'Ah,' said Norman the Second, 'magic.'

The room was nothing more than a cell, happily unoccupied. Black walls, floor and ceiling. A cunningly concealed light source illuminated a centralized computer terminal, bolted to the floor. 'And people have the gall to ask me why I never take employment,' said Omally, parking his bike. 'Imagine this place nine to five.'

The robot faced the console and cracked his nylon knuckles. 'Now,' said he, 'only one small problem. We do not possess the entry code.'

Professor Slocombe handed him a folded sheet of vellum. 'Try this.' The automaton perused the paper and stared up at the old man.

'Don't ask,' said John Omally.

'All right then.' With a blur of digits the robot punched in the locking code. The words 'ENTER ENQUIRY NOW' sprang up upon the now illuminated screen. Norman's hand hovered.

'Ask it for permission to consult the main access body,' said the Professor.

Norman punched away at the keyboard.

Professor Slocombe stroked at his chin. 'Ask it for a data report.'

Norman did the business. Rows of lighted figures plonked up on to the monitor. Row upon coloured row, number upon number, little illuminated regiments marching up the screen. 'Magic,' crooned Norman the Second.

'Looks like trig,' said Jim disgustedly. 'Never could abide trig. Woodwork and free periods, but trig definitely not.'

'The music of the spheres,' said Norman the Second.

Professor Slocombe's eyes were glued to the flickering screen. His mouth worked and moved, his head quivered from side to side. As the projected figures darted and weaved, so the old man rose and fell upon his toes.

'Does it mean something to you?' Omally asked.

'Numerology, John. It is as I have tried to explain to you both. Everything, no matter what, can be broken down into its base elements and resolved to a final equation: the numerical equivalent; all of life, each moving cell, each microbe, each network of cascading molecules. That is the purpose of it all. Don't you see?' He pulled Omally nearer to the screen, but John jerked away.

'I'll not have it,' said he. 'It is wrong. Somehow it is indecent. Obscene.'

'No, no, you must understand.' The Professor crouched lower towards the screen, pushing Norman's duplicate aside.

Pooley was jigging from one foot to the other. 'Can't we get a move on. I'm freezing to death here.'

The room had suddenly grown impossibly cold. The men's breath steamed from their faces. Or at least from two of them it did.

Omally grasped Pooley by the wrist, for the first time he realized that the Professor was no longer wearing his helmet, and hadn't been since they had joined him on the landing. 'Oh, Jim,' whispered John, 'bad Boda.'

The 'Professor' stiffened; slowly his head revolved a hundred and eighty degrees upon his neck and stared up at them, sickeningly. 'Learn, last men,' he said, clearing his throat with the curiously mechanical coughing sound John and Jim had learned to fear. 'It is your only salvation. Humble yourselves before your new master.'

'Oh no.' Omally stumbled back and drew out his crucifix. 'Back,' he shouted, holding it before him in a wildly shaking fist. 'Spawn of the pit.'

The Professor's body turned to follow the direction of his face. His eyes had lost their pupils but now glowed from within, two miniature terminal screens, tiny figures twinkling across them in hypnotic succession. 'Behold the power,' said he. 'Know you the number of the beast, for it is the number of a man.'

'By the Cross.'

The thing which dwelt in the Professor's image thrust a hand into its trouser pocket and drew out a small black box with two slim protruding shafts.

'Head for the hills,' yelled Pooley, as the clone

256

touched the nemesis button and the black rods sparkled with electric fire.

Omally flattened himself to the wall as the thing lunged towards him. A great explosion tore the world apart. Shards of glass and splinters of burning circuitry spun in every direction, spattering the walls and the two cowering men; flame and smoke engulfed the room. The Professor's duplicate stood immovable, his synthetic hair ablaze and his clothes in tatters. Norman's double drew a smouldering fist from the shattered terminal screen. He leapt forward, grasping the Professor's *doppelgänger* about the throat, and dragged it backwards. 'Out!' he shouted. 'Run for your lives, lads.'

Pooley and Omally bundled out of the door. John leapt astride Marchant and Pooley clambered on to the handlebars. At very much the hurry-up they took to the retreat.

In absolutely the wrong direction.

Omally's feet flew about and Marchant, realizing the urgency of the situation, made no attempt to ditch its extra rider. With its bell ringing dramatically it cannoned forward up the corridor. Figures appeared before them, dressed in grey uniforms and carrying fire-fighting equipment. Pooley struck aside all he could as the bike ploughed forward. As he cleared a path between several rather sloppy versions of himself, a thought struck him. The great machine for all its dark magic certainly lacked something in the old imagination department. Obviously when idling and stuck for something to do, it just kept turning out the same old thing.

'Do you know what this means?' Omally shouted into his ear. Pooley shook his terrified head and lashed out at another robot duplicate of himself.

'It means that I am the last Catholic on Earth.'

'Well, some good came out of it all, then.'

As Omally's hands were busily engaged at the handlebar grips, he could do no more than lean forward and bite Pooley's ear. 'Jim,' he shouted, 'Jim, as the last Catholic, I am Pope! Jim . . . I . . . am Pope. I am Pope!'

31

Some distance beneath the pedalling pontiff a great cry broke the silence. 'Fe . . . fi . . . fo . . . fum.' Neville the barbarian barman had finally reached a wall. And at long last he had found something he could thump. The thrill of the prospect sent a small shiver up his back which finally lost itself amid acres of straining muscle fibre. Neville ran his hand across the barrier blocking his way; hard and cold as glass. An outside wall surely? The barman pressed his eye to the jet crystal surface and did a bit of squinting. Something vague was moving about on the other side. People in the street? Neville drew back for a shoulder charge, and he would have gone through with it had not a sensible thought unexpectedly entered his head. He wasn't exactly sure which floor, or wherever, he was on. With his track record the movements were likely to be those of roosting rooftop pigeons. It could be a long hard fall to earth. Neville pressed his ear to the wall of black glass. He couldn't hear a damn thing.

Bash out a couple of bore holes to see out through, that would be your man. The barman drew back a fist of fury and hurled it forward at something approaching twice the speed of sound. With a sickening report it struck home. His knotted fist passed clean through the wall, cleaving out a hole the size of a dustbin-lid. 'Gog a Magog!' Neville took an involuntary step backwards. An icy hurricane of fetid wind tore out at him shredding away the last vestiges of his surgical smock and leaving him only his Y-fronts. Neville stood his ground, a great arm drawn over his face to shield his sensitive nostrils from the vile onslaught he had unwittingly unleashed. 'Great mother.' Tears flew from his eyes as he forced himself onward. With his free hand he tore out a great section of the wall, which cartwheeled away in the stinking gale. With heroic effort he charged forward into the not-so-great beyond.

The wind suddenly ceased and he found himself standing in absolute silence and near-darkness. It was very very cold indeed. 'Brr,' said Neville. 'Brass monkey weather.' To the lover of Greek mythology, what next occurred would have been of particular interest. But to a Brentford barman in his present state of undress, the sudden arrival of Cerberus, the multi-headed canine guardian of the underworld, was anything but a comfort.

'Woof, woof, and growl,' went Cerberus, in the plural.

'Nice doggy,' said Neville, covering his privy parts. 'Good boy, there.'

The creature tore at the barman, a blur of slavering mouths and blazing red eyes.

Neville sprang aside and ducked away beneath it as it leapt towards his throat. 'Heel,' he said. 'Sit.'

The thing turned and stood pawing the ground, glowing faintly, its scorpion tail flicking, low growls coming from a multiplicity of throats. By all accounts it made Holmes' Baskerville growler seem pretty silly.

'Grrrrrrrrrrs,' went Cerberus, squaring up for the kill.

'Grrrrrrrr,' went Neville, who now considered that thumping a multi-headed dog was as good as thumping anything. 'Come and get your Bob Martins.' With a single great bound it was upon him, heads whipping and snapping. Neville caught it at chest height and pummelled it down with flailing fists. It leapt up again and he caught at a scaled throat, crushing his hands about it until the thumbs met. The hell-hound screamed with pain as Neville dragged it from its clawed feet and dashed it to the ground. Roll on chucking-out time, thought the part-time barman. With one head hanging limply but others still on the snap, the fiend was on him once more, ripping and tearing, its foul mouths snapping, brimstone vapour snorting from its nostrils.

The two bowled over again and again, mighty figures locked in titanic conflict. The nightmare creature and the all-but-naked barman. The screams and cries echoed about the void, the echoes doubling and redoubling, adding further horror to a scene which was already fearsome.

Roll over and die for your country Rover, was not in there.

'I'm not doing it, John, and that's the end of the matter.' Pooley clung precariously to his handlebar perch as Pope John the Umpteenth freewheeled down a deserted corridor. 'I am not a Catholic and I utterly refuse to kiss your bloody ring. The thing came out of a Jamboree bag for God's sake.'

'Let me convert you, Jim, come to the Mother Church before it's too late.'

'Let me down from here, I want a drink.'

'Drink?' Omally tugged on the brakes and sent Jim sprawling. 'Drink did I hear you say, my son?'

Pooley looked up bitterly from the deck. 'Popes don't drink,' he said. 'Such is well-known.'

'A new Papal bull,' his Holiness replied.

'All right then, but no ring-kissing, it's positively indecent.' Pooley unearthed the hip-flask and the two plodded on, sharing it turn and turn about.

'It's getting bloody cold,' Pooley observed, patting at his shirt-sleeves. 'And the pong's getting a lot stronger.'

'What do you expect?' Omally passed him back the hip-flask. 'Roses round the door?'

'Are you sure we're going the right way?'

'The passage is going down, isn't it? Would the Pope put you on a wrong 'n?'

'Listen, John, I'm not too sure about this Pope business. I thought you lads had to be elected. White smoke up the chimney or the like?'

'As last Catholic, I have the casting vote. Please don't argue about religious matters with me, Jim. If you let me convert you I'll make you a cardinal.'

'Thanks, but no thanks. God, it stinks down here. Couldn't you issue another Papal bull or something?'

Omally halted the infidel in mid-step. 'Would you look at that?' he said, pointing forward.

Ahead of them loomed a great door. It seemed totally out of context with all they had yet seen. At odds with the bland modernistic corridors they had passed down on their abortive journey of escape. It rose like a dark hymn in praise of evil pleasure, and hung in a heavily-carved portico wrought with frescoed reliefs.

Omally parked his bike, and the two men tiptoed forward. The hugeness and richness of the thing filled all vision. It was a work of titanic splendour, the reliefs exquisite, carved into dark pure wood of extreme age.

'Fuck me,' said John Omally, which was quite unbecoming of a Pope. 'Would you look at that holy show?'

'Unholy show, John. That is disgusting.'

'Yes, though, isn't it? And that.' Jim followed Omally's pointing finger. 'You'd need to be double-jointed.'

'There's something inscribed there, John. You know the Latin, what does it say?'

Omally leant forward and perused the inscription, 'Oh,' said he at length, his voice having all the fun of herpes about it, 'that is what it says.'

'Exit does it say?'

Omally turned towards the grinning idiot. 'Give me that hip-flask, you are a fool.'

'And you a Pope. Drink your own.'

'Give me that flask.'

'Well, only a small sip, don't want your judgement becoming impaired.' Pooley began to hiccup.

Omally guzzled more than his fair share. 'It's in

there,' he said, wiping his chin and returning the flask to Pooley.

'What is?' Jim shook the flask against his ear and gave the self-made Pope a disparaging look.

'The big It, you damned fool.'

'Then next right turn and on your bike. We don't want to do anything silly now, do we?'

Omally nodded gloomily. 'We must; stick your tattooed mitt up against it.'

'I can think of a million reasons why not.'

'And me. For the Professor, eh Jim?'

'For the Professor, then.' Jim pressed his hand to the door and it moved away before his touch.

Omally took up his bike, and the two men stepped cautiously through the opening.

'Oh, bloody hell,' whispered Jim.

'Yes, all of that.'

They stood now in the vestibule of what was surely a great cathedral. But its size was not tailored to the needs of man. It was the hall of giants. The two stared about them in an attempt to take it in. It was simply too large. The scale of its construction sent the mind reeling. The temperature had dropped another five degrees at least, yet the smell was ripe as a rotten corpse.

'The belly of the beast,' gasped Pooley. 'Let's go back. The utter cold, the feeling, the stench, I can't stand it.'

'No, Jim, look, there it is.'

Ahead, across an endless expanse of shining black marble floor, spread the congregation, row upon regimental row. Countless figures crouched before as many flickering terminal screens, paying obeisance to their dark master. For there, towering towards eternity, rising acre upon vertical acre, spreading away in every direction, was the mainframe of the great computer. Billions of housed microcircuits, jet-black boxes stacked one upon another in a jagged endless wall. Upon giddy stairways and catwalks, minuscule figures moved upon its face, attending to its needs. Feeding it, pampering it with knowledge, gorging its insatiable appetite.

I AM LATEINOS, I AM ROMIITH.

The Latin, the formula, words reduced to their base components, stripped of their flesh, reduced to the charred black dust of their skeletons; to the equations which were the music of the spheres, the grand high opera of all existence. Omally slumped forward on to his knees. 'I see it,' he whispered hoarsely, his eyes starting from his head. 'Now I understand.'

'Then bully for you, John. Come on let's get out, someone will see us.' Pooley fanned at his nose and rubbed at his shirt-sleeves.

'No, no. Don't you understand what it's doing? Why it's here?'

'No. Nor why I should be.'

'It is what the Professor told us.' Omally struck his fist to his temple. 'Numerology; the power lies in the numbers themselves. Can't you see it? This whole madhouse is the product of mathematics. Mankind did not invent mathematics nor discover it. No the science of mathematics was given to him that he might misuse it to his ruin. That he might eventually create all this.' Omally spread out his arms to encompass the world they now inhabited. 'Don't you understand?'

Jim shook his head. 'Pissed again,' said he. 'And this time as Pope.'

Omally continued, his voice rising in pitch as the revelation struck him like a thunderbolt. 'The machine has now perfected the art. It has mastered the science, it can break anything down to its mathematical equivalent. Once it has the formula it can then rebuild, recreate everything. An entire brand new world built from the ashes of the old, encompassing everything.'

'But all it does is churn out the same old stuff over and over again.'

Omally clambered to his feet and turned upon him. 'Yes, you damn fool, because there is one number it can never find. It found the number of a man, but there is one more number, one more equation which never can be found.'

'Go on then, have your spasm.'

'The soul. That's what the old man was trying to tell us. Don't you see it, Jim?'

'I see that,' said Pooley, pointing away over John's shoulder. 'But I don't believe it.'

Omally turned to catch sight of a gaunt angular figure clad in the shredded remnants of a tweed suit, who was stealing purposefully towards them.

'The Saints be praised.'

'Holmes,' gasped Pooley. 'But how . . . ? It cannot be.'

'You can't keep a good man down.'

Sherlock Holmes gestured towards them. 'Come,' he mouthed.

Jim put his hand to Omally's arm. 'What if he starts clearing his throat?'

Omally shrugged helplessly. 'Come on, Jim,' he said, trundling Marchant towards the skulking detective.

Holmes drew them into the shadows. There in the half-light his face seemed drawn and haggard, although a fierce vitality shone in his eyes. 'Then only we three remain.' It was a statement rather than a question. Omally nodded slowly. 'And do you know what must be done?'

'We do not.'

'Then I shall tell you, but quickly, for we have little or no time. We are going to poison it,' said Sherlock Holmes. 'We are going to feed it with death.' The cold determination of his words and the authority with which he spoke to them seemed absolute.

'Poison it?' said Jim. 'But how?'

Holmes drew out a sheaf of papers from his pocket, even in the semi-darkness the Professor's distinctive Gothic penmanship was instantly recognizable. 'Feed it with death. The Professor formulated the final equation. He knew that he might not survive so he entrusted a copy to me. What he began so must we finish.'

'Hear, hear.'

'Computers are the products of diseased minds, but they will react only to precise stimuli. Feed them gibberish and you will not confuse them. But feed

267

them with correctly-coded instructions and they will react and function accordingly, in their own unholy madness. Professor Slocombe formulated the final programme. It will direct the machine to reverse its functions, leading ultimately to its own destruction. This programme will override any failsafe mechanism the machine has. I must, however, gain access to one of the terminals.'

'And how do you propose to do that?' Jim enquired as he slyly drained the last drop from his hip-flask. 'They all seem a little busy at present.'

Sherlock Holmes drew out his gun. 'This is a Forty-four Magnum, biggest . . .'

'Yes, we are well aware of that. It might, however, attract a little too much attention.'

'My own thoughts entirely. I was wondering, therefore, if you two gentlemen might be prevailed upon to create some kind of diversion.'

'Oh yes?' said Pope John. 'What, such as drawing the demonic horde down about our ears whilst you punch figures into a computer terminal?'

Holmes nodded grimly. 'Something like that. I will require at least six clear minutes. I know I am asking a lot.'

'You are asking everything.'

Holmes had no answer to make.

John stared hard into the face of Jim Pooley.

The other shrugged. 'What the heck?' said he.

'What indeed?' Omally climbed on to his bike. 'Room for one more up front.'

Jim smiled broadly and tore off his metallic balaclava. 'Then we won't be needing these any more.'

'No,' said John, removing his own. 'I think not.' Raising his hand in a farewell salute he applied his foot to the pedal. 'Up the Rebels.'

'God for Harry,' chorused Pooley, as the two launched forward across the floor, bound for destiny upon the worn wheels of Marchant the Wonder Bike.

A strange vibration swept up the mainframe of the great computer. The figures moving upon its face stiffened, frozen solid. Diamond-tipped lights began to flicker and flash, forming into sequences, columns, and star-shapes, and pyramids, veering and changing, pulsing faster and faster. A low purr of ominous humming rose in pitch, growing to a siren-screaming crescendo, as the machine's defence system suddenly registered the double image coursing across the floor of its very sanctum sanctorum. A ripple of startled movement spread out from the base, as the terminal operators took in the horror. Their heads rose to face the mainframe, their mouths opened, and the curiously mechanical coughing sounds issued forth, swelling to an atavistic howl.

'Do you think they've tumbled us, John?' Pooley clapped his hands across his ears and Omally sank his head between his shoulders as the two zig-zagged on between the sea of terminals and their shrieking, howling operators. The robots were rising to their feet, stretching out their arms towards their master, their heads thrown back, their mouths opening and closing. They stormed from their seats to pursue the intruders.

At the back of the hall a stealthy figure in shredded

tweed slipped into a vacant chair and flexed his long slim fingers.

'Get away there!' Pooley levelled his travelling hobnail towards a shrieking figure looming before them. He caught it a mighty blow to the chest and toppled it down across the face of a terminal, tearing it from its mounts amidst a tangle of sparking wires and scrambled mechanisms.

'Nice one, Jim.'

'Hard to port, John.'

Omally spun a hasty, wheel-screeching left turn, dodging a cluster of straining hands which clawed towards them. They dived off down another line of abandoned terminals, the robots now scrambling over them, faces contorted in hatred, anxious to be done with the last of their sworn enemy. Small black boxes were being drawn into the light, emitting sinister crackles of blue fire. The chase was on in earnest. And there were an awful lot of the blighters, with just two men to the bike.

The figures on the high gantries now ran to and fro in a fever of manic industry. They worked with inhuman energy, tending and caring to their dark master. The lights about them streamed up the dead black face, throbbing in 'V' formations, travelling down again to burst into pentacles and cuneiform. They became a triple-six logo a hundred feet high which reformed into the head of a horned goat, the eyes ringed in blood-red laser fire. Blackpool illuminations it was not.

Holmes laboured away at his terminal, but here and there his trembling fingers faltered and he punched in an incorrect digit. Cursing bitterly, he was forced to erase an entire line and begin again.

'You bastard.' A clawed hand tore off Pooley's right shirt-sleeve. 'I'm down to the arm. Let's get out of here, John!'

'Strike that man.' As a foaming psychotic rose up before them, Pooley levelled another flailing boot. The floor was now a hell-house of confusion. The robots were fighting with one another, each desperate to wring the life from Pooley and Omally. The cycling duo thundered on. Omally wore the orange jersey. The tour de Brentford was very much on the go.

'Get a move on, your Popeship, they're closing for the kill.'

John swung away once more, but the road-blocks were up. He skidded about, nearly losing Pooley, who uttered many words of justifiable profanity, and made hurried tracks towards the door. The androids encircled them, black boxes spurting fire. The circle was closing fast and every avenue of escape was blocked as soon as it was entered. Omally drew Marchant to a shivering halt, depositing Pooley on the deck. 'If you know how to fly,' he told his bike, 'now would be the time to impress me.' Sadly, the old battered sit-up-and-beg showed no inclination whatsoever towards sudden levitation. 'Well,' said John, 'one must never ask too much of a bike.'

Pooley rose shakily to his feet. To every side loomed a sea of snarling faces, surrounding them in an unbreakable circle. It was many many faces deep, and none looked amenable to a bloodless surrender.

'Goodbye, John,' said Jim, 'I never knew a better friend.'

'Goodbye, Jim.' Omally pressed his hand into that of his lifelong companion, a tear rose in a clear blue eye. 'We'll go down fighting at least.'

'At the very least.' Pooley raised his fists. 'Beware,' he cried, 'this man knows Dimac, the deadliest martial art known to . . . well, to the two of us anyway.'

The crowd rose up as if drawing its collective sulphurous breath, and fell upon them; cruel hands snatched down, anxious to destroy, to draw out the life. Omally struck where he could but the blows rained down upon him, driving him to his knees. Pooley could manage but one last, two-fingered expression of defiance before he was dashed to the deck. The writhing mob poured forward, thrashing and screaming, and it seemed that nothing less than a very timely miracle could save the dynamic duo now.

A great tremor rushed across the floor of the unholy cathedral. The lynch mob drew back in sudden horror, the black marble surface upon which they stood was being jarred as if by some great force battering up at it. Pooley and Omally cowered as the floor moved beneath them. A great crack tore open, tumbling androids to either side of it. Shards of sparkling marble shot up like some black volcanic eruption. An enormous fist thrust up from the depths. Another followed and, as the crowd backed into a growing circle, crying and pointing, a head and shoulders emerged from the destruction, rising noble and titanic amongst the debris.

'Fe . . . Fi . . . Fo . . . Fum.' As a great section of flooring smashed aside, Neville scrambled up through the opening. He was bloody and scarred, with great wounds upon his arms and legs, but his face bore an old nobility. He was indeed a Titan, a god of olden Earth. Yes, there were giants in the Earth in those days, and also after that. Neville stood, a Hercules in soiled Y-fronts. 'All right,' he cried. 'Who wants a fight then?'

'Not us,' cried Jim Pooley.

'Hello, lads,' said the bulging barman, sighting the cringing twosome, and flexing a selection of chest muscles. 'You appear to be somewhat unfairly outnumbered.'

'A bit of assistance would not go amiss.'

Neville flexed shoulders which had previously only been flexed by the Incredible Hulk, and even then to a minor degree.

'The rest has done him good,' said John. 'He looks well on it.'

Amidst a roar of green flame, Cerberus, the hound of hell, sprang up from the netherworld beneath to confront the barman. Its three heads, one now shredded and dangling, worked and snapped, saliva drooled from fanged jaws, and the stench of brimstone filled the already overloaded air. The scorpion tail flicked and dived. 'Come on, doggy,' called the barman. 'Time for a trip down to the vet's!' The creature launched itself towards him, passing over two terrified human professional cowerers. Neville caught it by a throat and the two crashed back into the crowd.

'On your toes, Jim,' called Omally. 'I see a small ray of light.' Shrinking and flinching, he and Jim edged away.

Neville swung the beast about, bringing down a score of robots. Others snatched at him but he swept them aside. Above, the mainframe pulsed and flashed, the moving lights forming obscene images. Pooley and Omally backed towards it, the exit was thoroughly blocked and the only way seemed like up.

Neville drove his fist through a plasticized face, sending up a cascade of synthetic blood. The hound of hell fell upon him once more but he tore down a lower jaw with a rending of bone and gristle. He was quite coming into his own.

Pooley and Omally gained a first staircase. 'Not more stairs,' gasped Jim.

'Pull the plugs out,' screamed Omally. 'Pull it to pieces. Follow me.' He thundered up the steps on to the first gantry. A vista of housed microcircuits met his gaze. Omally thrust forth his hand and tore out a drawered section, punching the things free. Pooley followed suit. Faces turned from the *mêlée* below, a group of androids detached themselves from the throng. Pooley ran along, drawing out random circuit patterns. Omally followed on, punching them from their housings. They gained the second level. Ahead stood a robot barring their way. 'You duck, I'll hit it.' Omally pressed Jim forward. The robot swung its hand at him but Jim ducked out of reach, grabbing at the knees. Omally drove a fist over his diving back, and the thing lurched off the gantry to fall into the chaos which now reigned below.

Neville stood defiant, taking on all comers. Cerberus with but one head left snarling, snapped at his ankles. A ring of shattered pseudo-corpses surrounded the combatants. John and Jim gained the third level. They were making something of an art out of dispatching the face-workers to whatever fate their microchipped god had in store for them.

'Pull it to pieces, Jimmy boy.'

'I'm pulling, I'm pulling.' Jim ran forward, dragging out segments, Omally came behind, kicking and punching. Microcircuits fell like evil snow upon the ferocious crowd welling beneath. Up another stairway and beyond.

Below them the lights exhibited a jumbled confusion. Great battle waged upon the floor. Neville stood head and shoulders, and a good deal more, above the great ring of his attackers. Blue fire sparkled as they strove to apply their killing weapons to his naked flesh, but Neville snatched out the arms from their silicone sockets and flung them high over his head. Cerberus had barked his last, but from the great chasm yawning in the marble floor other horrors spilled, spinning and thrashing, whirling out of the pit. Barbs and spines, close balls of fur, animals and swollen insects with the heads of infants. A darkness was filling the air, as if it were a palpable thing, felt as much as seen. A fog of hard night.

'Bandits at six o'clock,' shouted Pooley. 'Get a move on, John.'

Omally applied his boot to the face of a pursuer as it loomed up from a stairwell. 'Onward and upward, Jimmy.'

The two men struggled in an unreal twilight world. Below, Neville's great warcries and the dull thuds of falling, broken bodies mingled with the unholy screechings of the monstrous obscenities pouring up from the pit. The siren had ceased its banshee wail but voices issued from the computer's mainframe, sighing and gasping from the circuitry, whispering in a thousand tongues, few ever those of man. A hand fastened about Pooley's ankle, drawing him down. Omally turned, sensing rather than seeing his friend's plight. He wrenched out a drawer-load of circuits and swung it like an axe, severing the clinging hand at the wrist. The thing remained in its deathlock about Jim's ankle, but the hero clambered on.

They were by now high upon the computer's great face. The air was thin but sulphurous. John clutched at his chest and strained to draw breath. Pooley leant upon his shoulder, coughing and gasping. 'We're running out of stairs,' he croaked. Above them now was nothing but darkness. They stood engulfed in it, breathing it. The sounds of battle echoed below but nought could now be seen of the conflict. 'You don't happen to see any daylight lurking above?' Jim asked. 'Fast running out of wind this man.'

'I can see sod all. Get off there.' A hand had John by the trouser cuff. He squinted down in horror to see no other face than his own, leering up. Without thought or feeling he tore out another section of circuitry and thrust it down into the snapping mouth which sought his leg. Sparks blistered the visage, and the thing sank away into the darkness.

Pooley clung to a further staircase, his energy, such as it ever was, all but gone. 'About making me a Cardinal?' he gasped.

The Pope followed him up. 'Bless you, my son. Popes and Cardinals first. Press on.'

The two thrust blindly onward; there was nothing left to do but climb. The metal handrails were like ice and their hands were raw from the clinging cold which tore at the flesh. Their attackers poured at them in an unceasing horde. They called to them in voices which were their own, jibing and threatening, crying out explicit details of the fate which they intended for them.

'I'm gone,' said Jim. 'I can climb no more, leave me to die.'

Omally fumbled about with numb and bleeding fingers. 'I will join you,' said he. 'There are no more stairs.' Pressed back against the icy metal of the mainframe the two men stood, alone and trapped. The mob surged up beneath them, swarming over the catwalks and gantries. There was finally nowhere left to run.

'I don't want to die here,' said Pooley, his voice that of pitiful defeat. 'I'm not supposed to be here, amongst all of this. This isn't true, this isn't right.'

Omally clung to the cold hard wall. They were neither of them supposed to be here. They were alone, two men, leaning now as in a time long past, upon the parapet of the canal bridge, above the oiled water of the old Grand Union. They looked down into their own reflections and those of the old stars. The stars always had much to say to drunken men, although none of their counsel and advice was ever heeded upon the cold, cruel, hangover-morning. But the truths lay there. For ordinary men, the truths always lay there upon that very moment before falling over. It was there at that instant a man was truly himself. The truth lay in that netherworld between drunkenness and oblivion, and dwelt where no sober man could ever grasp it. Only the drunken taste reality, and that for an all-too-fleeting moment. Removed from all sensible thought they made their own laws and moulded futures unthinkable at sunrise. Ah yes, John and Jim had tasted the truth upon many many an occasion.

'I see the light,' shouted Omally.

Jim craned his head. Above them a torch beam shone down.

'Get a move on lads,' called a voice. 'You're late as usual.'

'Norman,' called Jim, squinting up at the flashlight. 'Is that you?'

'Sorry, were you expecting someone else?' Norman stretched down an arm towards them. 'A stitch in time never won fair lady you know. Get a move on will you.'

'At the hurry-up.'

Omally shouldered Jim, who took Norman's hand and struggled up through the rooftop opening. The screaming swarm beneath were hard upon the Irishman's heel, he stretched up his hand towards Jim and Pooley leant down, fingers straining to reach. Their fingers met, but with a cry of horror Omally was gone. The screams of the mob welled up and the shouts of Omally as he battered down at the creatures engulfing him were nothing if not ungodly. Their fingers met again and Jim drew him up through the opening.

'That was quite close,' said John, dusting down his trousers. 'But where now?'

Norman's impossible machine was parked near at hand. An icy wind screamed over the rooftop, howling and moaning. 'This way,' cried Norman. With tears flying from their eyes, they followed the shopkeeper. Pooley shielded his face and moved with difficulty, the gale near tearing him from his feet.

The sky above was black and starless. The blank vista of the rooftop seemed to stretch towards impossible extremes in every direction. Beyond, in the vertical seas which girded the borough, strange images burst and sparkled projecting themselves as if on three vast screens. But the panorama was shrinking, the streets still dimly visible below were diminishing. The building was shuddering beneath them, rising like a lift in a shaft. Its distant edges were becoming ever more distant. The building was duplicating itself. Time had run out, Holmes had not been successful, the Professor's programme had failed.

'The Millennium!' cried Norman, as he forced himself into the driving seat. 'Hurry!'

Pooley clung to the handrail of the time machine. The duplicates were pouring through the roof opening, a screaming mass tumbling towards them through the smashing firmament.

'This helicopter will never fly,' Jim told the shopkeeper.

'You have lost the last of your marbles.'

'All aboard now.' Omally did just that, as the satanic horde engulfed them.

Norman turned the ignition key and engaged reverse.

32

Neville, the new part-time barman, pushed the two brimming pints of Large across the polished counter-top and chalked the difference on to Pooley's slate, a mistake he would soon, through experience, come to rectify. He studied the two men who now sat before him. The sudden change in them was dramatic, it was as if they had aged by twenty years, literally overnight. And the state of them, their clothes hung in ribbons. Evidently they had taken work in the building profession and experienced a hard morning's graft.

The two men stared beyond his crisp right shoulder as if not noticing him. Their eyes seemed glued to the brewery calendar which hung unobtrusively amongst the Spanish souvenirs. Yet there was nothing strange to be seen in it. A simple cardboard rectangle with the brewery's name surmounting an out of register colour print of Constable's 'Haywain' and the hanging tab: June 6 1969. What could they see in it?

As if suddenly aware of the barman's scrutiny, the two men drew themselves away to a side-table, glasses in hand.

Omally studied his pint. 'And so, what do you propose we do now?' he asked.

Pooley sucked beer froth from his upper lip and made smacking sounds. It really did taste better back in those days. He tapped at his nose. 'I have a plan,' said he.

'Oh yes?' Omally's voice lacked enthusiasm.

'Indeed. Don't you understand? We've been given another chance to stop it all. At this moment, the Professor toils amongst his books and Holmes lies sleeping in his mausoleum. Norman chats, no doubt, with Leonardo da Vinci. Or has. I can't be certain exactly how it all works.'

'So what do you intend to do?'

'Down a few more pints for a first off. Drink up, John, you haven't touched yours.'

'I am not thirsty. Don't you understand? We are in an even worse position now than ever we were. We know what is to come, but we can do nothing whatever to stop it. We know that it cannot be stopped.'

'Oh fish,' said Jim Pooley. Delving into his trouser pocket he drew out a bulging drawstring pouch. 'Didn't know I had these, did you?' he asked, weighing it in his hand. 'Pooley's ace in the hole.'

Omally extended his hand but Jim held the thing beyond reach. 'No touching,' he said. 'All mine, but you can have a peep.' He loosened the neck of the pouch and held it tantalizingly apart.

Omally peered forward. 'Diamonds,' he gasped. 'A king's ransom.'

'I should say at the very least. I was going to have some cufflinks made up, but in all the excitement I completely forgot. I have no doubt they are synthetic, but nobody in this day and age is going to know that.'

'So what do you intend to do with them?'

'I am going to become a philanthropist,' said Jim. 'I am going to build a church.'

'A church?'

'A cathedral. And do you know where I'm going to build it?'

Omally nodded slowly. 'On the bombsite.'

'Exactly. No dirty big satanic buildings are going to come springing up from consecrated soil. What do you think, brilliant, eh?'

Omally leant back in his seat, his head nodding rhythmically. 'Brilliant, you almost cracked it.'

'I don't know about almost.'

'I do.' Omally's eyes flickered up towards Jim's. His hand moved towards his trouser pocket wherein rested a small black box, attached to which were a pair of wicked-looking rods. John Omally cleared his throat with a curiously mechanical coughing sound. 'Hand me the diamonds, Jim,' he said in a cold dead voice. 'We have other plans for them.'

Pooley's mouth dropped open in horror. Clasping his diamonds to his bosom, he kicked over the table on to the robot double of his dearest friend and made for the door.

'You're both barred,' screamed Neville, finding his voice, as the sleeveless Jim passed him by at speed, a raging Irishman with a black transitor radio close upon his heels.

As the two pounded off up the Ealing Road they all but collided with a brace of young gentlemen, who were strolling towards the Swan, studying a racing paper.

'Did you see what I just saw? asked Jim Pooley, rubbing at his eyes and squinting off after the rapidly diminishing duo.

John Omally shook his head. 'No,' said he. 'I am certain that I could not. How do you fancy Lucky Number for the three-fifteen?'

'What, out of that new Lateinos and Romiith stable? I wouldn't put any money on that.'

THE END

SPROUT⟨P⟩LŌRE

The Now Official
RŌBERT RANKIN
Fan Club

Members Will Receive:

Four Fabulous Issues of the *Brentford Mercury*, featuring previously unpublished stories by Robert Rankin. Also containing News, Reviews, Fiction and Fun.

A coveted Sproutlore Badge.

Special rates on exclusive T-shirts and merchandise.

'Amazing Stuff!' – Robert Rankin.

Annual Membership Costs £5 (Ireland), £7 (UK) or £11 (Rest of the World). Send a Cheque/PO to: **Sproutlore, 211 Blackhorse Avenue, Dublin 7, Ireland.**

Email: sproutlore@lostcarpark.com WWW: http://www.lostcarpark.com/sproutlore

Sproutlore exists thanks to the permission of Robert Rankin and his publishers.

THE SPROUTS OF WRATH
by Robert Rankin

Amazing, but true: Brentford Town Council, in an act of supreme public-spiritedness (and a great big wodge of folding stuff from a mysterious benefactor) has agreed to host the next Olympic Games. The plans have been drawn up, contracts, money and promises are changing hands. Norman's designed some stunning kit for the home team, and even the Flying Swan's been threatened with a major refit (gasp!). But something is very wrong . . . primeval forces are stirring in ancient places . . . dark magic is afoot in Brentford and someone must save the world from over-powering evil . . .

. . . Jim Pooley and John Omally, come on down!

This must be the daring duo's toughest assignment yet. No longer can they weigh up the situation over a pint of lager at random moments during the day. No, this time, to save the world as we know it, the lads must contemplate – nay, undertake – the most horrible, the most terrifying, the here-tofore untried – REGULAR EMPLOYMENT!!!

'A very funny book . . . a brilliant and exceedingly well written series'
Colin Munro, *Interzone*

The fourth novel in the now legendary *Brentford Trilogy*

0 552 13844 4

THE BRENTFORD CHAINSTORE MASSACRE
by Robert Rankin

'Jim took himself to his favourite bench before the Memorial Library. It was here, on this almost sacred spot, that Jim did most of his really heavyweight thinking. Here where he dreamed his dreams and made his plans . . .'

There is nothing more powerful than a bad idea whose time has come. And there can be few ideas less bad or more potentially apocalyptic than that hatched by genetic scientist Dr Steven Malone. Using DNA strands extracted from the dried blood on the Turin Shroud, Dr Malone is cloning Jesus. And not just a single Jesus, he's going for a full half-dozen so that each of the world's major religions can have one. It's a really bad idea.

In Brentford they've had a really good idea. They're holding the Millennial celebrations two years early to avoid the rush and it promises to be the party of this, or any other, century. Unless, of course, something REALLY BAD were to happen . . .

'Stark raving genius . . . alarming and deformed brilliance'
Observer

The fifth novel in the now legendary *Brentford Trilogy*

0 552 14357 X

A SELECTED LIST OF FANTASY TITLES
AVAILABLE FROM CORGI AND BLACK SWAN

THE PRICES SHOWN BELOW WERE CORRECT AT THE TIME OF GOING TO PRESS. HOWEVER TRANSWORLD PUBLISHERS RESERVE THE RIGHT TO SHOW NEW RETAIL PRICES ON COVERS WHICH MAY DIFFER FROM THOSE PREVIOUSLY ADVERTISED IN THE TEXT OR ELSEWHERE.

☐	13017 6	**MALLOREON 1: GUARDIANS OF THE WEST**	*David Eddings*	£6.99
☐	12284 X	**BELGARIAD 1: PAWN OF PROPHECY**	*David Eddings*	£6.99
☐	14255 7	**ECHOES OF THE GREAT SONG**	*David Gemmell*	£6.99
☐	14256 5	**SWORD IN THE STORM**	*David Gemmell*	£6.99
☐	14274 3	**THE MASTERHARPER OF PERN**	*Anne McCaffrey*	£6.99
☐	14762 1	**THE CRYSTAL SINGER OMNIBUS**	*Anne McCaffrey*	£8.99
☐	14614 5	**THE LAST CONTINENT**	*Terry Pratchett*	£6.99
☐	14615 3	**CARPE JUGULUM**	*Terry Pratchett*	£6.99
☐	13681 6	**ARMAGEDDON THE MUSICAL**	*Robert Rankin*	£5.99
☐	13823 0	**THEY CAME AND ATE US, ARMAGEDDON II: THE B-MOVIE**	*Robert Rankin*	£5.99
☐	13923 8	**THE SUBURBAN BOOK OF THE DEAD, ARMAGEDDON III: THE REMAKE**	*Robert Rankin*	£5.99
☐	13841 X	**THE ANTIPOPE**	*Robert Rankin*	£5.99
☐	13842 8	**THE BRENTFORD TRIANGLE**	*Robert Rankin*	£5.99
☐	13844 4	**THE SPROUTS OF WRATH**	*Robert Rankin*	£5.99
☐	14357 X	**THE BRENTFORD CHAINSTORE MASSACRE**	*Robert Rankin*	£5.99
☐	13922 X	**THE BOOK OF ULTIMATE TRUTHS**	*Robert Rankin*	£5.99
☐	13833 9	**RAIDERS OF THE LOST CAR PARK**	*Robert Rankin*	£5.99
☐	14212 3	**THE GARDEN OF UNEARTHLY DELIGHTS**	*Robert Rankin*	£6.99
☐	14213 1	**A DOG CALLED DEMOLITION**	*Robert Rankin*	£5.99
☐	14355 3	**NOSTRADAMUS ATE MY HAMSTER**	*Robert Rankin*	£5.99
☐	14356 1	**SPROUT MASK REPLICA**	*Robert Rankin*	£5.99
☐	14580 7	**THE DANCE OF THE VOODOO HANDBAG**	*Robert Rankin*	£5.99
☐	14589 0	**APOCALYPSO**	*Robert Rankin*	£5.99
☐	14590 4	**SNUFF FICTION**	*Robert Rankin*	£5.99
☐	14741 9	**SEX AND DRUGS AND SAUSAGE ROLLS**	*Robert Rankin*	£5.99
☐	14742 7	**WAITING FOR GODALMING**	*Robert Rankin*	£5.99
☐	14743 5	**WEB SITE STORY**	*Robert Rankin*	£5.99
☐	14897 0	**THE FANDOM OF THE OPERATOR**	*Robert Rankin*	£5.99
☐	99777 3	**THE SPARROW**	*Mary Doria Russell*	£7.99
☐	99811 7	**CHILDREN OF GOD**	*Mary Doria Russell*	£6.99

All Transworld titles are available by post from:

Bookpost, P.O. Box 29, Douglas, Isle of Man IM99 1BQ

Credit cards accepted. Please telephone 01624 836000, fax 01624 837033, Internet http://www.bookpost.co.uk or e-mail: bookshop@enterprise.net for details.

Free postage and packing in the UK. Overseas customers allow £1 per book (paperbacks) and £3 per book (hardbacks).